BY THE SAME AUTHOR

Love Letters to Sports: Moments in Time and the Ties that Bind

SIMPLE GLORY

The Search for the Soul of an American Town

A Novel

JOHN CLENDENING

SIMPLE GLORY
THE SEARCH FOR THE SOUL OF AN AMERICAN TOWN

iUniverse books may be ordered through booksellers or by contacting:

iUniverse
1663 Liberty Drive
Bloomington, IN 47403
www.iuniverse.com
1-800-Authors (1-800-288-4677)

ISBN: 978-1-5320-5683-3 (sc)
ISBN: 978-1-5320-5682-6 (hc)
ISBN: 978-1-5320-5684-0 (e)

Library of Congress Control Number: 2018910841

Print information available on the last page.

iUniverse rev. date: 10/09/2018

To Caroline, Jocelyn and Cameron

If there is one thing that is forever it is my love for you

TABLE OF CONTENTS

Cattle per Year

A Good Remuda

Like a Longhorn

Sign on a Chuck Wagon

"The stage directions set the time as 'Not too long ago.' It might have been yesterday. It could have been tomorrow."

— INTRODUCTION TO THE PLAY, *INHERIT THE WIND*

PROLOGUE

LEMONADE

It was not too long ago when it all happened.

It all started when I decided to do nothing less than live my dream. I wasn't alone in having a dream, of course. I firmly believe we all have one. But I just as firmly believe we all arrive at a point in our lives, sometimes consciously and sometimes not, when we decide to try and live it. Or decide we can live without it.

What's better for a young man trying to make his way in a new century in a new world: to remain where he is, where he knows things, or to go where he doesn't?

When it all happened, it did so in an old train town.

In an old train town where some were embracing change, while others were doing all they could to hold it off for as long as possible.

It did so, too, in an old company in an old industry.

In an old company in an old industry where, to a certain degree at least, embracing change meant giving in to it.

What's better for an old train town trying to make its way in a new century in a new world: to remain one, to maintain its small-town soul, or to strive to become a bigger, more modern one?

What's better for an old company in an old industry trying to hang on for dear life in a new century in a new world: to keep doing what it's been doing for so long and hope things change, or accept that they won't?

When I think about these questions now, I think back to that lemon summer, that bite-into-the-pith summer, that summer when the new century and the new millennium were as shiny and as gleaming as a bike the day it's finally and triumphantly brought home from the store.

It was the summer when I went to this old train town from my big city home, a half-a-country and a world away, to live out my dream.

It was the summer that, at a certain point along the way, took on the zest of the peel.

And became lemonade.

Sometimes, I think everything in my life seems so different now.

Sometimes, I think everything seems the same.

Most of the time, I think it's both.

What is void of internal dispute is this: I remember. I remember it all. And when I remember the wonders of summer, the wonders of love and of baseball and of ice cream that all converged on me in that moment in time, I smile, for I know these are wonders that never cease. Because as much as things change, whether it's yesterday or tomorrow, it's nice to know that some things, some small-but-precious things, can always be counted on, counted on to smell, to taste, to be, the same.

*"350,000 cattle per year were driven up
the trails from Texas for 28 years"
– The Trail Drivers by Hunter*

Etched into stone at the northeast corner of Parkwood
and Warren, in front of the Holiday Inn in the
heart of the Frisco Bridges office park

CHAPTER ONE

SOMEWHERE EAST OF EL PASO

My car careened headlong into the darkness. I was basting in oil. My eyes darted up and to the right to meet the gaze of the rear-view mirror. The truck was still there. Its lights, its brights, mocked me, dared me to avoid them. The faster I drove, the more ground the truck seemed to gain. The brighter the lights, the harder the glare.

How all of this had started was a whodunit. I had veered into a left-hand turn lane. I hadn't known where I was going. Unsure I should be taking the left in the first place, I had decided against it and merged back into traffic on the two-lane highway along which I had been traveling. One of the cars behind me didn't like my decision. And it was that car, a white pick-up, now on my tail. The feeling was like being inside a video game, the outcome artificial at best. Yet the fear was real, on your skin, a calf separated from the herd.

1

When I first realized the truck was practically on my bumper, and conscious of the fact that I was in a far-off place that I still didn't know well, I had first tried diplomacy. I had pulled the car onto the dirt shoulder in order to let the truck pass. My offer had been rejected; rather than passing and continuing down the highway, the truck had swerved onto the dirt and pulled up in front of my car.

There had been no exchange of heated words, no gestures, no honk. I sat and waited. The wait was interminable, each second ticking off with the speed of a sundial.

All of a sudden, a figure emerged from the truck. It was of a man, tall and gangly, looking to be in his mid-30s. He had a dark brown, almost auburn, mustache and beard, with long, stringy, lighter brown hair flowing down his back. He was not just striding toward my car. He was stalking toward it, beer bottle in hand. His t-shirt was white, and looked to be singed with soot. His blue jeans were not blue anymore, but off-white remnants of years of hard use.

I was tempted to wait to see what the man had to say. Part of me was more curious than anything. What had I done to offend him?

I analyzed the man as he approached the car. The skin just under his lower lip bulged both outward and downward, a horizontal checkerboard of charbroiled beef brown-tobacco and watermelon-colored gum tissue revealing itself more and more with every step. With his lip swollen and protruding, the hair under it sticking out like toothpicks, he could have passed as a silver arowana.

But the real cue, the true sign of the danger I now knew I was in, was the man's eyes. They were disturbingly small, virtually colorless. They were vessels of anger, contagions of hate.

That was it. I slammed my foot on the gas and spiraled the car forward. I narrowly missed hitting the man as the car lurched to the left toward the highway. I could see him spewing venom, the ends of his hair flying in all directions, sweat emptying from him like that of a victimized boxer in a wire service photo, as he dove for cover. I was screaming now, screaming expletives I never knew were in me, screaming so loudly I could feel the shape of my ribs.

I exploded back onto the highway and pushed the gas pedal down even further. I was speeding now, frantically speeding. The truck had bounded onto the highway, was already gaining on me. I had succeeded in creating some distance. But the truck was still there, still had me in its sights.

I stopped screaming. I was taking deep breaths now, trying to focus, not let my emotions take over. I wondered if my California plates had invited the situation. Was I being chased because I looked like a tourist? Was I a sitting duck on this dark road in North Texas?

Then another thought struck. It arrived in my brain, settled in my gut. Could it be, could it possibly be, this chase was not an accident? Was it possible the man behind the wheel was after me because of my story? All I had done was report what I had seen. Nothing more. Nothing less. It was my job. It was a job I had dreamed of doing since I was old enough to remember. It was a job I was now doing as best I could.

My forehead still felt porous. Yet my extremities were cold, like something was siphoning them of warmth while replacing them with a blast of icy air.

Through the rushing night, I could see a T approaching in the road. The road I was on was about to end.

Left or right?

Right or left?

The entire interview process took place over two phone calls, in great part because, as Rip Skimer, the Frisco Evening Outlook's managing editor, said, "I can tell if someone's got what it takes just by hearing the questions they ask. Don't matter what you look like in this business, and I don't care whatcha wear. Besides, the last time we had a travel budget here, I was in high school. In other words, basically, never."

The job, as I understood it in this first call with Skimer, was to be the Evening Outlook's education reporter. That meant I would be responsible for covering the education "beat," as reporters called it. I knew this meant I would be responsible for covering the Frisco school district, but not much else.

But there was the name. Frisco.

For starters, the very name of the town made me squirm. Being from California, I knew that people often shortened the name of San Francisco to just "Frisco." This had always irked the native in my mom to no end. She was fond of saying that if someone called San Francisco "Frisco" that probably meant they rode a motorcycle or, God forbid, had a tattoo.

Then there was the location. From my initial golf clap of a research effort, which was all I could muster in my less than overwhelming exuberance for the opportunity, I knew Frisco was somewhere north of Dallas. But either I was getting desperate or something about Skimer's demeanor had challenged me to do more.

So I began digging a bit deeper. Frisco, I came to know, was a nearly-hundred-year-old town located about 30 miles north of downtown Dallas somewhere called Collin County along the old Preston Trail, a main north-south artery of 19th-century Texas that followed the earlier cattle line known as the Shawnee Trail. The town of Frisco had officially been born in 1902 when a train depot was built in town amid the rolling prairie land of the area. As for the town name itself, it had evolved from the Saint Louis and San Francisco Railway Company, which had been organized in 1876 and operated an east-west line through town commonly called FRISCO.

By 1910, Frisco had "grown" to 332 people. Over time, while its population had steadily increased, Frisco had remained a small farming town. As recently as the 1970s, it boasted of only 1,000 residents, and by 1990 was still quite modest in size at just over 6,000. In recent years, however, the town had gone on a binge, and was now truly burgeoning with a population that as of the new Census had reached 30,000. The nation's population had long been moving toward the Sun Belt, and in turn states like Texas had experienced major population growth. The Dallas version of this trend was that of the ongoing migration of the populace from the city to the ever-expanding suburbs to the north.

I was starting to actually consider the possibility of starting my career as a journalist not at the L.A. Times – the only paper I cared to read, let alone work for – but of all places at the Frisco Evening Outlook. After all, I only had a week-and-a-half at this point until graduation, and if there was a thought I could not handle, it was that of graduating without a job. That, to me, was license for my father and anyone he could enlist to turn up the heat on law school. This was not an option. This was defeat.

If I were to allow myself to get fully sucked in, and the second call with Skimer was approaching within days now, I still needed further inspiration. I needed something, someone, to tell me it was okay.

Woodward.

Even before I scorched my palm with the scalding hot iron that my professional bent was not the family business of law but journalism, I had worshipped him. The fact that the Watergate affair had all occurred before I was born was immaterial. I had watched "All the President's Men" enough in recent years, starting even before I joined up with the USC J-school, it had gotten to the point where I could almost mute the TV while reciting the lines in full lip sync with the characters. Then there was, to me at least, the big reveal of the term "ratfuck," my now-favorite term ever, which while it might have been primarily a noun in its original sense carried endless potential for other uses. A word which could also take on a life of its own as a pre-fix to other words, for example, with ratfucking and its semantic cousin, ratfuckingly, becoming adjectives in my personal vernacular to describe any action in the extreme. And don't even debate me about the greatest scene of all, the one where Bradlee, standing on his lawn in his bathrobe, looks at Woodward and Bernstein and says, "Nothing's riding on this except the First Amendment to the Constitution, freedom of the press and maybe the future of the country. Not that any of that matters, but if you guys fuck up again, I'm going to get mad. Goodnight." The movie had become, in fact, my anthem.

As much as I had consumed, dissected and analyzed each and every move he and Bernstein had made in chasing down the greatest story of all time, pored over every digital inch of their Washington Post ink I could get my eyes on, it had never occurred to me to look at where Woodward had come from, how he had gotten his foot far enough in the door to position himself for the same type of eternal journalistic renown for which I believed I was destined.

What I found was that Woodward had somehow started out at the Post, producing 17 stories. None of them were printed, however, and he was sent packing, professionally exiled to the likes of The Montgomery County Sentinel. Only after spending a year there did he return. The answer was clear: for the chosen few, the truly great, there was romance in that first stop, that initial way station on the way to journalistic heaven. All of a sudden, Frisco, Texas didn't seem so bad after all. The Plan was becoming easier to forecast by the day. I'd be in and out. I'd be back in Los Angeles within two years, three years tops, settled in for a long and decorated career at the Times, my seat on the aisle below Tunnel 9 in the Coliseum secure in perpetuity, the grains of sand from Santa Monica Beach never to be far from being nestled comfortably between my toes after yet another futile attempt to catch the flash of the sun at that fleeting moment when it dips below the horizon over the Pacific.

On my way…to something big.

"Frisco may not be Hollywood, and sorry to let ya know but no one here's gonna call ya dude, but you'll get all the hustle and bustle you'll have time for less than an hour down south in Dallas," Skimer said in closing our second call. "Red River, divides Texas and Oklahoma, just over an hour to the north. All sorts of stuff to do up there including some real serious duck shooting. I even hear sometimes you can get yourself one of those red-tailed hawks.

"Heck, I'm not suggesting you make a habit out of it or nothing, but they tell me they got some of them art galleries out there in Ft. Worth, and that's only an hour or so to the west, at least the way the catbird flies.

"But listen, you wanna be a reporter, and we're looking for one, a hungry one. If you're interested in us and can be here by June 18, the job's yours, kid. You get here and decide you wanna go back to the beach, well then, maybe we'll at least get a coupla good stories out of you. Don't matter to me if you're big, small, fast, slow, right-wing, left-wing, a bull or a heifer. Just wanna know you like news. I like news. Like it a lot. You like news, you call Lane in my office and let her know by the end of the week. You coming, we'll see you at 8 a.m. that morning. And don't be late."

By the time I hung up with Skimer for a second time, I was already there.

Did $800 a week sound like much of a salary?

Did writing for a 19,000-circulation daily sound like the way to the big time?

But if I was going to earn my stripes as an ink-stained wretch, as a Defender of Truth, as a standard bearer of nothing less than the Fourth Estate, this was my chance. How many times had I practiced holding the phone like Redford-as-Woodward and answered the imaginary phone with a curt, "McDougal," like, hey, unless you're a key source on a really important story, how dare you dial my number? How many times had I been back to At-Ease in Westwood Village to eye the toffee coat that most reminded me of Redford's Woodward character before actually buying it?

Now, finally, I was ready to face down my destiny as The Next Great Journalist head on. I was so ready I could taste it. I was going to see it through, see it through as best I could.

And then get the ratfucking hell out of there at the first call.

Somewhere east of El Paso, I dialed the phone.

"Happy Father's Day."

"Thank you, Marshall," my father replied. "So where are you now?"

Vintage. Cut to the chase. Get to the facts. My father had never been much of a conversationalist. In fact, I was shocked he had answered the phone at all. That task, by silent treaty, had long been assigned to mom.

I had put off the call for as long as I could. But I was way geeked up on Dr. Pepper by this point, having downed it like spring water since the truck stop outside of Las Cruces, and the inner tug of my bladder was quickly descending into a yank. I needed a distraction.

"I just passed some town called Wild Horse. Know where that is?"

"No idea," he said. "Honey, you ever heard of Wild Horse? Isn't that a winery up there by Santa Barbara?" he asked my mom, and I could envision the blank stare she was returning from the laundry room.

He turned his attention back to me.

"Is that in Texas? Are you in Texas yet?"

The geographic answer was yes; I had crossed over into Texas about an hour before. Of course, by the time I passed the state line, I had already decided I was on The Drive That Would Never End.

It wasn't just the time it had taken me to get this far that was working my nerves like a box grater does cheddar. It was the alarming shortage of memorable sights along the way. Neighbors of ours from Los Angeles had moved to San Antonio a few years back. The directions they had left behind for everyone, in case anyone wanted to visit, was "10 East, exit Huebner," Huebner being the 10 exit on the west side of town where they had rented an apartment. And it was, they assured us, amazingly true. If you want to drive from Los Angeles to San Antonio, even if you start all the way from the Pacific Ocean, all that is apparently required is to board the 10 Freeway, pass the sign less than five minutes later proclaiming you are on the Christopher Columbus Transcontinental Highway, and, literally, stay on it heading generally southeast. At which point roughly 19 driving hours later you find yourself peering down upon the River Walk.

My own route to Texas could not boast of such violent simplicity. I had followed the 10 through Palm Springs, past the either-misnamed-or-misplaced Salton Sea and through the nothing to Phoenix and then Tucson. And I had stayed on it for hours on end, through the mountains and deserts of eastern Arizona and New Mexico all the way into West Texas.

That's where I found myself now. The latest Dust Bowl image I had muscled my way through aside, the more relevant question really revolved around my state of mind. The answer was that I had been on familiar turf for too long. And already in Texas for as long as I could remember.

I talked to my father, then to my mom and sister, for just a few more minutes. It was another 73-degree day in Los Angeles. I hung up and pressed on. I needed to focus on getting to where I was going as quickly as possible. After all, the faster I got to where I was going, the faster I could get started on executing The Plan. I was on what to me was a sacred mission, one that felt almost pre-ordained in its clarity, and casual banter with the family was not about to get in my way.

Highway 20 was beckoning. Time to veer from the trusty 10. Time to explore the mystery of a new highway on which I never before had traveled. With a quick glance into the rear-view mirror, I hit the gas.

CHAPTER TWO

WELCOME TO FRISCO

I awoke in a stale funk. I had slept like a log in water, my torso a sausage that had been left in the pan long after the simmer, the grease having dried and formed on my candlestick skin.

No matter. At this point I was more wide awake than a truant teen at a peep show.

Once out of the shower and cleaned up, I faced a major, admittedly somewhat metrosexual dilemma: what to wear. My first call was to throw on a pair of ratty cords and what I had already assumed would be my signature: my Woodward coat. But what if I showed up underdressed? No way in hell I was going to take Skimer at his word. I raised an eyebrow toward the light gray, Brooks Brothers suit. It was the one and only suit I owned, the one I had worn all of six weeks prior at graduation, the off-white smudge on the left cuff a reminder of the Coors Light that had overflowed as I tried to balance it between my feet during the valediction.

On went the suit. On went the black dress socks with the tack-sized, white triangle designs in them. On went the black Bostonian shoes. On went the white dress shirt, over which went the crimson-based tie with the gray paisley design. Twenty minutes later, after I had gone through my traditional morning gyrations of patting my hair countless times and tucking and re-tucking my dress shirt over and over again for no apparent reason to anyone including me, I was ready for my close-up.

New maple syrup briefcase with the letters "MJM" imprinted in gold – my graduation gift from my parents?

Check.

New silver Mount Blanc pen, also with my initials imprinted in it – my graduation gift from my sister?

Check.

A minute later, and more than a bit full of myself now, there I was, jumping into my smoky gray 1997 Toyota Tercel hatchback and bounding out of my apartment complex parking lot onto Stonebrook Parkway. The dreaming, the planning, the imagining, had all come to this.

I took a left onto Preston Road. Where I was greeted by more nothing, the only difference this time being that this version had the gall to masquerade as something. Everything I passed reeked of the mundane. The Collin County Community College District, Preston Ridge Campus. Staley Steel. Hutson Industries. The only thing that turned my head was the sign advertising the "luxury attached villas" at the Preston Vineyards Villages being offered in the $150K-$160K range. Even as someone who had never owned real estate, as a Southern Californian I immediately realized how cheap the price was. For that kind of price back home, you'd be lucky if you got a couple of square feet within walking distance of something you didn't want to live within walking distance of.

But then I passed the Prestonbrook Crossing apartment complex, by which point it was already occurring to me that half of everything around me had the word Preston attached to it, and I encountered something so fascinating I had an ADD moment and pulled the car over.

It was the Donut Palace.

This was, this must be, I thought, the establishment of all Frisco establishments. On the north side of the small yellow brick building – a building about the size of an in-the-middle-of-the-parking-lot-of-the-corner-strip-mall Kodak one-hour photo store – the word "Donut" was printed, implying that if one were to be hungry for one donut, they would be in luck, whereas if one were looking to consume more than one donut, perhaps not. On one front window, the words "Donut," "Gourmet Coffee" and "Kolaches" were painted. On the other were the words, "Checks Cashed" and "Money Orders."

The Donut Palace's idea of cross promotion aside, I was captivated by the serious lack of commercial activity that permeated the scene. Dirt lots surrounded the building. A friendless car sat in the lot, a forest green Chevrolet Metro LSi with a "For Sale -- $1900" sign in the front window, and my first thought was why anyone would choose this spot to showcase something for sale.

I got out of the car and approached the window. A quick peek inside revealed, in fact, zero donuts. Meaning that, on first glance, even the singular use of the word "Donut" painted on the window appeared to be an overstatement. Shaking my head in amusement, I walked back to the car. At the red light now with the allegedly singularly-stocked "Donut" shop to my right, I glanced forward and to my left. Even if I hadn't already been seated and strapped into a cramped compartment, what I saw staring back at me from the opposite side of Preston Road would still have stopped me in my tracks.

I was staring at a beige water tower, likely no more than 30 feet high, a modest height compared to the eclectic mix of others I had driven by on my way into town. Painted on it was the large face of a raccoon. Above the raccoon's face was painted a single word, in large, blue block letters with a maize-colored outline: FRISCO. Below the raccoon's face, also painted in the same style, but in a smaller font, were five words: HOME OF THE FIGHTING COONS.

The Fighting Who?

I wasn't really reading this, was I?

I was.

The Frisco Fighting Coons.

Clearly the term "Coon" carried a negative connotation. Mean-spirited slang for a person of African-American descent. I wondered if I had ever actually heard anyone use the term to describe a black person, and I was sure I hadn't. I hadn't exactly been surrounded by black people as a rule growing up, and despite the fact that I had grown up in the melting pot of Southern California, I had still led a fairly sheltered life. So perhaps I wasn't the best judge as to what was offensive and what wasn't.

Even so, the term immediately jumped out at me as not just offensive, but obscenely so. I had driven through a town called White Settlement the day before. I wouldn't have noticed it, but my eye had caught a matching pair of stonewash blue, drum-shaped water towers obscured on a slope off to the left after Highway 20 had turned into Highway 30 just west of Ft. Worth. They had first reminded me of the two white ones in San Onofre, just along I-5 on the way to San Diego, the ones that look like a pair of finely-crafted, after-market breasts. But a closer inspection, done as best one can while zooming down the road at 70, revealed them to be different, the one on the left promoting one's arrival in White Settlement, the one on the right blank, yet joined at the hip like one of those comedy teams where one does all the talking and the other stays silent yet they play off of each other's cues as well as or better than any two people could in full conversation.

Upon digesting the White Settlement water towers, I had made a snide comment to myself that I was surprised that it was now the 21st century, as opposed to the 20th – or even, hell, the 19th. But this one, this water tower in front of me, this latest signpost to an earlier time, a different way of thinking, had a visual attached to it, that of an animal, a seemingly friendly animal taking a break from the day to welcome one to town.

The Frisco Fighting Coons?

The longer I stared at it, the longer the raccoon seemed to stare back at me, follow my eyes with his.

Welcome to Frisco, Texas, Marshall McDougal.

The horn in my ear blared me back to reality. I had no idea how long the light before me had been green. I gathered myself and kept driving. As I continued northbound on Preston, my mind was racing, outpacing with room to spare whatever speed my car may be capable of on its best day. In neither of the curious cases I had encountered was anyone trying to hide anything. In neither case, as far as I could tell, was anyone trying to offend anyone. In neither case, for all I knew, were people having a problem with it.

Then why, I asked myself, was I?

I looked for Main Street. Once I saw the sign, I noticed it had a second, alternative name: Farm Road 3537. I turned left on Main and started proceeding westerly, the morning sun nearly blinding me from behind via its reflection in my rear-view mirror.

I was all eyes now. On the right, at the northwest corner of Preston and Main, I passed the Big Tex Mart, and forgetting the taunting raccoon for the moment I crowed at the big news on the board out front that one could buy a Fanta drink for only 99 cents. I wasn't laughing at the fact that one could buy a Fanta drink for less than a dollar; I was laughing at the fact that such a development was big enough news to warrant a public proclamation.

I kept moving. On the left, just across the street, I passed the Randy White Hall of Fame BBQ & Grill. The building was constructed of dark wood, so dark it almost looked like it had been burned. I quickly assumed the restaurant was owned and/or operated by former Dallas Cowboy great and NFL Hall of Famer Randy White, and though I was typically as helpless as a malnourished bee to a steaming pot of honey when it came to sports, I quickly decided that my longtime hatred of the Cowboys would preclude me from paying the place much heed.

What I was now experiencing was Main Street USA. On the south side of Main stood Frisco Jewelry & Loan, Compass Bank and Frisco Sports Center; on the north side, Main Pet Medical Center, Frisco Used Car and Frisco Plaza, which I could see consisted of stores ranging from Palladium Tan to Teresa's Beauty Salon to Hair Design by Michele. Before I could blink, adjacent to the Frisco Plaza, there it was: the Frisco Evening Outlook. I had tried to ignore my gutteral wince at the notion that I was starting my award-winning journalism career on a farm road. I was now, however, in full cringe.

The building, one story and about the size of a small bank, looked like it had been there for as long as the town, and my willful imagination penalized me with a stereotypical vision of it having been built to serve as a hitching post during the heyday of the covered wagon. To make matters worse, if that was possible, the paper didn't even have the building to itself; a sign in the window announced that it shared the building with none other than Wilson-Monroe Realty.

Of course. Everyone wants at least one glimpse of Wilson-Monroe Realty before they die.

I pulled into the lot, parked in the first available spot, turned off the ignition and stared ahead. What had been unbridled enthusiasm all of 15 minutes before had disintegrated into full-blown buyer's remorse. Striding toward the door, I noticed a sign heralding the Evening Outlook as "Your Community Newspaper." What a shame that was for the people in the community, I muttered to myself, because said newspaper was being published out of a glorified mobile home.

I had about 10 seconds before I could be considered guilty by association on both counts, and all I could do was gird myself for what I was about to find on the inside of the shoe box. I reached for the door, fighting the demons with all I could muster. Remember, Woodward did it. So could I, dammit. But what had I done? Had I traveled back to the 1950s? And what about my skills? It's one thing to love writing. But that didn't make one a great reporter. What if I failed? Worse yet, what if I was good enough, but didn't like it? That would mean that every hope I had built, every instinct I had followed, had been wrong.

"May I help you?" said a surprisingly pleasant-looking woman behind a desk with easily the tightest bun of blond hair I had ever seen.

Despite the fact that I was the one who had just entered the building, I was a bit startled by the question. "Uh, yes, my name is Marshall McDougal," I offered, the words barely breaking through the Berlin Wall of phlegm in my throat. "I'm here to see Mr. Skimer?"

"Oh yes, Mr. McDougal. We've been expecting y'all. My name's Lane Sunnivan. I'm Mr. Skimer's assistant."

"Nice to meet you, Ms. Sunnivan. Do you double as the receptionist?"

"Oh, we don't really have a receptionist. Depends on who's closest to the door, hun. Why don't you follow me to Mr. Skimer's office."

I nodded. Though I felt like I already knew him from our phone conversations, I was about to meet my first editor in person.

"Mr. Skimer, Mr. McDougal is here to see you."

This was my moment; I didn't hesitate.

"Good morning, Mr. Skimer. I'm Marshall McDougal, and I'm ready to go."

A man behind the desk looked up. His appearance surprised me. I had been unable to stop myself from expecting him to look like Jason Robards, who had played Bradlee in "All the President's Men." I wasn't far off on age, but he was taller than I expected. He actually bordered on lanky, and I thought he might be as tall as 6'4". He looked to me to be in his mid-50s, with a full head of brown though gray-streaked hair, and a bushy mustache that was more cinnamon than anything. I quickly concluded he was much closer to Hal Holbrook in appearance, the irony hitting me immediately: it was Holbrook who had played Deep Throat.

His most powerful feature was his eyes: hotel pool-blue, so brightly and summer-sun blue they disarmed you. Especially when they're giving you the once-over on your first day on the job.

"Look like you're here for a board of directors meeting for Bank of America."

"Uh, well, I had a feeling this might happen. I can change if you'd like."

"Nah, don't worry about it. They might laugh ya out of the newsroom, but it's not worth changing over. Let's get you going. Got a story for you to cover today."

I had figured I would spend the first day filling out forms and meeting the staff.

"A story?"

"Yep, a story. You see, son, that's what newspapers do. We write news stories."

I wasn't laughing. I was still trying to get a handle on what was happening.

"Ain't what we call front page stuff. But it's a good way to get your feet wet, see. Have Lane here get you set up, and we'll meet in my office in an hour. Don't get your hopes up, kid. It's not like five burglars broke into the headquarters of the Frisco Democratic school board committee last night. Well, as far as we know they didn't, right Lane?!"

Sunnivan hee-haw'd in a way that was loud enough to give Skimer his due, all while motioning me to follow her. Did Skimer know of my fascination with Watergate? Had I said something about it during my interviews? Dear God, I thought, I hadn't said anything about Woodward, had I? As I silently strode down the hallway with Sunnivan, I found myself wondering why I had ever gone to journalism school in the first place.

"Now, I'm telling you what, Marshall, don't you worry about Mr. Skimer," Sunnivan said, massaging my discomfort.

"Any tips on how to work with him?"

"Just be honest and work hard. He can be hard on folks, but ultimately, he's fair. If you listen, you'll learn a ton."

"That's just what I'm here for."

"Awesome possum!"

I shook my head. This was, without question, not the term I thought I'd hear on my first day as a journalist. An hour later, paperwork mercifully out of the way, I found myself sitting in Skimer's office awaiting my first assignment. The roller coaster of emotions I had been riding was moving back toward the high end. My horror at seeing the paper's offices had now given way to the same nervous excitement I had woken up with.

It was summer, and just the beginning of it, so I figured my duties on the education beat wouldn't quite hit yet. Maybe someone had been killed? A controversy at City Hall? Fuck you, law school!

I studied Skimer's office. It was one man's tribute to two things: journalism and war. The desk, the file cabinet, the book case – all were covered with newspaper sections in various stages of dismemberment. Looking at the walls, I gathered, and his apparent age supported the theory, that Skimer had fought in Vietnam. I recalled Skimer using war analogies in our initial conversations, and it occurred to me that he likely saw the daily battles of a newsroom through the eyes of a soldier.

Skimer strode in and sat down, barely breaking stride in the process. "Welcome to the Frisco Evening Outlook, son," he said.

"Thank you, sir."

"Okay kid, here's the deal," he said, getting right to the point, and who did that remind me of. "I'm sure you've spent your share of time in grocery stores. There's a grocery store in town that today is holding some promotional event for baggers, you know, the kids that stuff the groceries in those bags. Basically, if I understand it right, they're gonna have some contest to see which bagger can pack the most groceries into the most bags without dropping anything, breaking a bag, whatever. Again, we're not talking the Saturday Night Massacre here, okay? But I figured this would be a good way to get you up to speed before we take those training wheels off."

I was nodding, I was nodding, I was nodding. I was waiting for the punch line.

"That's all I know. Contest starts in a half hour. Lane here'll getcha directions. You'll need to tell our readers who won the contest and why. But this ain't big news, right? Give us some color. Give us some human interest! Force your readers to care. I can assure you, Mr. McDougal, school board meetings ain't fun. Especially when they're still going on at midnight on Tuesday night. So have fun with this one."

I got up to leave. Part of me was pleased at being handed something to cover on my first day. A larger part of me was back to being pissed.

"Not exactly what you were bargaining for, I gather?"

"I, uh, well, I'm just a little surprised I guess that you've got me covering that type of story. I mean, is that really, you know, news?"

"Well, lemme tell ya something, and let's all make sure we don't forget it. Yes, as we discussed education will be your priority, see. But you also will be responsible for helping on other stories as they come up. If a building's burning down or someone's been shot, put it this way: whoever's closest to me when I take the call needs to be ready to jump in their car. That's the way it is with us small papers. No fluff here. You don't have no dirt under your nails when you get here, you will in a hurry. Any problem with that?"

Yes, there was a problem with that. I swallowed hard.

"No, sir."

"Excellent news, my dear Mr. McDougal. And if a grocery bagger contest breaks out in one of our fine local establishments, well, the same principle applies then. Today, that principle finds you. Any problem with that?"

A smile began to emerge from Skimer's mouth.

"No, sir."

"Alright then. Let's go write some news stories, ok? And welcome to the Frisco Evening Outlook. We are, after all, your community newspaper!"

Skimer let go with the full smile now, and it was wide and gummy and toothy enough that he looked like a full-grown bengal tiger with the scampering hind quarters of yet another outclassed zebra in full view, and no competition in sight. Either that, or said full-grown bengal tiger just having dipsticked its claws into said zebra, dragged it to a skidding stop and devoured it like a roast beef on rye, a mouth moist, a quest successful, a need met, a stomach full.

Or, in this case, a little bit of both.

"Places everyone, please!"

I eyed the woman on the mike with barely concealed disdain. From the look of intensity on her face, this was the Games of the twentysomethingth freaking Olympiad.

The contestants stood at their respective posts, heads down, arms outstretched, fingers nervously wiggling with anticipation, hollow-eyed moray eels poised to strike at their prey from the darkened corridors of a jagged reef.

"Go!"

With that, a flurry of motion was unleashed. Behind each counter stood three young men, each looking to be about 17, each ganglier and more pimply-faced than the last. In front of each of them lay an identically arranged, technicolor smorgasbord of common household goods, ranging from forest green Haas avocados and stop sign-red cherry tomatoes to the traditionally metallic blue and silver, rectangular dispensers of Reynolds Wrap to the tall, sponge-yellow containers of Sun Light dishwater detergent, all the way to the more muted tones of 12-packs of Ozarka water and boxes of Cream of Wheat.

Theirs was a two-legged race. The first was the paper portion. The challenge was to place as many of the items before them into the numerous brown paper bags stacked perfectly flat before them, and to do so as quickly as possible without breaking or otherwise sabotaging their natural shape. The second was, of course, the plastic portion. The objective here was harder to discern.

I was watching, but only because I had to. I was taking notes, too. For the same reason.

What appeared to be a panel of judges stood in the concourse area between the counters and the exit, walking to and fro, surveying the scene. Every few seconds, they would look down and scribble something on a piece of white, legal-sized paper on the top of a clipboard.

"One minute, one minute!" shrieked the woman, and the way she was talking way too loudly into the mike I decided that, slightly graying hair and a rather plump midsection aside, she resembled a testosterone-permeated teenager guzzling his first beer.

The pace quickened. Once they completed all or at least part of their paper exercise, the contestants next began shoving heretofore gently handled pieces of fruit into clear plastic baggies. I almost managed an actual smile watching the middle contestant thoroughly unable to navigate any of his five baggies, those incredibly irritating ones you find in the produce section that refuse to open no matter which end you try by rubbing your thumb and forefinger in opposite directions.

"30 seconds! Let's go, guys!"

What was once controlled motion was quickly careening toward the spastic. Limbs flew in every direction. Animals violently thrust vegetables and minerals of all kinds into brown paper bags, now standing at full attention on each counter like overstuffed sacks of toys ready for transport on Santa's sleigh. The baggies, by comparison, sat strewn about on the counters in virtual heaps, each with a size and shape all their own, and because they were all so clear and malleable they looked like platoons of jellyfish washed ashore in a summer storm.

"10 seconds left!"

The audience, maybe two dozen strong, was screaming, clapping, waving hands over heads. I glanced over at them, not understanding for the life of me who could even begin to get this excited about something so, you know, like this. I quickly determined that at least half of the poor suckers were store employees, with the other half most likely friends and family members, and that I pitied them all.

"Time!"

With that, the clutching and the squeezing and the stuffing came to a screeching halt. The contestants each took a step back and tried to catch their breath. Contestant #1 lifted an arm to wipe his brow, revealing in the process a mezzaluna of perspiration oozing through his short sleeve, sky blue, button-down shirt. The audience converged on the counters to offer encouragement to their chosen contestants, and the judges shuffled into Aisle 6 to confer.

What I had just witnessed, in all of my exasperated disbelief, was the first, theoretically annual Tom Thumb Grocery Bagger Contest of Frisco, Texas. My disgust was not so much a result of the contest itself, which admittedly had included more action than I had predicted. Besides, I was still chuckling at the clear plastic baggies getting the best of Contestant #2. Misery loves company, I guess; my amusement was undeniably connected to my memory of the time I got so frustrated by one of those damn things that I actually got removed from a supermarket for screaming an obscenity while hucking a Gala apple at the lobster tank.

No, it was that covering the Tom Thumb Grocery Bagger Contest of Frisco, Texas was the featured "news" event of my first day as a reporter. Beyond asking myself what the hell kind of name for a supermarket chain was Tom Thumb, which I had never heard of growing up in Southern California, I had spent the entire time driving to the event spewing frustration. Was this the type of thing they had in mind for me? Was this what I had driven halfway across the country for? Was this what I had dreamed of, trained for and dreamed of some more, ever since the first time I heard the name Bob Woodward?

The judges were ready to unveil their decision. Contestant #3 had prevailed. The woman on the mike breathlessly announced the decision as if she were proclaiming that the Great State of Mizzurah had cast all of its votes for the NEXT PRESIDENT OF THE UNITED STATES. Contestant #3's family and friends approached, and I knew that it was now my turn to step in. I had scribbled a series of questions I knew I should ask, starting with something to the effect of, "How does it feel to have achieved local if not national or even international supermarket industry immortality?" Oh, I figured I would at least try to be nice, though I doubted I could ignore the temptation to go with the "Paper or plastic?" one that I had continued to sarcastically mumble to myself throughout the morning.

I gathered my manners and approached the winner.

"Hi, Marshall McDougal with the Evening Outlook," I said, extending my hand. "Mind if I ask you a few questions?"

I was being nice. And I even tried to look interested. Not an easy thing to do when you're busy scoffing inside.

Thirty minutes later I walked out of the Tom Thumb and looked around the strip mall in which I had been imprisoned for much of the morning. I had been surrounded by food for the last 90 minutes, but for the first time all day I was hungry. It was almost lunchtime, and now that I was finally free to do so, it was time to get the taste of the grocery bagger contest out of my mouth.

The local choices I had noticed on my initial drive up Preston Road the night before had left my palette yawning. In fact, upon entering Frisco, I felt like I had entered Chain Restaurant Central. IHOP. Red Lobster. Applebees. Schlotsky's.

In short, culinary boredom.

The strip mall was checkered with businesses offering everything ranging from pool supplies to dry cleaning to orthodontics services to home loans. They all featured a red, faux brick façade, a nice try by the developers to attach a homestyle touch while masking the fact that the proliferation of such elements were threatening to turn 21st-century America into a giant 7/11.

A storefront on the left caught my eye. Scotty P's, the place was called. It was a burger joint, and it looked like a true burger joint, which at this point was cause for true celebration. A quick scan of the menu revealed a problem, albeit a good one. I was so hungry, I could envision myself ordering – and actually consuming – each of the 17 burgers, hot dogs or sandwiches seeking my affection. Just when I thought I couldn't make up my mind, I went with the Warren Burger: a 1/3-pound slab of fresh ground chuck, covered with supposedly tangy barbeque sauce, mayo, pickles and cheese. A side of Cardiac Fries and a large, make-it-yourself soda rounded out my order.

I staked out a spot at one of the few empty booths. I glanced at the black-and-white photo on the wall beside me. It was a photo of a storefront, with the caption entitled, "Foncine General Store, c. 1920." I glanced at the next closest wall; they, too, revealed touches of Frisco's past. The Curtsinger Drug Store, c.1923. The Sapp Café, c.1923. Main Street Frisco, c.1915.

In short, civic boredom.

But Scotty P's seemed different. It had been established in 1967 by whoever the Pontikes Brothers were, how many of them there were I couldn't tell, and not only were they cooking burgers, they were also offering something called Tommy P's Ice Cream Shakes. "No one knows ice cream better than our brother Tom. Try chocolate, strawberry, vanilla or oreo cookie," read the teaser, and I was already starting to believe. I noted the black and white tiles on the ceiling, counted the eight black ceiling fans I assumed were there to help provide relief throughout the summer months. I counted the 15 black leather booths and brown formica tables in front of them. Two TVs hung from the corners, four neon beer signs adorned the walls. I nodded in appreciation at the do-it-yourself soda machine and Iced Tea area, and I was flummoxed by the fact that you were free to retrieve your own clear plastic forks and knives, but you had to ask for a spoon.

Just enough time for a quick stop in the restroom. Here I found perhaps Scotty P's best feature of all: the TV. It's one thing to post the day's sports page so men visiting the urinal can read while they do their business. It's an entirely different thing to provide a TV in the men's room. Even better, since the door could be locked behind you, you could sit there for as long as you wanted and watch sports in complete privacy and, at the least, relative peace. Maybe this town had something of value to offer after all.

The burger itself. Perfection. Forty-five minutes later, after filling up one last time on Dr. Pepper, I stumbled outside. On the way back to the car, I realized I had passed a Hong Kong Express on my robotic march toward Scotty P's. I liked Chinese food, but given the fact that I had just consumed enough Cardiac Fries to induce cardiac arrest, the sight of the place made me turn away. A minute later, sweating both from the heat and from the pint of cholesterol I had just cocktailed into my bloodstream, I weebled into my car and pulled out of the strip mall.

Back at the newsroom now. Time to settle in with my first story, no matter what I really thought of it.

"Just in time for lunch, kid," Skimer said as I walked in, and after the morning speech I was surprised to see him respond to my presence so positively.

I didn't have the wherewithal to tell him I had already taken the liberty of eating. Maybe I had broken some sort of unwritten rule about lunch. Which would be a pretty stupid rule given that I didn't know anyone. And had been starving.

I looked at my watch: 12:45. When was I going to get to my story? My spirits sagged; my stomach followed suit. Skimer motioned toward a couple of colleagues to follow, and we all filed toward the door.

"Team, let me introduce you to Marshall McDougal here, our new education reporter. Marshall here's a big college boy, right outta school. And believe it or not all the way from California. So y'alls be nice to him, okay now?"

"Marshall, Chris Short," said a portly, black-haired, black-bearded man from behind a pair of Coke bottle glasses. He extended his hand. "I'm the sports guy around here. Not like all you serious news types. Live and breathe sports, except for when Rip here makes me cover the cop beat."

"Sounds interesting."

"Yeah. Means I gotta show up at 6 in the morning and do the

rounds to look at the logs. See if anybody killed anybody overnight, basically. Can't stand that. Way too early."

"Nice to meet you, Chris," I said. "Love sports. Could talk about it all day."

I was relieved. Short seemed like a regular guy.

"Well, I'm sure there will be lots of time for that," Short said. "California, huh? What part?"

"L.A. Huge Dodger fan. Chavez Ravine's a second home."

"Beautiful stadium, so I hear. We'll have to get you out to The Ballpark here. You know, where the Rangers play."

"Yeah, I think I passed The Ballpark. Arlington's pretty far out there, though. Drove through yesterday on the way into town."

"Yeah, but we don't care much as long as we've got our Trailblazers."

"Who?"

"Okay, enough you two," Skimer interrupted. "Geez, enough about sports, unless of course you're talking about the 'Boys."

Skimer motioned the group over to his Jeep Cherokee, which as far as I could tell through its screen of grime was white. "Football's the only game in town here as far as I'm concerned. Let's eat."

"Hey Rip, when's the last time the Cowboys had a winning season?" asked Short, buckling his seatbelt in the back seat. He flashed me a sly smile.

So that's what Skimer meant by the 'Boys.

"How 'bout them Blazers?!" Skimer said, saluting Short's effort.

"Okay, enough about sports already," said the woman in the front seat, peering around the front passenger seat. "Hi Marshall, I'm Tanya Costin," she said. "I'm the Evening Outlook's community editor. Y'alright?"

"I'm sorry?"

"It's so very nice to meet you."

A double-take was not enough. Her eyelids were marinating in periwinkle powder, the margins of which extended far enough outside her eyes to umbrella the deep wrinkles beside them like a porte cochere over a driveway. She was offering what appeared to be a friendly smile, and maybe I was just too jaundiced from the environs of Los Angeles but its key components, with the size and whiteness of the teeth overpowering the reed-like lips, almost made it seem too big, too wide, too friendly. No one, without wanting something, smiled that fully. But what really struck me was her hair, raven black, so black it was almost purple, and since it was backcombed into a nest of aquanet spray, it seemed disproportionately large in its circumference to that of her head.

"Hi Tanya, nice to meet you," I replied. I was trying hard to relax my stare. "You not a sports fan?"

"Oh, it's Tanya."

"I'm sorry?"

"Tanya, honey. Like Stan, but with an 'uh'. Like Stan. Rhymes with Stan. You know."

I had known a couple of Tanyas in my time, and neither of them pronounced their name to rhyme with Stan.

"Hello...Tanya."

Costin just kept moving. "When it comes time for football season, I'm as big a Cowboys fan as anyone, even Rip here. I've had me a real hoot out there at a couple of those games."

Skimer chortled and kept driving. "McDougal, you never had a burger in Texas, you're gonna start now."

He wheeled the Jeep into the parking lot of the Frisco Plaza. "Welcome to Scotty P's, McDougal," Skimer said, slowly angling his frame through his door like a slithering tuna. "Best damn burger in all of Texas, and it's right here in Frisco."

"Actually, I've—"

"Burger's up to you, but I highly suggest the Cardiac Fries," Skimer bellowed. He entered the restaurant with the air of a man walking into his own home. "You too much of a California boy, well, last time I checked we don't have much sushi here. Burgers and dogs. Not much in between."

I bit down on the inside of my lip. I had a feeling I was going to get to know the Scotty P's menu quite well. I was also beginning to get the picture that being The Lone Californian Lost in Texas had both disadvantages and advantages. The former seemed plentiful. The latter, I was still waiting to see one emerge.

"I'll take a Warren Burger, Cardiac Fries and a soda," I said.

"Nicely played," Short said. "You should try Dr. Pepper. You'll get to like it here real fast. National drink of Texas."

Chalk one up for the advantages. "Oh, I've had it a coupla times before."

"Cool. You should try the sauce then. They got their own barbeque sauce. Cooking. Baking. Just dipping. Awesome good."

"So what brought you to Texas?" Costin asked in mid-bite.

"Journalism," I said without hesitation. "I've wanted to be a journalist for as long as I can remember."

"A noble profession, in my mind."

"Well, I think it is."

"Oh, it is. I agree. It's not an easy one, though."

"I'm sure you're right. I suspect I'm just going to have to learn that for myself."

"You will, Marshall. An old editor of mine told me something about journalism I never forgot: it's like the graduate school of life. You learn how everything works, from the police to schools to the government. Everything. And you learn it all up close and personal, with a responsibility to educate the public about it. If you want to teach other people about something, you have to know it really well yourself."

"And just when I thought I was finally done with school," I said, grateful for the chance to stare at Costin's hair. "But the main thing I want to do is write."

"Do plenty of that," Skimer piped in. The cinnamon was spewing ketchup. "Do even more reporting."

"I admit it's the writing that first attracted me to this. I could write all day."

"Now what does daddy do?" Costin asked. "I suppose he's a writer? He write for one of those shows out there?"

"My father? Oh, he's a lawyer."

Skimer could barely contain himself. "Pops is a lawyer, huh? And son didn't wanna follow in his footsteps? Hate to break it to ya, but you'd make a lot more money as a lawyer than you ever will doing this."

"Well, my head tells me the same thing. I just couldn't do it. My grandfather was a lawyer, too, and my dad took over my grandfather's practice. I suppose I could still go to law school someday, but I can't imagine not writing for a living."

"And the reporting part?"

"That'll come, I really believe that. I really enjoyed interviewing everyone at the market this morning." I was lying through my ground chuck-laced teeth.

"Difference is, they were happy you were there," Skimer countered. "Things'll change when you're dealing with the school board."

"Do they not want coverage?"

"They want coverage as long as it's their coverage. You're writing good things about 'em, they're your best friend. You're not, they're your biggest enemy."

"I'm not trying to make any enemies."

"They'll be plenty of times you'll be their enemy. Part of the job," Skimer continued. "All we ask as a news team is, you're fair and objective. They don't like that, they can pound sand."

"Hey Rip, you had a chance to talk with Marshall about the, well, you know. The Coon thing?"

It was Short. I tensed up. Please – please – tell me I do not have to get involved in anything having anything to do with whoever or whatever the hell the Frisco Coons are. The taunting raccoon popped back into my head.

Welcome to Frisco, Texas, Marshall McDougal.

"Haven't had a chance yet," Skimer said. "Tell ya what kid, let's you get your grocery bagger story written today and a good night's sleep under your belt tonight. We'll talk about the Coons tomorrow."

"Sounds good, Mr. Skimer."

"My father was Mr. Skimer. Call me Rip."

"Uh, okay Rip," I said uneasily. I had finished nearly all of my second Warren Burger of the day, though I had succeeded in getting by on only a few Cardiac fries. "Thanks for lunch."

"Yep, time to get back," Skimer pronounced to the crew. "Let's go write some news stories."

"Rip, there's a school board meeting next week," Costin interrupted. "We really should brief Marshall on all that. You know, the issues?"

"Issues?!" Short cut in, barely able to contain himself. He let out the type of laugh only someone who was paid to write about sports could let out. "Yeah, I'd say they have some issues over there."

"Alright then," Skimer said. "New day tomorrow. We better get back to the ranch or some real news'll happen. Hell, another grocery bagger contest may break out."

We walked outside. "Welcome to Texas, McDougal," Skimer said. "By the way, hope ya like heat, 'cause summer starts this week. Real cooker out here. Should be north of 95 the next three, four months. Sure you're up for this, right?"

"Yes, sir."

"How's it going, McDougal."

It was 5:00. Outside of two trips to the bathroom, each of which had required the execution of a number two, the swell of my innards reminding me of my new personal single lunchtime record for fat gram consumption, I had been working on my story all afternoon.

All the while, I kept reminding myself of two things. One, no matter my belief to the contrary, the paper considered this story actual news. So I had to stay focused, bring the story out. Two, treat the story as it was: a lighthearted feature story. The last thing I wanted to do was overdo it or I might be on my way toward a long career of writing obits. And I wasn't here to write obits. Not in The Plan.

"I've got 'til 6, right?"

My eyes and tone were cohabitating, panic the welcome mat.

Skimer chuckled. "Yes, you got 'til 6."

Six o'clock was later than your average daily newspaper deadline, which was usually more like 5, Skimer explained as he walked off, because the Evening Outlook – as the name suggested – was an evening paper. While copies were made available on news racks in the morning, subscribers did not receive the paper until late afternoon.

"Let's not try and cut it too close, okay now?"

"Okay."

I kept at it. At five minutes to 6, I pressed send.

Twenty minutes later, I pretended I didn't see him coming. "Well, not bad, kid, for your first time out," Skimer said. "C'mon over here to the copy desk and let's have a run at it."

I was confused.

"Not bad?" I asked no one in particular.

"Pull up a chair, kid. Marshall, right? Jan Bennie. Nice to meet you."

"Hi Jan. How does it look?"

"Well, I'm the copy editor, which means two things. One, I'm your best friend. Two, I'm your worst enemy."

Bennie peered up at me from over her dark brown bifocals. She was diminutive, with her sandy blond hair tied up in a bow, the top of which sprouted like a dragon tree. Her eyes were bright green, linx-like in their gaze. Under them were chalky gray pouches, veterans of one too many dangling participles.

"Anyway from the looks of things so far, I'm closer to being your enemy on this one."

For someone who had never before had a true enemy, I was starting to think I might soon be gaining more than my share.

"Mr. Skimer said it looked pretty good though, right?"

"If I heard him right I think he said it wasn't bad. That means he thinks there's something there to work with. And he's gonna give you the benefit of the doubt while you're still so new. Let's start with the lede, which by the way we spell—"

"I know. 'Lede' as a way to distinguish it from the regular 'lead' in editing."

"Okay fine, so you've got all the answers. But here's the real question you need to answer: what's the single most important thing you want to say to your readers? What is the one thing, the one thought that you took away from this event that you think your readers need to know? Well, let me back up. This is hardly need-to-know stuff. This is a feature story, and even that's a bit of an overstatement."

I was crushed. I had written and re-written my lede at least 20 times before I turned it in. I loved my lede, however the ratfuckers spelled it.

"It was a contest, so I thought the readers would first want to know who won."

"Well, normally I would agree with you. If this was about the Frisco High football game, yes, the readers want to know who won. If it was against Plano West, they'd want to know by how much. But that's big, important stuff around here. This was a promotional event at a grocery store. So you gotta be a bit more, you know. Creative, right? Grab that chair and let's work through it."

Her quick dart up to the clock told me she meant business. We sat together and worked on the lede for several minutes. The pace, the process, was frenetic. She would type in a few words, I would react. She would type in a few more, I would react. Over and over, until she was finally comfortable. I was learning, literally, on the job. When we were done, as much as I hated to admit it the story was stronger than before.

"Rip, can you take a look?"

I noticed Bennie called Skimer by his first name. He sauntered over.

"Alright, guys, whatcha got?"

Skimer peered over Bennie's shoulder.

"Like it. Much better. Not there yet. Keep at it. Keep at it."

We did, for 30 minutes more. Final deadline was fast approaching. Bennie's eyes were like a reflection on a wall from a wristwatch based on the movements of one's arm, darting this way and that, from the screen to the clock and back again, up and down, from side to side, from this angle to that. With less than five minutes to spare, we were done.

"Congratulations Marshall. Your first story's in the bag."

"Does Mr. Skimer not look at it again?"

"Well yeah he does. But he doesn't get too worried about the details if he knows we nailed it. The essence, I mean. What's the essence of the story? It's like I was saying earlier. Don't worry, you'll learn. In the meantime, I need to be the enemy."

"I understand. I think the story reads well."

Bennie didn't buy a word of it. "Believe me, it's not easy to watch someone else take over your copy. I know that."

"It's not easy, no."

"Just wait 'til you get your hands on a real news story, then we'll really have some fun. In the meantime, picayune. You'll get used to it."

"The annual grocery store bagging contest isn't the pinnacle, then?"

Bennie smiled at my sarcasm. "Cool the jets, Marshall. You'll get there. You just gotta bear with us first."

I looked at my watch: 6:57. Not only had I started my first day as a journalist, I had been assigned a story, reported on it and written it. Now my story had survived copy editing and was on its way to the presses. Never mind that a good two-thirds of my words had been changed. The story was going to appear in the next day's paper. And it was going to appear with my byline.

"Aren't we past deadline?" I asked Bennie as I headed toward the door.

"Yes, we are," she said. "Normally, we can't go this late on a story, unless it's a big one. Features should be in the can earlier in the day. But that's alright. Your first day."

My first day. Never again would I hear this. Time to reward my ass with its rightful place on my couch.

"Well you must be the one and only Marshall McDougal."

"Uh, yes?"

"From Circulation. Sammy Breaux. French spelling. Friends call me Sammy. Pleasure's mine."

I glanced at my car. The man was standing between the driver's door and me. It was clear I was going to have to deal with him before being able to drive off.

"Um, hello, Sammy," I said, stammering. "Did we meet today? I'm sorry, but I don't—"

"No, I don't believe we've had the opportunity, young man."

I gathered myself and studied him. He looked to be in his mid-30s and was tall, probably a good 6'3". His hair was dirty blond, actively receding before its time, and his attempt to make up for it with pretend muttonchops hadn't worked. His upper back and shoulders arched slightly forward, making his already lanky arms appear even longer.

"So what do I owe this pleasure to?" I wondered aloud. "I'd like to get in my car, if that's okay. Long day."

"Oh, no problem, no problem at all, Mister Marshall," Sammy said, moving to his left. "I just wanted to be sure to take the time to properly introduce myself."

"Nice to meet you, Sammy. You said you're in Circulation?"

"Yes sir. You reporting stars don't see us much. We're just the dumb guys out back. Then again, we don't do our jobs right, our Evening Outlook readers don't read all those fancy words you've all been writing up in the newsroom, right?"

I wasn't sure how to react.

"I suppose so."

"You know, back in Louisiana, if someone don't laugh at your jokes, well. I might just be offended."

"Is that where you're from?"

"Yeah, Lake Providence is in Louisiana, way up north up there in the corner. Might as well be in Mississippi, is what I like to say. Love my Rajun Cajuns, but fact is, I could get going real good on a Hotty Toddy. You know that Hotty Toddy song, Mister Marshall? All y'alls probably don't sing that one much out there in California."

"How do you know I'm from California?"

"Blue bird, Mister Marshall, blue bird. Fact is, lotta those around here, you might say. Tell ya what. You start writing up some of those fancy words, I'll make sure to get them to our fine readers. Ok? 'Course, before I do, I'll be sure to read what you're writing. New guy in town, we gotta be sure about ya first."

"Sure about what I write?"

"Just pulling your chain there, young Marshall. Pulling your chain. Gonna go back there now and get those papers ready. Speaking of chains, remember us Dispatch guys. Last part of the chain. Call ourselves the Chain Gang out back. Gotta get back to the gang."

Back at my apartment, I was essentially inanimate. Was every day like this? Would I be assigned a new story tomorrow? Was I expected to publish a new story every day? Would my copy be better received next time?

I had stopped for a slice of pizza on the way home. As I flipped on ESPN for the Dodger game, and despite the fact that I had already consumed not one but two large cheeseburgers for lunch, I declared it to be fact that the pizza I was eating was the greatest ever.

What? No Dodger game at 7:30? With the time difference, the game was not due to start until 9:30 Texas time. That was going to take some getting used to, especially since it meant the games would often end, local time at least, past midnight.

Welcome to Frisco, Texas, Marshall McDougal.

An hour later, long since nodded off, I jerked up from the couch and looked around.

The apartment was shaking. Did they even have earthquakes in Texas? Just my luck, I thought. I elude the reach of the San Andreas Fault for the first time, and I still end up in the midst of The Big One.

There was the sound of a whistle. I knew instantly it was that of a train, and I bounded to the window and peered outside. There it was, having seemingly arrived from nowhere, rushing by to the northwest. Its profile was long and dark and narrow, and it cut through the fields like a submarine slowly but purposefully making its way through the depths of a murky sea.

As the train passed and the shaking subsided, I watched the train rumble its way further into the darkness. Even when I could no longer see it, I could still hear the unmistakable drumbeat of the tracks as it pushed forward through the night.

Clackety clack, clackety clack.

I laid my head back down, the steady haunt of the rumble still in my head, and stared blankly ahead.

Clackety clack, clackety clack.

The baptism of a cub reporter was complete.

"A good remuda held five or six horses for each cowboy, it was each hand's responsibility to see that one of his mounts was saddled at all times to deal with stampedes..." – The Trail Driver by Hunter

Southwest corner of Parkwood and Warren,
in front of an apartment complex

CHAPTER THREE

TIME TO WRITE SOME NEWS STORIES

I wasn't sure of the medical definition of having crossed the line from heavy breathing to hyperventilating, but I was fairly sure I had done so. Not that that bothered me. It just made me drive faster.

I was about to buy a newspaper, something I had done many times before. Something people, even if their numbers continued to decrease on an annual basis, do millions of times each day. The difference in my case: the newspaper I was going to buy today was going to have a story in it that I wrote. Even better, that newspaper was going to have a story in it that I wrote – with my name on it.

I figured I could just pick up a free copy of the paper at the office. After all, I did work at the paper. But I wanted to see the fruits of my labor by myself. No one else, other than maybe Woodward in spirit, had been with me every step of the way on my journey to this moment. I had to do this my way. Besides, if I wasn't pleased with what I saw,

I didn't want Skimer to see my disappointment. He was to be my Bradlee. He had hired me, given me a chance for a byline on my first day on the job. The fact that it was to be associated with a story on a grocery-bagging contest was, I had rationalized, but an asterisk.

Where to get a paper? I realized I had no idea where a news rack might be. What happens when you're all dressed for your 15 Minutes of Fame, but have nowhere to go?

Pulling up to the light at Preston and Warren, I noticed a Starbucks on my right. I was very likely the last remaining human being over the age of 10 who had never, not even once, been to one. That was quite a feat on my part; I had, to date at least, resisted out of a sheer and utter distaste for coffee. I had tried a sip of a friend's cup once and sworn the stuff off on the spot. And I had for years now worn this anti-coffee stance on my sleeve. What I had never sworn off was sugar. So it didn't take me long to pull into the driveway anyway, because I had also noticed, right next door to the drive-through Starbucks, a drive-though Krispy Kreme. As I prepared to enter the drive-through Starbucks lane, I was confronted with a shocking sight: a line of cars not just in the drive-through Krispy Kreme line, but winding through the larger parking lot enveloping it.

I lost count at 20 cars. I liked donuts as much as the next guy. But I had never had a donut from Krispy Kreme, not having seen any in Southern California, so I decided to go to Plan B and make my way inside. Maybe they had a news rack in there, went my logic, the light from the red neon "Hot Now" sign in the window in my eyes, siphoning whatever was left of my willpower.

What I encountered was not a donut shop, but a fun zone. The line inside wound throughout the store. Wedged between the line and the window into the plant where the donuts were being manufactured with Six Sigma precision was a raised area roughly two feet high upon which the eager could perch themselves for a bird's eye view of the process. And what a process it was. From right to left on your radio dial, the donuts – still sugar-free at this point – were moving slowly, roughly eight across, on a conveyer belt-like, silver metal grid. At a certain point the donuts passed under a Niagara Falls of sucrose descending down upon them, transforming them all at once from round mounds of dough into round rings of pure, white sugar. Round rings of pure, white sugar with sheets of glaze draped over them like fluffy comforters, the shards dangling precariously from the sides like would-be icicles dripping from rooftops before they could fully form.

I got in line. They didn't seem that big, after all. And it was a big day. Who's to tell the next Pulitzer Prize winner he shouldn't indulge himself in celebrating his first byline? Besides, these may be the steamiest, the drippiest, the creamiest, donuts ever, but I was planning to down them with milk, and non-fat milk to boot.

I ordered one. Or maybe it was a box of six. I don't recall. Driven by a mixture of nervous energy and the power of the most legally addictive breakfast ever, I continued inhaling as I crossed the longest drive-through line in retail history on foot and walked into Starbucks next door.

Time to meet my destiny. I checked out the newspaper selection. On top was The New York Times; on the next rung down, The Dallas Morning News; on the next one down, the Plano Star Courier. Not an Evening Outlook in sight. I inquired with the attractive though greasy and over-earring'd girl behind the counter. Nope, they didn't carry the Evening Outlook. I slumped, an anemic polar bear, the pond frozen over before I could fetch my last seal for the winter.

But I was, at least in the short-term, still physically buoyed by my sugar high. So I decided to just drive toward the office until I noticed a news rack on the sidewalk along the way. Driving north on Preston Road toward Main Street, I saw a row of them up ahead. I veered into the parking lot, only to notice that the news racks were in front of no less than the very same "Donut" shop I had first encountered the day before. Even in the haze of the adrenalin-and-triglyceride cocktail in which I was currently fermenting, the irony was not lost upon me. In the donut world, I had just ridden the Matterhorn at Disneyland; I was now standing next to one of those purple and green horses outside the corner drug store. But I no longer cared about donuts; I could see that the news racks included one for the Frisco Evening Outlook, and that it had several papers inside.

I fumbled erratically for a stray quarter in the ashtray-turned-bank in my Tercel, a trembly teenager trying to unhook his first bra. Catapulting myself from the driver's seat, I strode up to the news rack and, all in one motion, inserted the quarter while opening the door. Out came an Evening Outlook. I was overcome at the mere sight of it. My eyes darted at the headline on the front page, then lasered throughout the page like a flashlight in the dark. Nothing.

Defeat? Never! I flipped the paper open, looking at page two. A quick glance produced more nothing. I wasn't actually reading anything now. I was in a hallucinogenic state, like a shark that can't really see much in front of it with any detail but smells a bloody morsel nearby.

Flip.

Fling.

Flip.

Fling.

Flipflingflipflingflipflingflipfling.

Several pages in, I gave up, literally tossing the front section on the ground. All of a sudden, staring up at me from the dirt lot, there it was. On the front section of page two, the "Community" section itself. My body tensed up. I glanced at the headline. Things were starting to slow down now. *Grocery Store Baggers Show Their Stuff.* My eyes moved slightly downward.

And there it was.

No.

There I was.

By Marshall McDougal.

Marshall McDougal himself stood and stared. And he was overcome. Tears started flowing from my eyes. I wasn't smiling. My mouth was open, stuck in a frozen, elongated, hanging position, like someone in mid-stroke.

I was swathed in victory. Damn the doubters to hell. There it was, black and white and read all over, and no one could ever take it away from me. As of today, I was a published author. In the family of journalists, I was a made man.

And so there I stood, Marshall McDougal, of Los Angeles,

California, white male, 22 years of age, on the sidewalk in front of the one and only "Donut" shop in Frisco, Texas, glaze encrusting my upper lip, my mouth still in mid-stroke, at 7:48 on an otherwise-just-another Tuesday morning. I was a young man who had just achieved a lifelong dream. I was, for just this one moment, a giant.

I looked up. The achievement of my dream had played out in full view of tens of cars as they passed me on the street. The only problem being, I wished there were more.

The cat that ate the canary? A poor man's steak dinner compared to the full stomach of satisfaction I walked into the newsroom with.

"Good story, McDougal," Skimer said. "Not bad for your first day. Good story."

"Thanks Rip, I—"

"Ending could have been better. No matter. Had to cut it anyway. Good story though."

I had been so excited about the story making the cover of the Community section, I hadn't yet gotten to the jump page. I sat down at my desk and started scanning with the intensity of a cost accountant looking for the error in a spreadsheet. Everything looked exactly the same way it did last time I saw it. I moved to the jump page. All of a sudden, I realized what Skimer was referring to. The last four paragraphs of my story had been cut. And because of that, the story had ended awkwardly. I had told a story, and now the ending to the story hadn't even made it.

"Morning, kid," Bennie said. "Good story. Whaddya think?"

"Well," I said, trying to form the right words. "It looks great. I'm really pleased with the placement."

I was trying to bite my tongue; the tongue was winning.

Bennie shook her head.

"Marshall? Problem?"

I looked around.

"Alright. Did the story really have to be cut like that? What about the stuff at the end? That was a good ending."

"Okay, now I get it. Your first time out. You know, it's pretty rare that an entire story, at least a feature story like that, makes it all the way to the end assuming we're short on space. Just remember what we talked about yesterday. Your lede is that one thing that, if you had 10 seconds to tell people what you want to tell them, you would scream from the rooftops. Everything else is second place. It's the roux. Thickens it."

"But what if your ending rounds the story out?"

"It shouldn't. No offense, but it's not a book report. You grab 'em in the beginning as opposed to building things up for the ending. Not that every word doesn't serve a purpose, because it does. Or at least it does in a perfect world, which reporting is anything but. It's just that you need to know that oftentimes space dictates things."

"Is that always the case?" I was calming down now. The sugar crash was not far off.

"Not always. But ads sell papers and pay us, not editorial. If the ads are there, sometimes we get squeezed. That's okay. Just part of the game. Don't worry about it."

An hour later, I was at my desk, just beginning to read up on Frisco history. With my first byline now part of that history, I was about to earn another, albeit far different, stripe.

"Truck's here," someone yelled from the back, and the stampede was on.

"Is it 9:30 already?" Bennie asked no one in particular.

"Where's everyone going?" I asked, and no one heard a word I said. Skimer wandered by. "Coffee truck. Comes every day at 9:30. Evening Outlook tradition. We don't pay much, and the work environment's fair to Midland, Texas. Make up for it with the coffee truck. C'mon, McDougal. Lemme show ya."

"Thanks Mr. Ski—. Uh, thanks, Rip. I must have been filling out paperwork yesterday morning when the truck came."

"Well, then consider today your second first day as the new reporter on the block," Skimer said. We walked briskly past the editors' area and periodical library along the back of the newsroom toward the side exit.

The scene before me was one surely being repeated outside of office buildings across the country. The truck parked in the side lot of the building was your average roach coach, the prototypical white truck with the silver aluminum top that rolls up to reveal the various and sundry pre-packaged weapons of mass preserved starch, sugar and chemicals better left unleashed. A virtual herd of reporters, editors, salespeople, administrative assistants and the like were lining up, their feet gradually inching forward, one by one filling their Styrofoam cups, on one hand human, purposeful, on the other, the silent trudge of the caribou across the tundra. To me they might just as well have been a family of piglets suckling up to the pink underbelly of their bulbous mother at the County Fair for all to see. Their actions were that rote, that automatic, they were like a herd of cows drifting its way through the day, the only difference being the lack of freely exposed genitalia and/or stringy tails swatting at the day.

"First cup of coffee as a reporter's on me," Skimer said, putting his arm around my shoulder.

"Thanks Rip. I'll take a pass on the coffee, but maybe I'll grab some juice."

Skimer was amused. "No coffee? All ya'lls get a load of this. McDougal here says he's not a coffee drinker."

"Good one, Marshall," Bennie said, and for the first time I actually saw her smile. I wasn't sure she knew how, and upon my first glimpse of the totem poles of dried rubber cement between her teeth I wished she hadn't.

Costin couldn't keep it in. "Marshall, you mean you don't want coffee? I mean...really? I mean, what a shame."

Her tone was one of hushed concern, that not drinking the coffee would somehow inhibit me from, well, I wasn't sure what.

"Oh, that'll change real quick," said a middle-aged man with blue, owl-style glasses approaching me. He was tall and thin to the point of being sinewy, and his graying and curly hair protruded from the sides of his head like they had been shot sideways out of his ears.

"Hi, Marshall, Ted Meesbruggan. Business editor. Good story today. Good story."

"Thanks Ted. I never expected to publish a story on my first day."

"Fair assumption, but that's the fun of this place. On any given day, well, you know."

He called out to Short, who was now in full waddle in my direction.

"So, not a coffee drinker, huh?" he said, laughing. "Tell ya what, Marshall. I said the same thing when I first started. Always hated the stuff. Seemed like brown water to me, nothing more. But the truck started calling me."

"The truck started calling you?!" I shot back, laughing.

"Well, we're not talking Son of Sam here. But it was calling me. You know."

"To drink brown water?"

"Yeah, basically," Short said. He took a long swig. "Good shit."

Meesbruggan was seeing where the conversation was going.

"The thing is, it's not so much about the coffee," he said. "It's about the coffee break."

Short leaned in, lowering his voice for effect. "Mees is right. I told Ted, there's just something about the morning coffee truck. No matter what kind of mood I'm in when I get here, when the truck comes it's like the day is finally starting. It's really our best chance to all take a deep breath as a team and talk up the day. Hell, I probably find out more about the Blazers out here than I do by covering the damn games. The coffee, it's the rallying point."

"Short, I trained ya well," Skimer said, re-filling his cup. "This coffee's downright awful. But I love it anyway. The daily holy water. Ain't no journalist I know who hasn't stared down the meanest deadline without it by his side."

Despite the fact I had not only been up for several hours now but also in fact had been inside a Starbuck's already that day, in a sense I was just starting to wake up and smell the coffee. I didn't want to be confused with someone not wanting to be part of the group. If this is what reporters did every day at 9:30, this must be what I should do every day at 9:30. I reached for the cup. Filled it up half way. Put it up to my mouth.

Petrol. Short must have thought this was about the funniest thing he had ever seen. "Try some creamer, man."

I reached for the creamer. I knew I had gone too far as soon as I poured it in the cup. What I was now staring down at was a pool of water that was more eggshell than brown.

"The last time I saw this much experimentation I was in high school chemistry," Skimer announced. "Whatcha got there son, some sorta beaker?!"

I had been vaguely aware that Skimer was standing nearby, but I was still startled by the proclamation. A little more actual coffee would make it just right. A couple more sips later, I found myself back at the truck, looking for more. I was like a sleepwalker wandering the premises under the cover of a self-induced darkness. I had no idea how I had ended up back there – but there the spigot hung, mocking me, a vertical steel temptress, buttoning one less button on its blouse than it should, daring me to forego its powers.

"Short, we're gonna have to start cutting the kid off," Skimer said, cackling. "Yep, that coffee's bad stuff, huh?! Good stuff. Good stuff."

I could only laugh. I was learning to, well, go with the flow.

"Time to talk about the Frisco Coons," Skimer said. "C'mon in and I'll give you the rundown."

Five minutes later, I was ready for my de-briefing. "Okay, so here's the deal," Skimer said, leaning back in his chair. "First, understand a bit about Frisco. Town's full of good people, you know? Folks here don't have a lot of mean bones. What they do like though is tradition, and tradition says Frisco High goes by the Fighting Coons. Now, their real name is the Raccoons, the Fighting Raccoons I guess. But bottom line, they're the Coons. Simple as that."

"But don't they see that some people wouldn't like the name?"

"Well, that's the rub, see. There's a grudging feeling the nickname's a problem. Actually, more than that. I think people do get it deep down, and they get it more and more all the time. What's changing is that Frisco's changing, and that's ramped up the pressure to get rid of it."

"Place doesn't look like it's changed much."

"You just got here. I'm here to tell ya, the Frisco of today ain't the Frisco of 30 years ago, of 20 years ago. Hell, of 10 years ago. Just ain't. Heck, the Frisco of today ain't the same Frisco as five years ago."

"So, the population is increasing, and the people moving to town have a problem with the name?"

"Yes, it's that. Most of the folks moving into town are not from

47

town. What I mean is, they're moving here from elsewhere. So they don't understand the damn nickname's been around forever. They don't understand people who grew up here, who've been here for awhile, a long while, they're used to it. Don't mean anything bad by it.

"They don't have roots here, is the thing. And I'm thinking that's not good or bad. I think it's good, 'cause it means the town is growing and guess what – for us, it just means more to write about. Which to me is about job security. It's only bad for the folks trying to hold on to the smaller town feeling of what Frisco's always been about."

"And this is something the school board is discussing?"

"That's where you come in, McDougal. School board's discussing it, you bet. Everything's really heating up, to the point where you've got folks debating it at meetings, writing us letters about it. The whole deal. School board's scheduled to vote on it, as soon as this school year."

Skimer sat forward and took a gulp of coffee.

"What I need you to do, son, is be all over this. May not seem like much to you. But here in Frisco, this whole Coon thing's a big deal. What I need you to do is get to know the issue. Get to know both sides of it. Get to know what folks in town think. They're the ones who've gotta live with this thing."

I was wanting to ask a question I wasn't sure I should ask.

"So why me? Why would you bring in someone from straight out of college to get in the middle of this? I'm flattered, I must say. I just hope I can do the story, you know. Justice."

"Good question, McDougal. Good, fair question. Reason I wanna throw you to the coyotes on this one is, well, two things. One, I believe in trial by fire. No sense in us babying ya too much. At a certain point, you're gonna have to sink or swim in this business. I did. So did everyone in that newsroom."

"And the second reason?"

"You're young, kid," Skimer said. "They won't open up as much to the others here. We're all a little too familiar. Best way to put it I can think of."

"Okay, but what about the fact that I'm an outsider?" I was pushing.

I wasn't about to pull a Woodward and write a handful of stores before getting shown the door.

"Doesn't that put me in a negative light with people who don't want to change the name? I want to be seen as objective."

Skimer nodded.

"Be your toughest task. No doubt. Best thing you can do is get to know the school board. Let 'em know you're here to be fair and impartial. That's all they can ask us for, to report the facts as we see 'em. Good thing though is none of 'em have any bad history with you. And you have no bad history with any of them. I like that. Last thing we want with a big story like this is for things from the past to get in the way of progress, and I define progress as good reporting. And selling papers. Plain and simple."

"Makes sense to me, Rip. You can count on me."

I rose from the chair and moved toward the door. And then I stopped. Perhaps I should have asked my next question earlier. Like several weeks earlier. Like before I accepted the job earlier. Like before I moved away from my family and friends for the first time in my life earlier. Like before I drove halfway across the country to a town I had never heard of earlier.

"By the way, I can't help but wonder -- what happened to the last education reporter?"

"Oh, we don't need to talk about that. Let's just say he wasn't up for the job."

"Anything I need to know about?"

"Nothing you need to worry about. We didn't go out on some limb and seek out somebody from a big J-school like the University of South Californians for nothing. We want some good new blood here! And you got a good story on your hands, Marshall, so go get it. 'Cause if you don't, those other goddamn papers around here'll be all over it in three shakes of a lamb's tail. And if you need to find a Deep Throat in a parking garage somewhere to help you get where you need to be, so be it."

Now I was sure Skimer knew about my Watergate thing. And I just knew he was baiting me on it. But that was tangential at this point.

More importantly, beyond briefly wondering how quickly a lamb's tail shook, I was permeated with a mixture of fear and energy. I was taken aback by the Coons issue in general. I felt Skimer's confidence. And I still couldn't help but wonder what it was about my predecessor that didn't work.

Remember, I kept telling myself.

Something...big.

Three hours – and four cups of coffee – later, I found myself at Scotty P's with Short and Meesbruggan.

"So all the way from California, huh?" Short asked. "Long trip, man."

"You're not kidding. It's a whole different world here."

"Yeah, I suppose it is. Me and Mees here, we can help ya adjust."

"Can you dial down the heat?"

"No can do."

"Too bad."

"So, coupla helpful hints, Marshall," Meesbruggan interrupted. "We can help with that, I guess. Let's talk weather. It's hot here, Marshall. I'm talking hot as hell. And you think it's hot now? What is it, 12:30? Let me ask you a question: what's the hottest part of the day in L.A.?"

"Probably about 1:00 in the afternoon."

"1:00? Okay so let's say it's 1:00 here, and it's 95. By 5:00, even hundred. That's right, Marshall. That's the hottest part of the day here, about 5."

"How do you get used to that?"

"You don't. It is what it is. It's Texas."

"Mees' right, Marshall. 100 at 5? Might go down to 95 by 8. Maybe 90 by 9. Know what you call that?"

"What?"

"A cold front."

Short let out a loud and long giggle, which soon morphed into a cackle. I shook my head and stared at him; the longer the stare, the harder the cackle.

"Okay Marshall. So that's hint number one, which seeing as how it's June and all I'm guessing you've already figured out," Meesbruggan said. "So let's get to the real stuff. Hint number two. What's our hobby around here? Too damn hot to do anything outside. And if it's not too hot, it's too damn cold. There's an old saying here: you don't like the weather, wait five minutes, ok? But either way it's biblical, I'm telling ya. This place is all about extremes. So here's this: I'm telling ya right now, our hobby is money. Cashola. Ain't nothing more Dallas than money. Okay so things are a bit different up here in Frisco. A whole lot different. I mean, you can actually live a normal life up here and not be surrounded by this and that. Take a walk one day down there in that Highland Park Village, and you'll see so much money around you you'll be wondering how all the blue bloods ended up with all of it for themselves.

"But okay, so that's down there in Dallas. Let's talk Frisco. I got two words for ya. Well okay three. You ready for this one?"

I was mowing through my Warren Burger with the precision of a cotton gin.

"Tax Free Day. No taxes! That's right: no taxes. What would you say if I told you there was a weekend out of the year – just one weekend now – that you could shop 'til you dropped and not be taxed on any of it? That's right. Tax Free Day. It's the first weekend in August, so your timing here is good. That's the weekend they opened the new mall here last summer. Over there at Preston and Highway 121. You probably saw it when you came into town. Stonebriar Mall, they call it, and the place opened to record crowds there, all because no one had to pay any taxes. Brilliant."

"I'm pretty sure I saw it. Looks huge."

Short couldn't contain himself.

"Huge? You better believe it. 'Course, we do everything big here, and I know they like to talk about 'Texas-sized' and all of that and sometimes it's just bullcrap. But this one's true. Something like 25 first-run movie theaters, a Nordstrom, stuff like that. You even got an

NHL-sized ice rink in there. And the food?! We're talking Cheesecake Factory, California Pizza Kitchen, Dave & Busters. Cool deal."

"Biggest mall in North Texas now," Meesbruggan said. "One point six million square feet."

I wasn't sure how big that was, but it sounded big regardless.

"It's all about Frisco being, as they say, 'The New Plano,'" Meesbruggan said. "No more room down there, so they gotta build up here."

"As opposed to the old Plano."

"Yep, that's right. And they've got the stats to back it up now, with all this growth. Ten years ago, that corner at the mall, Preston and 121. Surrounded by empty fields and ranch land, right? Last year? That corner had the eighth-most car accidents of any intersection in the country. Can you believe that? Read it in USA Today."

"So it must be true," Short said.

"It's in the newspaper, I believe it," Meesbruggan said. Even he was smiling at this point.

"But really, it's true. I mean, drive down Parkwood there by the mall. They got so many of those darn business parks going in there, they're multiplying like fruit flies. Funny thing is, you've got all these offices going up, and right next to 'em you've still got all these open fields. So you've got these BMWs and SUVs driving right past horses and cows and corn fields and into all these nice new parking structures. Sight to see, I'm telling ya."

I could only shake my head and keep mowing.

"Which brings us to the third and, by far, most important hint," Short said. "The single most important thing you need to know, Marshall, for living in Frisco."

"Can't wait to hear this one," Meesbruggan said.

"Which is?"

Short looked around and lowered his voice. "Don't ever reach into a shoe."

"Don't ever reach into a shoe?"

"Don't ever reach into a shoe with your hand, heck even with your bare foot, without first shaking it."

"And that would be…because?"

Meesbruggan was the one laughing now.

"Scorpions!" Short blurted out, and it was possible that I'd never seen someone so proud of himself.

"Scorpions?"

Short couldn't contain himself, so Meesbruggan chimed in.

"What Sport here is trying to explain, Marshall, is that it's common up here in these parts for scorpions to, shall we say, make themselves at home in our homes."

I leaned my head forward in disbelief.

"You see, it's because of all the ground they're tearing up out here to build these new homes. Scorpions used to be right at home in all the dirt. Now we're putting new homes on their homes. No worries though. Ya just gotta shake your shoes before you stick something in there. That's all."

I calmly placed what was left of my Warren Burger on the table. "You're kidding, right?"

"Like Mees said, it's Texas, man," Short said. "You got any high schools out there in California going by the Fighting Farmers?"

"The Fighting Farmers? Oxymoron."

"Should be, I suppose. Not over in Lewisville. Not when we're kicking everyone's asses while they're laughing. State champs, man. Says it right there on the water tower. Right next to 35."

"So you're a Fighting Farmer? And you can say that with a straight face?"

"You know it. Wasn't too bad on the O-line. Blew it out senior year. Tore the ACL and MCL all at once. Doc said he'd never seen anything like it. Never made it back on the field. Brutal. Had a free ride at Stephen F. Austin all set up. Was gonna be a Lumberjack."

"More than I can say for myself. But sorry to hear all that."

"No problem, man. Sucked at the time though. How do you think I ended up a sports hack? You talk to 10 sportswriters, and nine of us would rather be out there on the field. Most of us either got hurt or were too uncoordinated to get out there in the first place. I tried. Thought for awhile I'd be like a physical trainer or something. But that was too much work I wasn't good at. A sportswriting gig was way down the ladder for me. At least it was. I started by covering high school football as a stringer. Just kind of grew on me, I guess. Not a great writer, but I get by."

I reached for a Cardiac fry. "Back home, I guess we've got scorpions, but not in our shoes. Not in L.A., at least. I do know we don't have any Fighting Farmers."

I thought about what I had just heard. Beyond a weekend when I didn't have to pay taxes for anything, and since I didn't have any money anyway I wasn't sure how relevant for me that was, I decided there had to be something positive beyond Dr. Pepper in a geographic trade-off that at this point looked to have all the balance of the sale of Manhattan.

"So what about Plano? There some good spots to go to there to get a taste of Texas? I mean, I'm talking a real taste. Like can I go there and see the boots and the hats and all of that. Where's the big hair?"

"Oh that's a good one," Short said. "Pretty damn plastic down there, if you ask me." "Son," Meesbruggan said, "Let me sum it up for you in three words: Plano ain't

Texas."

"I'll try and remember that," and a comforting sip of Dr. Pepper, thankfully, was only inches away.

"So speaking of Texas and scorpions and high school nicknames," Short said, stuffing a fry in his mouth, "Rip wants us to see if you have more questions about the Coon thing. You ready for this one?"

"Sounds like I don't have a choice."

"Okay, so here it is," Short said. "First thing is, ya gotta understand two things. One, the South, and when I say that I include Dallas first, and Frisco second. And two, how different things are in Frisco today compared to the past."

"I'm all ears."

"Okay, good, 'cause there's a lot here. So basically let's look at the South. If you read your history books you probably think the Civil War was all about slavery, right?"

I hadn't seen that one coming.

"Um, yeah?"

"Wrong. It was about the South's right to live its own life. About its right to uphold its own ways, without the folks up North getting all up in their grill about it. And if you think about it, it ain't dead yet, and I'm not talking about Frisco. Look at South Carolina. There's some politician every time that gets into big-time trouble over the Confederate flag still flying down there. States rights, that's what they call it. I call it Stonewall Jackson bites."

"That would be a Southern perspective," I said. I was a bit confused over where the conversation was going. I was also starting to feel slightly pious. "I was a history minor, okay."

"Well, yeah, just like the Northern perspective, and I think the opinion of most people outside the South is that it was about slavery. Ultimately, yes, slavery was the huge thing. It was the lightning rod. But the issue is more basic than that, really. The South had a different way of life than the North, and the North didn't like it."

"Okay, but didn't the North not like it because it felt that slavery was wrong? I mean, isn't it wrong for one group of people to tell another group of people what to do based on skin color?"

"Yes, I do think it was wrong," Short said. "But even if someone were to agree with that, the issue for Southerners, it was more fundamental."

Meesbruggan jumped in.

"I think what Sport here is saying, Marshall, is that even if it was wrong in the eyes of the South, it wasn't the North's call to make. So ultimately it was a question of, does one region of the country get to tell another region of the country what to do?"

"In some cases it should."

"Maybe so. But welcome to Texas. You wanna get the hackles up of folks here? Marshall, lemme tell ya. There's three things you wanna do, see. One, state income tax. You got one of those out there in California? I thought so. And a pretty high one, I'm betting. Not here. And never here, I'm thinking. Politicians try to ram that type of thing through here gonna get lynched, and that's no racist comment.

"Two, guns. I'm talking guns, Marshall. You see any of those billboards for these local gun shows they got going? Always see the one out there in Mesquite. That's fine, just don't tell us to put 'em away.

"Anyway, three. Don't ever, I mean ever, tell us what to think. This Coon thing? That's just it, Marshall. New people coming in, telling folks around here what to think. That just doesn't fly. That's a no-fly zone."

Meesbruggan took a breath.

"You know, most folks don't think of us as being a Confederate state, but we were."

"Texas was in the Confederacy?" I asked. I was amazed I didn't know that. "I thought that was just the South."

"One of the original seven, guy," Meesbruggan said. "Why do you think the first Confederate flag only had seven stars? People forget that, 'cause the Navy Jack took over after awhile. That one's got 13 stars, and Texas is one of 'em."

Meesbruggan sat back and looked at Short. "You know, it's one of those things. Lotsa folks look at Texas as being in the South. Other folks look at us as being in the Southwest. Me, I've always looked at Texas as being its own place. Its own region, really."

"Big state."

"Absolutely. Look at Dallas, and I think this is where Sport here was starting to go. I'm actually the outlier in the group, being from Dallas and all. Grew up down there, right by Forest and Central. Hebrew Heights, as they call it. Got a place out in Santa Fe we get to whenever we can. But Dallas is home. It's where the money is.

"But look at the others. 'Ol Skip's from out there in East Texas. His assistant, Lane, you met her yet? Came in from Oklahoma. She's a real Sooner, that Sunnivan. Somewhere near Ardmore, I think, where they got that Three Frogs Inn spot. Though I guess she's got lots of family from Nashville, or maybe Memphis which is a lot closer to here. Jan, she's from down south there in Louisiana. You wanna learn about some of that brown gulf shrimp they got over there, she can talk your head off about it. Costin, you met her yesterday. She's from out there in West Texas. Well, Abilene. I suppose folks in West Texas wouldn't call Abilene West Texas, but it's a good 2-3 hours west of Ft. Worth. To me, sorry, but that's West Texas. And then there's Thornaker."

"Thornaker?"

"Oh, Marshall, I guess you'll meet Will," Meesbruggan said. "Not sure you'll get much beyond that, but anyway. Point is, he's from Arkansas. Somewhere up there near Springdale, I think. Might be Ft. Smith, but I'm thinking a little further up there in Springdale. About five hours from here. Not a real pretty drive up through eastern Oklahoma once you get through Sherman on 75. Until you cross the state line, I suppose. Unless you like trailer parks."

"And the point would be…" Short said. He looked at me. "Pardon our fine business editor here, Marshall. Sometimes—"

"Sometimes I get interrupted by our fine sports editor when I'm trying to make a point," Meesbruggan said, to which Short burst out in laughter. "Point is, Marshall, Dallas is the local hub. It's the magnet. Big D, right? So you've got people moving here from all over, or at least all over the area. You wanna job in these parts of the country, you're coming here. And that's so much of what's driving all the growth to Frisco, 'cause people who are moving to Dallas these days, they're moving to Frisco. It's where the action here is now. No trees, but we planted a few crate mertels. Not the live oaks they have down there in the city, but it works. Master planned, cookie cutter, okay. But stuff doesn't break. Never thought I could do it."

"Oh, so that's the point," Short said, and he shot me a wink. "Crate mertels, right Ted?"

"Point is, Marshall, back to what Sport here was talking about. Pardon the analogy, but what happened in the South with slavery isn't much different than what's happening here in the sense of, 'hey, whose call is it how we live?' What's happening here is that the teams have been called the Coons for as long as anyone in this town can remember, and some folks in town don't like the idea that they may have to change."

"But what if the term is offensive?"

"That's just it, though, that if the term is offensive today, and of course it is, it was offensive before," Short said, chiming in. "In other words, it's not the term that has changed. It's Frisco that has changed."

"So the folks in town that don't want to change are pointing at the changes in the town, and really the new people coming into town, as the problem."

"Pretty much," Short said. "If the name has been there forever, why should newcomers to town force the school board to change it? Or even more accurately, why should the town feel pressure just because it's changing? I'm not real sure where the actual pressure is coming from."

"Just so you know, the term is not meant as a derogatory thing at all," Meesbruggan added. "I mean, it's just a term you hear. Ever hear someone say they're going 'coon hunting'"?

"Nope," I said, shaking my head. "Haven't spent a lot of time hunting. Like never. I don't think I could ever even fire a gun."

"Well, that's a separate deal," Short said, laughing. "What Mees here is describing is someone saying they're gonna go shoot raccoons. To say they're going coon hunting doesn't mean anything. Just like someone calling the Frisco High Raccoons the Frisco High Coons doesn't mean anything. It's more of a term of endearment for a raccoon than anything else. That's it."

"So I'm starting to understand a lot more," I reasoned. "I can see both sides, really. One side says, hey, what's the big deal, no one is doing anyone any harm, it's always been that way. The other side is saying, you know, we oughta look at this name in a broader context, because it can be offensive to people."

"That's exactly right," Meesbruggan said. "And the driver here is that Frisco's just changing. Just look around at all of the construction. Drive through some of these new gated communities they've put in. The town is becoming bigger and bigger every day. It's just becoming a different place."

"Yeah," Short said. "Just yesterday our circulation was 18,900. Now it's 19,000."

"19,000's nothing to shake a stick at, I suppose. But remember it was 30,000 just a few years back. Had a lot more people around the building back then. Our industry's not exactly setting things on fire. Neither are we. You're the first new hire in I can't remember how long. At least in editorial."

Not that any of that made a difference to me. I wanted to write for a newspaper, period. If the larger industry in which I was a part was finding it hard to make money, that wasn't my problem. And the last time I checked, the Times' circulation was still north of a million anyway. What was my problem, I knew now, was what was going to happen with Frisco High and its nickname.

If I could have gone coon hunting at that moment, I would have.

"Oh, one more thing, Marshall," Meesbruggan said as we walked outside.

"Can't wait to hear this one."

"Booze. You like beer? Stock up on Saturday. First off, Collin County's dry. No booze here anywhere. During the week and on Saturday you can head over to Plano or somewhere else and get some. Not on Sunday though. 'I'm not saying we don't like drinking here, because we do. We just don't buy it on Sunday."

I climbed into Short's back seat and stared blankly out the window, trying in vain to assimilate what I'd just heard.

Short couldn't resist.

"So about this heat—"

"Give the kid a break, Sport."

"Just trying to make him feel a little better, Mees. Hey Marshall. I know it's hot now, and there isn't much relief in sight yet. But there will come a time when you'll wonder where the sun went. I got two words for ya."

I was too mentally exhausted to answer.

"Ice storms, Marshall. Ice storms. See, in the winter we get these really nasty ice storms where there's basically like sleet that freezes over. You can't drive on the roads. You can't do anything, really."

"Oh, that's the same way in L.A.," I mustered. "It rains there and the whole town shuts down."

"Marshall, my dear young Marshall," Sport continued, and another cackle wasn't too far off. "Rain? No, we're talking ice, man. They're not roads anymore. They're rinks. They're ice rinks, you're a Zamboni. You ever drive a Zamboni, Marshall? And sometimes the ice is black and you're sliding all over—"

"Sport…"

"And don't even think about trying to get across a bridge or overpass. That's where it's really—"

"Sport…"

"Hey Mees, you know there's more than a thousand of those things over there in Tarrant County? A freakin' thou—"

"Sport, how can you even think about an ice storm right now? It's 150 degrees outside."

"Wishful thinking, man. Wishful thinking."

I kept staring.

And didn't say a word.

CHAPTER FOUR

SHREVEPORT

"Fire at Baldwin Park!"

I looked up from my desk. The voice had come from the editing station. It was Friday, just after lunchtime. The newsroom was deserted.

Skimer came bursting out of his office in a lather. "Where the bird drop is everyone?" he asked, looking around.

He found only me.

He looked around again.

He still found only me.

"McDougal, you're on the story," he said, and I could almost see him pull a muscle.

Bennie rushed up. "Okay, the story is there's a fire at Baldwin Park. That's one thing. But the park is next to a neighborhood of homes and is threatening them as well. People are evacuating. Marshall, you need to get over there right away."

My heart was pounding.

"Best way to start is find the watch commander on site," Skimer said.

"What's a watch commander?"

"The guy in charge with the fire department. We know 'em all. Don't know who's there today. Just find him and get your information there."

I grabbed my coat and started toward the door.

"Color, local color," Skimer yelled behind me. "I want human reaction!"

"I'm on my way, too," screamed Pat Clarke, the photo editor, emerging from the photo lab. "I'll see you over there."

"Where is Baldwin Park?" I blurted out. I had no clue where to go.

"Just go up Preston and turn left at the first street. You'll run right into it. It's five minutes from here."

I flew through the front door – directly into the chest of a heavyset man in a dark, gray, pin-striped suit. I took the worst of it, the man's bulk sending me hurdling sideways, my keys shooting through the air like a spitball.

"I, uh, I'm sorry, sir," I offered as I tried to gather myself. "I apologize."

"No worries, son," I heard him say, and only once I had hopped into my Tercel did I notice that the man was being followed into the building by two other, younger but largely unidentifiable men in similarly dark suits.

I turned the key; my heart sank. Almost literally, I had no gas. I had been driving this car since high school. I knew it well enough to know when I couldn't take a chance. I had been surprised that I'd even made it to the office in the first place earlier that day. But I'd overslept and hadn't wanted to be late. I had to make the call. I couldn't afford to miss the story. But I figured running out of gas would be worse. I flew down Main Street and into the only gas station on the street. I stopped at five dollars and wheeled the car back the other way down Main toward Preston.

Less than five minutes later, I flew again, this time into the lot at the park. The scene was unbelievable. Much of the park was in flames, with what was left of the children's play area at the epicenter. The play area was made of wood as opposed to the metallic play areas I had grown up playing on in California. Almost as quickly as I saw the flames, I smelled them. They were outhouse strong, stronger than I would have expected, and it occurred to me that I had never been this close to an actual fire.

Clarke spotted me first.

"You take the long way?"

"Don't ask."

"See that man over there? He's the watch commander. He knows you're coming."

Christ. My first big news story, and I'm already behind the eight ball with the photo editor having to run interference.

"They think the fire was set by an arsonist," Clarke said. "You'll need to push on that angle. I'm running around the corner to get photos of the neighborhood. A bunch of homes are burning, and an entire block is in danger of being lost. Go!"

I approached the man Clarke had pointed to.

"Uh, excuse me, are you the watch commander?"

"Evening Outlook?"

"Yes, sir. Marshall McDougal, nice to meet you."

"Lt. Mike Sement," the main said, not turning his body toward me.

"What can you tell me?" I said, whipping out my blue ball-point pen and utility bill-shaped reporter's notebook. "So you think it was arson?"

"That is our belief, yes."

"Why would someone want to burn a park down?"

"Your guess is as good as mine. Real tragedy. Be with you when I can. We're not going anywhere for awhile."

With that, Sement went back to work. I looked around, surveying the scene. Instinct said to follow Clarke around the corner.

In the foreground, the street was pure Cecil B. Demille. Humanity was everywhere. Parents and their children scurried about. Police officers controlled the area, primarily to keep the crowd back. Firemen ran back and forth between their equipment and the front line closer to the fire. In the background sat a series of homes, all with their backyards facing the park, in various stages of distress. One house was completely engulfed in flames, with a row of six firemen furiously shooting water at it. Flames shot out of an adjacent home's window. Smaller flames scattered throughout the rooves of a third and fourth house. Police had already blocked the street with yellow tape.

I approached a young woman trying to corral her two young sons.

"Hello ma'am?" I asked gently. I could see she was upset. She glanced up.

"Yes, I'm Marshall McDougal with the Evening Outlook," I said. "Okay if I ask you some quest—"

The woman was too distracted to pay much attention. "Do I look like I want to talk?"

I took a step back; no grocery store bagging contest here.

"Sorry to bother you."

A few yards down the sidewalk, I stopped and watched a frantic conversation unfold between another local resident and a police officer. From what I could gather, the man lived on the street and wanted to get to his house to retrieve his belongings. I stood to the side waiting for the encounter to end. A heavyset man who appeared to be in his mid-40s, he was beyond frustrated.

"Hello, Marshall McDougal, with the Evening Outlook."

The man looked at me and sighed. "That's my house down there," he said. "They say there's no fire there but they won't let me past."

"Do you mind if I quote you?"

I wasn't sure I needed to ask the question. But I knew the man was in an emotional state.

"Yeah, sure," he mumbled. "All I know is that the police won't let me get to my house."

"Why do you need to get to your house?"

"I run my business out of there. That fire gets to my house, I lose my business. I lose my business, I lose everything."

"What do you do?"

"Sales. Pharmaceuticals. I just can't afford to lose my business. I've got product in there, files, you name it. I've got written orders in there from customers. I've got my entire business on my computer system."

"So you want to retrieve your computer, the files and things right, and the police won't let you in?"

"Yes. But I also want to grab some pictures. My wife gave me a list of which ones to get and wants me to get inside. She's in a complete panic."

"Where is she?"

"She's at the kids' school. She's a volunteer. I'm just relieved this is happening with no one home. That's the most important thing."

"How many kids do you have?" I was taking notes to the point of cramping in a desperate attempt to keep up.

"Three, two daughters and a son. If this had hit a couple of hours later, they might be in there. I can't believe this is happening."

"Can you tell me your name?"

"Sure, Brook. Dick Brook."

"Thanks Dick. Hope you get your stuff out."

I kept moving. The conversation had energized me. This is the stuff Skimer wanted to see.

"How's it going?" Clarke yelled, motioning me over.

"Good. I got some great quotes from a guy whose entire business is in one of the houses on fire. I need to find some others to talk as well."

"I think I have enough on my end. Stay close with the watch commander. See you back."

I was on my own now. I quickly spotted a woman standing by herself. She was crying.

"Uh, excuse me?"

The woman looked up at me, startled. She didn't say a word, didn't need to. The look on her face spoke volumes.

"Hi, I'm Marshall McDougal, with the Evening Outlook. I know it's probably a bad time, but do you mind—"

"That's my house over there," she said, pointing to another house in flames. "We built that house, my husband and I, from scratch. That home is our life."

"How long have you lived there."

"We moved here from Oklahoma City after the bombing. Just too many bad memories there. And my husband had a great job offer in Dallas. We were one of the first families in the neighborhood here."

"When was that?"

"'96. Year after the bombing."

I had been in high school when it happened. I recalled being upset about it, but thinking that a place like Oklahoma City, especially when you're living in Los Angeles, seemed so remote.

"Why did you settle in Frisco?"

"We thought it was a wonderful community. Still do," she said, fighting back more tears. "We love Frisco. The only problem is my husband's commute to Dallas is too long. It used to be a half-hour. Now with all these new folks moving to town it's a full hour. I call him 'The King of the Tollway.'"

"Where is he now?"

"He was at the office, but he's on his way home now," she said. "I can't believe this is happening."

I knew right away, hearing the woman say those words, that the man I just interviewed had said the exact same thing. I circled the statement and drew a star by it.

"Your name?"

"Yes, it's Ann, Ann Morgen."

"Thanks Ann. Hang in there. I'm sure your husband will be here soon."

I approached the watch commander. "Not yet Evening Outlook," Sement said, seeing me coming his way. I didn't argue, and turned around to walk back toward the flames.

Just as I turned the corner, there was a boom. A second story window had exploded in the home closest to the crowd. What had appeared to be a manageable situation for that house, with small flames moonwalking across its roof, was worse than it had appeared. All four homes were now ablaze, an interconnected inferno of bricks, wood, paint and dying dreams.

The explosion had terrified the crowd. A group of children in wet bathing suits stood in a semi-circle screaming, with others running toward their parents for safety. The crowd moved back, with others running for any cover they could find. One of the police officers in the street lifted his megaphone.

"For your own safety, please evacuate the area," he said. "Again, for your own safety, please evacuate the area immediately."

I motioned to the police officer. "Officer, Marshall McDougal with the Evening—"

The officer shot back. "Afternoon, Mr. McDougal. I need you to evacuate the area immediately."

"Yes, but—"

"I'm sorry, but you need to evacuate."

"Officer, I'm with the—"

"Need you to back up, sir."

I was overheating. How could I write a story if I couldn't see what the hell was happening? I turned and started walking back toward the park. I only had quotes from two homeowners, and I knew that might not be enough. I looked at my watch. It was 2:30. I'd already been there for more than an hour. I needed to get to the office.

One more time, I tried to catch the watch commander's eyes.

"Evening Outlook," Sement said, seemingly sight unseen.

"We believe it is arson," he started in, clearly having done this before. "There will be a full investigation of course, and we have no details on suspects, motives, anything like that."

"What tells you it might be arson?"

"We found some lighter fluid by the playground," Sement said, pointing toward the far end of what remained of it. "That's a pretty sure sign right there."

"Any details on damage?"

"None definitively yet. What we can say is that four homes are burned completely, with three others being fought right now. We think we have the fire under control beyond that. That is all we have for now."

I kept scribbling and looked up at Sement. He was again busy motioning to someone else.

"Thanks a lot, appreciate your help," I volunteered, stuffing my notebook in my shirt pocket.

Within minutes, I was careening again, this time back into the Evening Outlook lot.

"Welcome back, McDougal," Skimer said. "Pat says it was pretty bad, huh?"

"I'd say so."

"Okay, then, let's really make this one sing. You got color, McDougal?"

"Got it. Talked to two people whose homes were burning down. One guy's whole business is in his house. Got good quotes. The whole bit."

"You talk to the watch commander? Which one was it?"

"Yes. Sement. He thinks it's arson. They found some lighter fluid at the scene."

"Alright, we got ourselves a real a big one then. Let's make it happen team."

I started pounding away at the keys. It was 3:00 now. I still had three full hours to file something for Bennie to work with.

Nearly two hours later, I was still at it. I had at first led with one of the quotes I got from the homeowners. Bennie had reminded me this was the lead news story for tomorrow's paper. So the news had to come first, followed by the color. I had felt the quotes were the best part. For the moment, we had agreed to disagree.

All of a sudden, Bennie came running into the newsroom.

"It's 10 to fucking 5!" she shouted. "Marshall, two minutes. We gotta get this in."

"What?!" I shot back. "I thought I had until 6?"

"Normally yes, but today is Friday. We have to put the paper to bed earlier."

"What?"

Bennie was ignoring me, her focus on her screen unbroken.

Meesbruggan looked over.

"We put together both weekend issues in one night here so we don't have to run the press on Saturday for the Sunday," he said. "It's a money thing."

I wasn't listening.

"Almost done," I screamed.

One minute went by. Two minutes. Three.

"Marshall…"

"Almost done!"

"One minute."

"Coming your way," I shouted to Bennie a minute later as I pressed the send button.

"Got it."

I took a deep breath. It had been 1:00, my Scotty P's lunch just starting to settle in my ever-expanding stomach, a theoretically quiet Friday afternoon of research and writing ahead. I looked around and noticed nearly all of my colleagues at their desks, most with their heads down working on stories. I wondered where everyone had been a few hours earlier.

Short toddled by. He looked far too relaxed to be on deadline.

"Guess nobody told you Friday deadline was an hour earlier."

"Nope."

"Marshall, come on over," Bennie shouted.

"Good luck, kid," Short said. "Don't mind me. I'm going back to the toy department."

"The toy department?"

"Yeah, that's what you cityside guys like to call the sports department," he said. "You know, like we got it easy. Like there's no deadlines after high school football games. Like you're not tired going through your notes at 11:00."

"Marshall…"

I parked myself next to Bennie's screen.

"So the lede isn't bad. But we need to play the arson angle higher," Bennie suggested, cutting and pasting while she talked. "We talked about that, right?"

"Well, we did, but the quotes—"

"The quotes are great. But this is arson, Marshall. I mean, right? Arson's pretty shitty.

We can do a pull quote or something on your guy."

"What about—"

"Also let's move this guy's quote up. To me it's more powerful to have a guy saying he's gonna lose his whole business with his home than just someone saying they're gonna lose their home."

"But isn't the woman's story about moving here from Oklahoma City powerful?"

"Belongs in the story. Let's see what Rip says."

Skimer approached Bennie's desk. "Where are we team?" he said, rubbing his hands together.

"We're ready for you," Bennie said. "Final deadline in 15."

"Okay, then, let's take a look."

He lowered his voice and leaned closer, like a doctor examining a bodily injury. He read quietly for a minute. It seemed like an hour.

"Arson thing needs to be stronger. Mucho stronger. Got the watch commander saying they found evidence of arson at the scene. Doesn't always happen like that. Make it stronger. And the part about the explosion – gotta move it up."

Bennie pushed back. "Marshall's got some great quotes here, Rip."

Skimer was hearing nothing of it. "Let the layout guys work with that," he said. "For us we need to tell people somebody set their park on fire, and we need to do more to describe the scene. Yes, the color is important, but in this case we gotta get the facts out first. We got an arsonist running around here."

Bennie continued cutting and pasting.

"How does that read?" she said, glancing up. I scanned the lede quickly.

"I like it." I was surprised that I did.

"Done," she said, firing the story off to layout. She leaned back in her chair and exhaled. "And people expect me to stop smoking. Speaking of which."

She got up and started heading to the back lot.

I took a deep breath. "What an afternoon."

"Sorry I jumped down your throat on the deadline," she said. "We should have told you about Friday deadline."

"I didn't realize you put together two papers in one day. That's gotta be tough."

"Yeah, it's tough, but it's either that or come in on Saturday to put the Sunday paper together, so I'm happy to have Friday be lousy. It's really all about money, though. They don't want to have to pay to have the hourly folks come in on the weekend."

"I had no idea."

"Stick around for layout and Rip to take another look."

That was fine with me. I had nowhere to go. The Dodgers were playing that night. But as I had already come to realize, the game wouldn't start for several more hours anyway. My favorite game's poetic flow, always so soothing anyway, would have to become my lullaby.

Thirty minutes later, Skimer approached me at my desk.

"McDougal, nice job on that fire story. Wasn't easy, I know. Quotes are good though and that helps a lot. Next time we'll need to be more clear about deadlines. Worked out alright this time."

I nodded. "You got it, Rip."

I allowed myself a moment of reflection. I had just covered my first big story. The editor had tapped me on the shoulder, and I had come through. Had I known upfront what the Friday deadline was, I would have likely delivered a story that have would required less re-work. But the story was done now and on its way, I assumed, to the front page.

I got up to leave. Passing the photo room, I happened upon Clarke.

"Read the story Marshall," she said. "Good story. I got some great photos. It'll be a nice package when they're done with it. Have a good weekend."

My first week as a reporter was in the books, my first front-page news story on the way. I managed a lukewarm smile as I pushed the door open and greeted the glare.

"Well now hello there Marshall McDougal."

"Hello? Sammy. How's things in Circulation?"

"Gang's having fun. What we do best."

"Have a good weekend, Sammy."

"Aim to, my good man. No better place to start than Shreveport."

"Shreveport."

"Gonna play me some cards. You like cards, Marshall? Something tells me you're a card guy. You a card guy there, Mister Marshall?"

"Played a little in Vegas."

More like lost a lot in Vegas. What happens when I go to Vegas is that at a certain point I realize I have been stupid enough to get suckered into getting into a car and driving five hours through the tumbleweeds, the endorphins converting me as the inelastic consumer like the most effective end-aisle display ever all the way through the sales funnel, all for a rush that lasts roughly 45 minutes as I valiantly try to hold off this miserable excuse of a human behind the table, this guy whose nametag says he's from Carson City and who smiles a lot and who starts off as my bud when he busts on the first hand but whose heart, I come to believe as my second-and-last free drink vaporizes faster than liquid helium as he pulls his third consecutive 7 to his 14, has not only shrunk to less than the size of that of The Grinch but in fact was never a match in the first place, the sonofabitch bastard of a ratfucker.

"Las Vegas, Nevada?! Now that's the real deal out there. Sin City, I do believe they call it. Shoulda known, big-time California guy like you. Tell ya what, Mister Marshall. Meet me here in an hour. Gang'll be done getting those papers out."

"I don't know. Long week, you know."

"Just what the doctor ordered then, that's what I say."

"I don't know."

"Now you just let 'ol Doctor Sammy here help ya out. We'll see you back right here. Three hour drive. Two hours plus the way I do it. Back by breakfast."

An hour later, we were off.

"Assume you've never been out to Shreveport, good sir?"

"Never been there. Been to Vegas a few too many times. Most of the time we don't leave 'til late. We'd drive all night, four or five hours. Finally, just when you think you're never going to see civilization again, all of a sudden you see this faint line of light in the distance. The closer you get, the brighter it becomes. Next thing you know, you're in a sea of lights."

"Mister Marshall, you've been livin' the high life out there in Cali. Cajuns like me though. We go to Shreveport."

"Always been that way out here?"

"Never been that way until a few years back now. Maybe five, six, seven years ago. They started putting all these boats in. My dad's been involved, you might say. That's a nice business, lemme tell ya. Turned the whole town around."

"How's that?"

"Way back when, Shreveport was all about manufacturing. But you're a smart guy. Manufacturing ain't where it's at no more, right? Was like the Rust Belt had come to the South. Sad, ya ask me. So they started looking at bringing in those casinos. Riverboats used to go through there. Just passing through though. Casinos? Now there's some money. Shreveport's been on a roll ever since. Folks like to gamble, I guess.

"Every town has a calling card, I say. You know, something that makes it different, right? Big ones, small ones. Before we get to Tyler out there, we'll hit Grand Saline. Salt capital of the world, they say. Always liked that. Heck, even big towns reinvent themselves when they need to. Look at Louisville. Was reading up on that. The Derby, right? Mint juleps, pretty ladies in those hats. Well, that's great, but that's one day a year. Doesn't put enough people to work. So a year or two ago, they opened up some bourbon thing. The Bourbon Trail, or something like that. They got all these bourbon farms or bourbon joints or bourbon mills. Whatever it is they call places that make bourbon. Now they got all these tourists. Folks like drinking, too.

"It's all about the money, I say. You need more, you do what you gotta do. You got the money already, you do what you gotta do to get more. The American Way."

We kept driving through the night. Sammy seemed nice enough. I was trying not to over-think things. I'd been in Texas less than a week now, and I was already on an all-night gambling trip. Did I have a chance in hell of winning? Maybe it was Vegas. Yeah. Maybe it was Vegas all along. Maybe there was better karma elsewhere.

"You know where you're going, right?"

Sammy laughed.

"My good man. Could do this here drive in my sleep. Might say I have, coupla times."

"You okay to drive? I mean, you need a soda or something?"

"Adrenaline's all I need. Loaded up on it right about now. Once we get through Terrell here, just open space. Can count off the towns real easy after that. Kilgore. Longview. Heck, Marshall, we're gonna go right through a town called Marshall. Howdya like that?"

My turn to laugh. I was settling in.

"Hey, sounds like a great town."

"Great town to drive through, as long as Shreveport's the target, I say. Just a straight shot on 20. You'll see. We're just racing through the longleafs. Like they frame ya. Guide ya, all the way there. Then you hit Carthage and Jefferson. By the time you get to Waskom, you're at the border. And then it's Bienvenue, you're past the big-ass water tower and the fairgrounds and you're home in 15."

We kept moving. The conversation was mainly one-sided, me telling Sammy all about my life in L.A., all about why I wanted to be a journalist, all about how I ended up in Frisco. And all about the Fighting Coons and what it looked like my main assignment was to be. At a certain point we honed in on the art and science of black jack, and I somehow felt the need to let go and reveal to him that, if I admitted it in the most private of moments, the only thing harder for me than being too far from water for too long was saying no to a gambling road trip, even though I generally know the outcome in advance.

We arrived somewhat suddenly. The sign welcoming us to Louisiana had come out of nowhere, and sure enough 15 minutes later we were on the off-ramp at Spring Street, then taking a quick right at Crockett, a quicker left on Clyde Fant and circling for a spot in the Sam's Town structure.

"Prefer Sam's Town, if that's ok with you," Sammy said. "Something about that name, I guess."

"I'm just along for the ride, Sammy."

"Things go bad, we can hit the El Dorado down the street there.

Things go real bad, we can hit the other side over there in Bossier City 'cross the river."

"Bojer City? Never heard of it."

"Other side of the tracks, basically. Got the Horseshoe. Couple other ones, too. It's alright over there. All part of the same deal. Just like it better over here."

We glided like rays across the third-floor covered bridge and into the lobby of the hotel. Down the escalator we went, past Smokey Joe's Cafe, past the disturbingly long line for the buffet, Sammy in the lead, me a stride or two behind, two people who know what they want, the only lapse being the momentary one when the toothless man with the pine needle whiskers sticking out from his porcine jowls, his belly like a bag of feed suffocating his belt buckle below and his fly undone pressed us in the elevator about how sure he was that we would take the spot we did and then whose wife insisted her husband did not in fact have a heart condition like the doctor thought but in fact was better off staying active. By the time we had descended into the catacombs of the property down by the water, into whichever of the three floors of the boat we started at, we had the passive-yet-focused, been-there-done-that of a team of surgeons scrubbing in.

"Time to play some cards," Sammy says, and it's all I can do to keep up. We find a couple of free seats at a table, and it's only seconds until I'm reaching for the bills whose stay in my pocket is about to come to a stunningly premature end.

I'm trying to stay focused, but I'm a dervish compared to Sammy. He is all business, engaging in little small talk with anyone other than the cocktail waitress whose bust line was so deep it was like peering down a dark alley and whose breasts would have been way more attractive had their mass not been matched by that of her midsection and whose fingers, I decided in a fit of bitterness at a push when a 20 should have been more than enough, were swollen and ruddy enough they could have been baby back ribs without the sauce.

At one point in the night, Sammy still in full play, my money long gone, I ended up wandering up and down the noticeably rickety stairs on the east end of the casino, the ones that through the glass of the non-exitable doors you could glimpse the river just outside. The more I did this the more I came to believe that despite it being called the Red River the water was really much more brown, and when the moonlight was shining on it before the red neon lights on the Texas Street Bridge went out it looked like a giant trough of gravy under a heat lamp.

The drive back is a skit on survival. My navigating is much more active this time, Sammy having inhaled an entire oak cask of Gentleman Jack since we'd first sat down, but somehow we arrive back in Frisco in one piece, the only substantive discussion point being the discovery of our shared dislike of the Cowboys, mine stemming from my dislike of Troy Aikman since he was a Bruin, his coming from the fact that his fellow Louisiana Tech guy was Terry Bradshaw, he being a Steeler and all, and well it was the Cowboys that had gone up against Bradshaw and the Steel Curtain in all those Super Bowls way back when.

As I began to doze off, I realized I smelled like the smoke my lungs had been injesting all night. And I remembered I owed Sammy $200. My luck had been even worse than usual, something I didn't think possible. This was always the worst moment of the gambling all-nighter: the next morning. The next morning, when the casino buildings look like starlets without their make-up looking straight ahead in line at the grocery store and just hoping you don't notice, when the whole joint looks like a back lot where all the backs of the buildings are as hollow, as sunken, as the eyes of those who more shuffle than stride. The next morning, when the matte of day signals to all who have the energy left to listen that the luster of night has given way.

CHAPTER FIVE

TASTE OF THE SOUTH

I t was a water color day, the air so still, the canvass freckled by lonely pillows of cotton, the sky looking like a facsimile of itself, a mural hand-painted on a domed ceiling in an ornate dining room.

Time to work off the stress of my first week as a journalist. Driving north on Preston, I began looking for signs for the Warren Sports Complex. Short had said it was a great place to get some fresh air and exercise. Heading west on Main Street, I took a right on North County Road, taking note that, if one were to turn left, one would be on South County Road. I wondered if that meant what it appeared to, that Main Street served as the halfway point of Collin County. Not having been north of Main Street yet save my experience at Baldwin Park, I was surprised at the thought of another half a county still to come.

As soon as I turned right, however, I realized immediately how uninformed that thought was. What I was entering was a different Frisco, a different world than the highly commercial one I had so far experienced. I looked up and down each block, down Oak, down

Walnut, down Maple. The homes were bandbox small, almost all made of wood, a painter's box of little boy blue and of Easter egg yellow and of mauve. Most were old, some looking to be quite old, with many long having fallen into disrepair. Long, lonely St. Augustine weeds listed in front yards. Rusted pick-up trucks convalesced in driveways.

What I was now experiencing was the oldest part of Frisco's many residential neighborhoods. It had grown back in the early part of the 20th century, back when Main Street was all there was. In recent years, the neighborhood had become home to many of the farmers who labored on the ranches that still made up much of the land throughout the region.

A few blocks up North County Road, I passed the Frisco Independent School District's athletic complex. The most prominent of its several features, which included a natatorium and a baseball field, was the football stadium, and I took note that the scoreboard at the far end of the field featured the words "Frisco Coons" centered at the top.

Continuing up North County Road, I passed a sign for the complex. I didn't know it at the time, but I would surely have appreciated that the complex had been named after the same Bob Warren who had once served Frisco as mayor and whose namesake burger I had consumed way, way too many times already at Scotty P's – thus prompting the morning jog I was now endeavoring to pull off despite the general yawn my expanding body was still experiencing.

The Warren Sports Complex was a modern-day suburban mecca. Football fields. Soccer fields. A baseball field, complete with an outfield fence. Basketball courts. Tennis courts. The works. The complex, and it truly was a complex more than a park, was the biggest single weekend activity center in town. On Saturday mornings in the spring and fall in particular, it was typically abuzz with activity. Soccer tended to be the sport of choice, not only for the legions of kids running in no particular direction but for their soccer parents as well.

What I saw as I jogged around the perimeter of the park, both literally and figuratively, was a porridge of modern-day family dreams. Children looking to be between the ages of five and eight were running and jumping and kicking and heading and screaming their way through youth soccer games across an antipasto of several fields. Moms and dads and sisters and brothers and aunts and uncles and grandmothers and grandfathers stood along the sidelines, encouraging and cajoling and pleading with the young ones on the field before them to run faster and kick harder and just, well, try. At times these calls were heeded – with young Mia Hamms and Landon Donovans throwing themselves into the scrum, awkwardly emerging with the ball and descending toward the other end, their mouths hanging open in a mixture of terror and glee, the goalie-less nets inviting them to experience a glory they were just beginning to grasp. At times these calls were not – with various six-year-olds kneeling down, picking grass at one end of the field, with the action all at the other.

It was Americana that I saw on those fields, not necessarily at its best or finest, but at its truest.

"Isn't it great?"

I looked to my left. I had been so enthralled by the scene before me that I was idly standing between several fields, surrounded by hundreds but in a world to myself.

"I'm sorry? What?"

"The soccer, I mean. Isn't it great? It's a lot of fun to come out here and just take it all in. You look like you're doing just about that."

I was still gathering myself.

"You a soccer fan?"

"Well, not really. I just kind of stumbled onto it this morning during my jog."

"Well, the soccer quality isn't exactly world-class. It is entertaining, though. I call it bunchball."

"Bunchball?"

"Yeah. Look at that game over there. You see how all the kids are in a big group in the middle? They're all bunched together. I'd be surprised if half of them even know the ball is in there. And those that do, half of them aren't sure what to do with it."

"Sounds like torture to me."

"Torture? Oh, it's harmless fun."

"For the parents or the kids?"

"Jaded much?"

There was a pause. I didn't know what to say.

"My name is Marshall, Marshall McDougal."

"Well hello, Marshall McDougal. Sabrina Sapphire."

She grasped my outstretched hand. It was at this point that I first realized I was talking to a highly attractive young woman. I took my eyes off of hers quickly.

"Nice to meet you, Sabrina Sapphire. Anything else I should know about soccer?"

"Sure. You see that goal down there? The one none of the kids are kicking the ball toward?"

"Yep."

"That's called a goal. If you kick the ball into it, you get a point. If any of the kids make that happen, let me know. You can tell me in person tonight at the Double Dip."

"The Double Dip? You couldn't have made that one up."

"Well, I didn't make it up, but it pays the bills. I'm on shift tonight there. If you show up I might even serve you some frozen custard. If you don't laugh at the name, of course."

She smiled as she said this. The look on her face implied that she was playing with me.

"Uh, yeah. Maybe I'll see you tonight. Double Dip."

Sabrina looked around.

"What is it?"

"Smells like smoke. Just seeing if someone around us is smoking. Shouldn't do that around the kids. It's gross anyway. But, you know. The kids. Anyway."

I took a step back. Shreveport.

"Yeah. Was thinking the same thing. Double Dip."

With that, she disappeared into the throng of the big people rooting on the small people, regardless of whether the small people scored any goals. The point, I could see, was to be there, win or lose, goal or no goal, tears or more tears. I kept walking toward my car, still tired from my first week on the job, still sweating profusely from both my jog and the gathering heat, still smelling like smoke, still impressed by the humble grandeur of the scene around me, still a bit baffled by my brief-but-entertaining conversation with the all-too-engaging Sabrina Sapphire.

I spent the rest of the day catching up on the countless moving details that had been put aside during my first week in town, all of which reminded me of how much I hated moving. It had been just a week, but as I waded through the already-mushrooming mounds of unidentified laying objects in my midst, it felt like longer.

Main Street. The allegedly-named Double Dip was in my sights. I had finally regained control over the minutia around me. And eliminated the stench. Good excuses both, I felt, to take Sabrina Sapphire up on her offer.

I could not believe how hot it still was. I looked at my watch: 7:12 p.m. The temperature must be 95, I thought, probably more. But the issue at hand was not just the heat; that I was already, albeit grudgingly, getting used to. The more immediate concern was the extreme humidity. As hot and dry as the weather had been throughout the day, a storm had blown into town. The sun remained, somewhere, in the sky; the sky that was, only hours before, light blue in all its splendor was now, mostly to the north and west, obscured by a kaleidoscope of pure black to varying hues of darkened blue, a shiner under an eye, and the flashes of lightning that were cutting diagonally through the prism were like electrical beams in a syrupy swamp.

Perhaps as a symptom of the gathering moisture, a parallel universe of bugs had, literally in some cases, come out of the woodwork, and for the first time since my arrival in town I had become aware of their co-existence in what had heretofore outwardly presented itself as – outside of the scorpions having been evicted from their homes by the construction – an insect-free zone. Upon parking my car between the Double Dip and the hand car wash, I had engaged in a stare-down contest with the single biggest beetle I'd ever seen. It was so bulbous, so misshapen, it looked prehistoric. And if I hadn't next encountered without question the strangest-looking spider I'd ever seen, a virtual albino creation that had affixed itself to my windshield wiper, I'd still be staring at it.

I noticed the red and white "Frisco" water tower to my left. Modest in size and scope, its torso was weebil-shaped, with a rounded bottom, topped off by a red, beanie-cap shaped lid. Painted onto the center of the white body was a red, horizontally-tilted rectangle, inside of which the word "Frisco" was painted in white. Four white pillars held up the tower, which seemed to rise a good 100 feet from the ground.

The tower stood out as by far the tallest landmark for miles around. Regardless of its actual water content, if any, its purpose seemed to be that of beacon, the clock tower to the courthouse square, the lighthouse to the rocky point. As if to say to all around it, if you're looking for Frisco, Texas, look no further.

The Double Dip was hard to miss. Located in the shadow of the water tower, the building was modest but cheery in its appearance, yellow with a rounded pink arch in the middle, all covered with a garden hose-green, wood shingle roof. I wondered if it had formerly been a gas station. The parlor in front was framed by rolling glass doors that were rolled up to let guests in and were, in all likelihood, rolled down after closing.

Visitors arriving here in search of frozen custard have two choices: go through the drive-through on the right, or enter on foot to the left and sit at one of six round, metal tables, each of which is encircled by four purple stools, inside. Once inside the one-room parlor, the technicolor feel of the place only intensifies, thanks in great part to the collection of blue, red, green and yellow Christmas lights dangling from the 20-foot-high ceiling. A casserole of the increasingly heterogeneous blend of folks the town was attracting was on display. At one table sat a well-manicured, Polo-insignia'd family of four, at another an older, beefy man with a dark blue "USA" hat, long blue jeans, black boots and a long-sleeve black shirt.

I found myself in the back of a long line to order. Not yet seeing the still-mysterious Sabrina Sapphire behind the glassed-in counter, I glanced up at the menu. If I thought Scotty P's had an impressive array of menu choices, I had another calorie coming.

There was the "For Chocoholics Only": a rich brownie, fresh custard, extra hot fudge, marshmallow cream and pecans.

There was the "Mango Dango": fresh custard, fresh mangos, topped with pecans and cherries.

There was the "Big Dipper Sundae": scoops of custard with one's choice of toppings, covered with pecans and cherries.

If that wasn't enough, there was "The Gizmo": fresh custard, extra hot fudge, caramel, pecans and cherries.

"Taste of the South," said an older man with a protruding gut, apparently a veteran of more than a few Double Dip visits.

I was so caught up in the menu I had momentarily lost connection to my surroundings, a dynamic that appeared to be happening with increasing regularity.

"I noticed you taking it all in," the man repeated, smiling a generous smile. "You from 'round here?"

"No, I'm from California," I said, somewhat sheepishly. "My first visit to the Double Dip."

"Your first visit to the Double Dip?!" the man blurted out, still smiling. "Alright then son, let me welcome you. I'm the owner of this place. You let me know what we can do for you, okay?"

With that, the man was gone, off to wipe down another table with his white cloth. I looked up to see if I could locate Sabrina Sapphire. I was only two people from the window now. I glanced back up at the menu. The choices were good. Too good. All of a sudden there was nothing between the window and me. I looked up …and there she was. I froze for a split-second, the panic starting to set in. I approached gingerly.

"Well hello, Marshall McDougal," Sabrina said. Her smile was wide and bright, her two front teeth slightly oversized yet white as glue, her cheeks rounded like plums, her eyes big and oval and olive green.

I tried to get the words out. Any words would be good at this point.

Sabrina leaned toward the window. "This is when you're supposed to order something."

She said it quietly, but she might as well have blared it into a megaphone held directly into an open mike.

"Well, I have to admit I'm not exactly sure where to start. Lotta good choices."

I looked up at the menu, my desperation revealing itself more and more with each passing second.

"Well, what's your favorite flavor?"

"Not to sound boring, but I'm kind of a vanilla guy."

"Kind of a vanilla guy," Sabrina said, nodding her head. She had the same look on her face that she had at the soccer field.

"Well, we've got lots of things that will go with that. I'll start listing them, and why don't you stop me when something sounds good. Okay?"

"Okay."

"We've got almonds, we've got pecans, we've got pistachios, we've got Spanish peanuts, we've got pineapple and we've got butterscotch."

Sabrina looked up for a reaction. I wasn't about to get in the way of this. Now this was too good.

"Okay, well, you could try some blueberry, some Oreo cookies, some frosted mint, some cookie dough. Some raspberries even."

If she wasn't done yet, I still wasn't stopping her.

"I'll just read the rest of them off. Chocolate, caramel, cherry, chocolate chips, Reese's Peanut Butter Cup, Snickers, coconut, marshmallow, key lime, hot fudge, M&Ms, cheese cake, peaches, lemon, Heath, Butterfinger, Whopper Malt Balls, espresso, peanut butter, mango, strawberries, banana, Reese's Pieces, mint chips, green mint and, finally, ...espresso and cream."

She looked up, her work done. She had listed each topping more and more slowly as she read on, as if to tease both my senses and me more and more with each one.

"Anything there sound good?"

I had become more and more confused with each topping. Each one sounded better than the last. And I was even further mesmerized by her. She was cute when she got to butterscoth. She was really cute when she got to coconut. She was enormously cute by the time she got to espresso and cream.

Sabrina sensed I wasn't about to make a decision.

"Let me make a suggestion. I know you're kind of a, you know, pardon the pun, vanilla guy and all, and that works just fine here at the

Double Dip. How about we start you slow with some vanilla custard with pecans and cherries on top?"

Relief. "Sold. But why pecans and cherries?"

"There's nothing better than pecans and cherries on frozen custard, especially on a hot summer night," she said, smiling again. "But if you don't like it, you'll just have to come back and order more vanilla with a different topping-to-be-named later. Sound like a plan?"

"Sure," I said, reaching into my wallet. I knew I had just been outplayed.

"Nope, you're money's no good here," said the owner, watching the transaction about to take place. "First time at the Double Dip, it's on us. Welcome to Frisco, Texas."

"Thank you, sir," I said, extending a clammy hand. "I don't know what to say."

"Don't say anything while you're eating your custard, unless you've got a napkin, of course," he said, laughing. "But make sure to tell all your friends about us."

"Wow. Thanks." I was already fairly sure this was the single friendliest person I'd ever met.

"I'll come say hi in a few minutes," Sabrina said, laughing.

I gathered my frozen vanilla custard with pecans and cherries on top, white plastic spoon and handful of small white napkins and found a spot at the only open table. From which I felt myself being transported. The creaminess, the texture, was irresistible. The pecans and cherries were the perfect complement, providing something both crunchy and chewy to offset – yet not overwhelm – the smooth softness of the custard. I liked frozen custard. I did like frozen custard.

"So what do you think of my recommendation?" Sabrina said, hopping onto the stool beside me.

"Unbelievable," I offered in mid-bite. "This has gotta be the best ice cream I've ever had."

"You mean custard."

"Yes, custard. By the way, what is custard, anyway? Is it a form of ice cream, or is there some fundamental difference between ice cream and custard?"

"I'm not really sure. I think it has to do with how much air is beaten into it, or something like that. It's very close to gelato."

I took another bite as I pondered my next question. I was calmer now, my forehead no longer a rectangular aquarium of batter.

"So you work here full time?"

"No, just part time. That's Daddy that offered you the free custard."

"Your dad owns the place? That's cool. What else do you do?"

"Otherwise I study for a living. This is just a summer job. I've got one more year at North Texas, up in Denton."

"Oh, you mean the Mean Green," I said, pleased that a lifetime of the previously worthless practice of memorizing college nicknames was finally paying off.

"You know us then? I'm impressed."

"Yes, North Texas I believe is the only school in the country whose nickname comes from one of its former players."

"Which would be Mean Joe Greene."

"Absolutely."

"Okay, here's one for ya. Besides yours, there are only about a dozen colleges in the country whose nicknames do not end in 'S.' Let's see how many you can name."

"Well, let me see. Of course there's the Notre Dame Fighting Irish, that's easy."

Sabrina kept thinking. I kept chewing. And staring.

"Okay, I can think of a few more," she said. "There's the Stanford Cardinal, the Illinois Fighting Illini and the Marshall Thundering Herd."

"I've always thought Marshall's was the best nickname in the country. Or maybe I just like schools called Marshall," I said, smiling. "You're up to four now. Not bad."

"Then there's the Cornell Big Red and the Harvard Crimson. That's six, I think. And there's the Crimson Tide of Alabama, that's seven."

"I'm impressed," I said, offering her a high-five. "I thought I was the only person who cared about that kind of thing."

"Well, I don't exactly spend a lot of time thinking about college nicknames, but I do love sports. More than anything, I love Mean Green sports, of course."

"Well, we'll just have to see if you can remember the other five or so," I said. I was just finishing my frozen custard now, the last spoonful in my hand.

"Daddy says you're new in town."

"Yep. I'm the new kid in town. Just got here a week ago."

"And what brought you here, Marshall McDougal? Or should I call you 'Thundering Herd?'"

"Journalism. I'm the new reporter at the Evening Outlook."

"Oh, a writer. Very interesting. I've taken some writing courses at UNT."

"You like to write?"

"I love writing. Problem is, I'm not that good at it. You must be good if you want to be a journalist."

"I am a journalist."

"Of course. I read the paper today about that fire yesterday. Awful. Just awful. Who would do something like that?"

"I wrote that story."

"You're kidding! Now that's cool. I'm talking to a big-time reporter."

"Well, maybe someday."

Sabrina looked over her shoulder. "I better get back to work before Daddy gets on me. Thanks for coming in, Marshall. Maybe I'll see you again. I'll be here off and on all summer."

I wasn't about to let her get away that easily. "So what's your favorite sport?"

"Oh, no doubt – baseball. There's nothing like going to a baseball game. It's so much more pleasant than other sports, you know, because of the pace. You can actually go to a baseball game and have a conversation at the same time."

I could hardly contain my enthusiasm. "I love baseball – played it my whole life. I'd really like to get out to a Rangers game but I guess it's pretty far out there."

"Yeah, but we've got our Trailblazers. I'd just as soon go to a Blazers game than a Rangers game any day. The stadium's just down the road from here."

"Well, I've never been to a Trailblazers' game. Maybe we get to a game some time."

"I'd like that."

I had one last shot.

"How about tomorrow?"

"Tomorrow? Sure, I'll talk to Daddy to see if I can get the night off. I'm pretty sure the game is a night game tomorrow."

"You already know that?"

"Once it hits June, it's too hot for a lot of day games. Believe me when I tell you you'd much rather spend an evening at the ballpark than an afternoon. Not that it cools down a lot after the sun goes down, but every little bit helps, I guess."

"So you are a big fan."

"I know everything about the Blazers. They are Frisco's finest, after all. I'm pretty sure night games start at 7. I'll meet you at the ticket counter and we can just buy tickets and go in."

"Sounds great. See you there at 6:45?"

"It's a date," she said. With that, she headed through the door and back behind the glass counter.

From where, I had no doubt, she would reduce at least a handful of others to butterscotch, likely long before she got to espresso and cream.

I looked around as I climbed off the stool and headed out. Color truly was the order of the day at the Double Dip. On each table stood a silver vase enveloped by a purple ribbon and filled with red, yellow, purple and orange daisies. Above the customers hung four overhead fans, whirling round and round in a spirited attempt to modify the effects of the heat. One thing that did help was the frozen custard, though a point could be made that the company, at least the company I had just shared, had had the opposite effect.

One of life's great truisms is that there is nothing quite like cold ice cream on a hot summer night. On this hot summer night at the

Double Dip on Main Street in Frisco, Texas, I didn't just live this truth; I reveled in it, for all it was worth and more. Later that night, the rain finally came down, pounding the earth around me, transforming in the process concrete desert into brackish marsh. And when it was done, as I listened to the armada of cicadas now seemingly surrounding my window like a swat team called to a scene, their collective screech a thousand tiny jackhammers strong, they couldn't drown out my renewed hopes for a better tomorrow.

CHAPTER SIX

SAME OLD WHEEZERS

I was grease-bound, a junkyard hound to a New York strip, having heard about this Chick-fil-A place over at 121 and Preston. I had never been to Chick-fil-A; my only loose recognition of the name resulted from its sponsorship of one of the many random bowl games that lead up to the ones people outside of the host committee actually care about. Yet upon seeing it I felt frighteningly comfortable. I pulled up, a scientist in algorithmic ecstasy, the sweet song of the waffle fries calling my name like an old friend.

Closed?

Closed.

I let out a cry of at least somewhat-righteous indignation. At this point, I could only assume I was the lone wallow to miss the memo, a tardy mosquito in full inhale only to be waylaid by the brick wall of a hardened scab.

A fast-food joint closed on a Sunday. I shook my head and marched on.

Northbound on Preston I drove. Where I ran into another brick wall: a traffic jam. On a Sunday. Straight ahead, blocking all traffic from either direction, stood a brigade of navy blue-clad officers, their arms bobbing up and down like buoys in an idle bay. I looked to my left. A long procession of cars was emanating from what appeared to be a church, though with its collection of low-lying offshoots it was more compound than a place of worship. I wondered if this was the local church that was so big people called its sanctuary the Super Bowl of God.

The Super Bowl. It was way too hot to think about something associated with winter. But it's never too hot to think about baseball, I said to myself as I sauntered into Scotty P's, unsure whether I should admit to myself how thrilled I was that it was the first open spot I could find. Baseball is among our most benevolent words. Its mere utterance conjures up an image uniquely summer-in-America, so much so that you could paint it in red, white and blue, drape it with bunting, hang the kids off the side of the fire engine as it chugs down the street, streamers flowing from behind, delight in the air, and the best part is it doesn't fade, doesn't tear, remains young-at-heart no matter how much the morning sun exposes the wrinkles around the eyes.

In Frisco, Texas, I had come to learn, these images have played out for five decades through the Frisco TrailBlazers. The TrailBlazers were one of six teams that competed in the Southwest Conference Baseball League, an independent league founded in 1952. The league's name had originally spawned from the Southwest Conference, or SWC, the legendary football conference that disbanded in 1995.

In the meantime, the Southwest Conference Baseball League had continued to thrive, in great part due to a surge in independent baseball league interest in recent years springboarded by, among other developments, the resurrection of the Northern League, which had long been out of commission, in 1993. Numerous other independent baseball leagues had also sprouted up in various parts of the country since then, but the Southwest Conference Baseball League had survived for half a century, gaining prominence in independent baseball circles across the country for its ability to survive the ups and downs of minor league life. In fact, the league's unusually long tenure as a surviving independent league had earned it the nickname the "Wheezer League," in mock deference not only to its age but also to its custom of employing older players.

Teams in the Southwest Conference Baseball League often employed older players, or at least those over the age of 35, because many of the players attracted to its league had already migrated through their careers in the big leagues and/or outlasted their opportunities in the minor leagues, and were just happy to still be able to get paid, even modestly, to play baseball for a living. While that was a common element to independent league teams nationally, what made the Southwest Conference Baseball League different from other independent leagues in the attraction older players had to it was that its teams played (with the exception of Frisco, which most assumed was not big enough to host an actual Texas League team) in the same markets as teams in the Texas League, whose teams were formally tied to major league franchises, most often at the AA level.

That meant that fans in North Texas and the surrounding area, if they wanted to watch younger players trying to make it to The Show, would typically attend Texas League games. If they wanted to watch younger players try and leverage a stint in a local independent league in attempting to ascend the baseball food chain, they had the option of following, for example, a strong independent league team such as the Fort Worth Cats of the Central Baseball League.

That left, more often than not, the leftovers to be picked from by Southwest Conference Baseball League teams just happy to have players representing them who, for the most part at least, knew how to hit or throw. If it wasn't exactly the last round of kids picked for basketball on the seventh grade playground, with only the fattest, the shortest, the geekiest and the generally least popular left in the end, standing side-by-side yet increasingly alone along the yellow painted line, it was close enough. All of which had always been fine with Frisco, whose residents commonly referred to the team as "Frisco's Finest" regardless of how the team was doing. If the team was bad, or perhaps a player made a bad play, the Wheezer nickname would emerge from the shadows. "Same old Wheezers" was a term often heard about town when the team was going especially bad. Which was, alas, a little too often.

Baseball. Exclusively a major league baseball attendee to this point in my life, with the Trailblazers and Frisco Field as host I was about to attend my first-ever minor league game. In the case of what I was about to experience, the word "minor" might be considered an exaggeration. Regardless, I was more than ready to turn off my brain and enjoy an evening of baseball. Even better, an evening of baseball with Sabrina Sapphire.

"Thought you weren't gonna show, McDougal."

"Sorry I'm late," I said, scratching my ear in embarrassment.

"No problem. But we're gonna have to re-think the whole Thundering Herd thing."

"I'll remember that."

We grabbed hot dogs and Dr. Peppers and headed to our seats. It had been since the previous summer since I had been to a baseball game, and as soon as I sat down I couldn't help but take it all in. For the home of a team in an independent league I had never heard of, Frisco Field was a marvel. It had been renovated and re-opened in 2000, still in its original spot across the street from what now was the Stonebriar Mall, as a true ballpark – a sparkling testament to the formula that had started with Baltimore's Camden Yards less than a decade back of combining modern amenities with old-time charm.

The seats, all green bean green, enveloped the crisply cut diamond between the French's Mustard container-colored foul poles. There were 26 rows from first to last, giving the ballpark the type of intimate feel only a minor league ballpark can offer. "Hey 23!" a young boy yelled to the visiting Arkansas MarVista left fielder from the 10th row back, and there was little doubt the player could hear.

Behind home plate rose the pavilion, built all out of wood but painted off-white. There were two rows in the pavilion. The bottom one was for press, the second for luxury suites. There were eight suites in all, and win or lose, each was filled with the faithful every night.

There were also smaller pavilions going down each line. Each of the pavilions was connected by wooden catwalks, which at first glance seemed to be the most social areas of the ballpark. People loitered on the bridges, sipping their soda or beer, with seemingly no worries, no agendas. Many of them did not seem remotely interested in the action on the field below.

But no ballpark worth its salted peanuts steps up to the plate without offering some distinctive detail, a seminal imperfection, a nook here, a cranny there, that sets it apart. And the two most distinctive parts of Frisco Field were what was behind the outfield walls and what was down each line.

The first was that behind the outfield walls, running from foul line to foul line, were not seats, but grass. Surely one should not throw around the term "grassy knoll" lightly in Texas, particularly not around Dallas. But essentially running all the way around the outfield behind the walls was, in fact, a grassy knoll. Fans could sit out there at their leisure. There were no seats. Typically families would lay out blankets and have a picnic. And then parents would allow their kids to run around on the grass once the moment would inevitably arrive when they were tired of sitting. The second was the fact that, down each line toward the foul pole, the bullpens were actually in the stands. At first glance, this should be worrisome to those seated in the vicinity, particularly since the seats are protected from wild pitches only by a three-foot-high concrete wall.

"There's nothing like an evening at the ballpark in Frisco," Sabrina said. "We may have more than our share of weird things going on in this town, but we do baseball pretty well."

Fourth inning. The TrailBlazers were up now. With one out, center fielder Nick Ross strode to the plate with the bases loaded. A murmur went through the crowd, like it has for the first time realized there is an actual game being played.

"Who's this guy?" I asked. "Everyone seems really excited that he's up."

"That's Nick Ross."

"Who?"

"Nick Ross. He's the center fielder. Fastest guy on the team. By far."
Sabrina hesitated for a moment.

"Well, the team's not real fast in general, but he's still pretty fast."

Ross grounded to short for a force, tying the game. The next batter, shortstop Gregg Rexfordson, whose father, the manager, and twin brother, the first baseman, also happened to be with the team, doubled up the alley, scoring two. A third batter in a row, second baseman Cesar Jeffrey, lined one into right, scoring another.

All of a sudden, the TrailBlazers were up, 5 to 2, and all was good at Frisco Field. The fans were cheering appreciatively, with the home team now in control. And it was a typical summer night at the ballpark in North Texas. The temperature was in the high 90s as the game headed into the bottom of the fifth. There was a breeze, inexplicably, miraculously, mercifully, but a hot one, and the sensation was like blow-drying your hair when it's already dry. You just wanted to jump into something wet, something with any form of liquid associated with it, so you could get some relief.

I looked at the ballplayers and wondered how they put up with it. The catcher in the bullpen for the MarVistas was grunting more and more loudly with each warm-up pitch. His thick, hairy, Popeyed forearms were dripping with sweat. In the meantime, he was barely moving.

"So what do you want to do when you finish college?"

"You mean other than go to Blazer games?"

"There's more than this?"

"Actually, I'm not sure yet. I was looking into teaching. I also know a few people at EDS so I thought I'd look into that."

"At EDS, huh? Why there?"

"That's where Daddy worked until he retired a few months back. He did all sorts of things there. He did sales for a long time, and then they wanted him to go into IT so he did some of that. He worked there for 30 years."

"That's incredible," I said, shaking my head. "I didn't think people did that anymore."

"It still happens, especially at places like EDS. It's really an amazing place. There are so many people there who have been there so long, it's a way of life as much as a job. I really admire that."

A poker face mine was not.

"What are you thinking about?"

"Well, I don't want to say the wrong thing, but that's just so...I don't know, I guess just foreign to me."

"What is?"

"What I mean is, my father did the same thing. He didn't work for a big company or anything, but he runs his own law firm. He joined the firm, which my grandfather ran, right out of law school. Other than when he was in the Air Force for a few years, he has been there ever since."

"Good for him. I'm impressed."

"The thing is, I never have been that impressed by it. I mean, there's nothing wrong with being a lawyer, but it's not like the firm is a big international firm or something. It's a small lawyers' shop in Santa Monica. My father likes to call himself a 'country lawyer.'"

"I assume he means that as a compliment?"

"I've never been sure."

"I mean, I don't know him of course, but he sounds like someone who has lived a good life, who has raised a family and who has carried on the tradition started by his dad of being a lawyer. There's nothing at all wrong with being, as you say, a 'country lawyer.'"

Sabrina hesitated again, and I could already tell that that meant some sort of summary comment was forthcoming.

"I think it sounds great," she said, gazing down at the field. "I think it sounds like the kind of life that one should want. You know, that one should strive for."

"Well, I've never been that one," I said. "And I thought about being a lawyer – it's kind of hard not to when everyone asks you growing up if you're going to be a lawyer like your father and grandfather. It just never has appealed to me."

"So you've chosen not to follow in your dad's footsteps, which has led you to Frisco."

"Yeah, you could say that," I said, chuckling. "Not quite sure yet what to make of that."

"Well, you'll do fine here if you work hard and are honest. Frisco's a good town. There are good people here."

"I can see that," I said, offering Sabrina my eye. "I guess I just had to get away from home. Someday I'll get back, I'm sure. I mean, unless you want to end up on the East Coast, which I don't, if you want to write for a big-time paper the Times is it."

"So that's what you want."

"That's what I want."

"Then Frisco is just a stop on the express for you, huh?"

"That's the plan. I mean, no offense, but it's not exactly the big leagues here."

In the baseball equivalent of being saved by the bell, the crowd erupted. Left fielder Thom Seacurg had just piled on with a mammoth shot to left. The Blazers were up now, 6-2. Fireworks shot off from behind the center field wall. Frisco Field was, literally, electric.

"Blazers are looking good tonight," I said.

"I'm not celebrating yet," Sabrina shot back, suddenly seeming less than thrilled with her surroundings. "Too many disappointments in the past. Besides, it's only the fifth inning."

We went back to watching the game. Two innings later, the MarVistas staged a rally. Trailblazer starting pitcher Dwayne Hodgekinz was laboring. He was visibly upset, having just taken a line drive off his thumb, and I was fairly sure I could make out the curse words he was spewing as he constrictored the life out of the rosin bag. A few seconds later, the MarVistas had recorded their fourth consecutive hit; they were now within two runs at 6-4, and the tying run was coming to the plate. I was now completely sure I could make out the curse words Hodgekinz was throwing around on the mound.

"Same old Wheezers," Sabrina muttered, shaking her head.

The elder Rexfordson waddled out to the mound for a chat with his pitcher. I couldn't help but notice he was wearing a green sweater over his jersey.

"Why is he wearing a green sweater? Is that allowed? I don't think it would be in the majors."

"He wears it most nights. It's kind of his signature. I like it."

"Are you serious? Look at that thing. I mean, who the hell would wear that?"

The hurler's evening was likely over, which would be the bad news for Hodgekinz. The good news would be that, if the TrailBlazers could protect the lead, he would still be in line for the win.

Rexfordson looked up and signaled for the pen. As soon as the fans saw the right hand go up, a rousing cheer filled the air. Almost on cue, in jogged closer Marcus Roodie, who happened to be not only the TrailBlazers' closer but the best one in the SWC. Roodie leaned in for each warm-up pitch, pushing his black wire-frame glasses back up the bridge of his nose between each one, and fired toward home. Catcher Don Sugimuri, a former star in the Japanese league, was practically driven backward on his feet by the force of the pitch.

"This guy's kinda scary," I said. "Reminds me of Gagne without the music."

"Who?"

"Eric Gagne. He's the closer for the Dodgers. Every time he comes in they play 'Welcome to the Jungle' in the stadium. It's great."

"We'd do that here, you know, if we had a loudspeaker."

"You have a loud—"

"Just kidding. Though it'll be really nice someday when we get plumbing."

"What?"

Sabrina stared ahead. "Come on Roodie!"

I leaned over. "Did I say something wrong?"

"Well, no," Sabrina said, pausing for effect. "Not really."

"You're playing with me again."

"Oh, so you noticed. Not bad for a country girl. That's alright. It's a minor league thing. You wouldn't understand."

I tried to respond, but the din was growing. The opposing batter was digging in. The bases were loaded. The fans wanted this rally stopped, and stopped now. I looked up at the catwalks; all eyes were focused on the field below.

Roodie wound up...strike one.

The flat-footed batter hadn't bothered to swing. Roodie leaned in again, squinting for the sign from Sugimuri.

The MarVista batter swung.

Strike two.

The din grew louder. Roodie was in control. Third baseman Doug Jinsberg approached for a quick chat, Roodie, with hand on chin, nodding his head with the confidence of an art bidder.

The suspense was building by the moment. It was Frisco Field in Frisco, Texas, it was the Southwest Conference Baseball League, it was June and it was the Frisco TrailBlazers against the Arkansas MarVistas in front of 1,500 people. Not exactly Dodger Stadium in October, the World Series on the line, 56,000 fans on their feet, a national television audience looking on. That's what I was used to; that's the world I had grown up in, had experienced, had known all my life. A different world, this was.

"C'mon, Roodie!" Sabrina yelled, her voice straining now with the others'.

Strike three!

Roodie had fanned the batter on three pitches. The TrailBlazers' lead was safe, at least for another inning. The fans cheered wildly. For an instant, I allowed myself to get caught up in the excitement. I wasn't convinced, but I was trying.

"Time for the best part of the evening," Sabrina said.

The seventh inning stretch. If it's true there is nothing like baseball in summer, it's as true there is nothing like the heavy sigh, the convergence of the believers, the hope for the retchid, the chance to pedestal the marrow of the game the seventh inning stretch represents. And all at once, as the crowd broke into song, I felt myself letting go. I was being transformed by this most familiar of tunes, transformed to Dodger Stadium in my beloved Los Angeles, transformed to the foot of the Green Monster at Fenway Park just off the Charles in Boston, transformed to the heart of the Bronx in New York at Yankee Stadium, transformed to the Friendly Confines of the North Side of Chicago at Wrigley Field, transformed to any and all of the iconic cathedrals of America's grandest and oldest of games. For no matter where you are when you're at a baseball game, there's always going to be the seventh inning stretch, the fans are always going to insert the name of their favorite team when proclaiming in unison who to root for, "Take Me Out to the Ball Game" is always "Take Me Out to the Ball Game" and, best of all, baseball is always baseball.

"I love this part," Sabrina said, swaying along with the others.

I was beginning to think I had perched myself a bit too high on my big city horse. I waited for the song to end and turned to her.

"I guess I need to explain myself. I didn't mean to put Frisco or the minor leagues down. I've only been here a week, and I have to say that everyone seems great. Sorry if I offended you. Things are just, well, different here, that's all."

"It's okay. Believe me, I understand Frisco is not exactly the be-all, end-all. I just think there are more important things than how big or important a place or a job is. What matters most to me is if you're doing something real, something that matters, something that, somehow, makes your community a better place to live. That you're doing right by your family, that you're caring for others. Simple, I guess. Simple doesn't have to be so bad."

"And that's your destiny? You know that?"

"I'm not quite sure yet. But I know it will come to me. And I know it will come to me because I know who I am. You've gotta start with that, I think."

I nodded. "I think I understand what you mean."

"Do you?"

"Yeah, I think I do. I think I do."

Twenty minutes later, the game was over. Roodie had preserved the victory for the Trailblazers with two-and-a-third shutout innings. Hodgekinz had earned the win. The team had now won four in a row, and had surged to within two games of first. Not too bad for a team for which losing was a way of being.

There was joy in Dr. Pepperville this season, at least so far.

"I enjoyed the game, Marshall, thanks," Sabrina said, as we walked into the parking lot.

"Well, hello there, pretty lady."

"Sammy?"

"And Mister Marshall, I see. Well, well. Small world."

Sabrina didn't seem thrilled. "Hi … Sammy."

Sammy looked at Sabrina.

"How are you?"

"Fine."

I was starting to feel invisible.

"Do you guys know each—"

"Might say so, Mister Marshall. Sabrina here's my girl."

"Oh, I uh …"

"Isn't that right Sweetie."

"Sammy, we had one date. I wouldn't call myself your girl, ok?"

I was starting to wish I were invisible.

"Sammy, Sabrina and I just met yesterday. Tonight's the first time we've spent together. Sorry if—"

"All good, Mister Marshall, all good. Tell you what. If you could just excuse yourself from the proceedings here for a moment it'll all be even better."

"Excuse myself from the proceedings?" I was becoming more and more confused by the minute.

"Marshall, we just need a second, ok?"

I stood back. "Ok, but I'll be right over here."

I watched as Sammy and Sabrina engaged in conversation. I still couldn't tell who was intruding on whose date, Sammy or me, but as the conversation went on it was clear that Sammy was more interested than Sabrina in continuing it.

Sammy looked over at me.

"Young Mister Marshall here says he's been to Las Vegas, Nevada a bunch of times. Now that I've seen him lose pretty much all he's got out there in Shreveport, I'd say gambling's not exactly his strong suit."

"What does gambling have to—"

With that, Sammy was gone with the crowd.

"You know him too?"

"Yeah, guy I work with."

'Oh, right. The paper. Small town is right."

"Small town, alright."

"And we know how much you enjoy small towns."

Neither of us knew what more to say.

"Ok Marshall, here's the situation. For a long time Sammy has, well. How do I put this. We had one date once, and I didn't even want to go. It was ok I guess, but that was it. Let's just say Sammy wanted more, and I didn't."

"How long ago was that?"

"Couple of years, two or three. I don't even know, really."

"And he still hasn't let it go?"

"You don't know Sammy. He doesn't let anything go."

"He seemed fine the other night in Shreveport. I mean, we had a good time."

"Oh, Sammy's all about the good time. Unless, of course, he's not getting his way. But he'll smile through it. At least while you're looking."

"He got his way a lot the other night with the dealers."

"Whereas you apparently did not."

"What did he mean with the gambling comment? Sounded like a threat."

"Don't worry about Sammy. Just stay clear of him, that's all."

"I thought he and I were becoming friends."

"Just stay clear, ok?"

"Advice accepted."

We each took a deep breath.

"Good night, Marshall. I enjoyed the game."

"I enjoyed the game, too, Sabrina," I said. "Look for me in the paper. Maybe I'll stop in for some frozen custard."

"I'd like that."

With that, she turned and walked away. I watched her until she was out of sight before turning to find my car. There was something to her stride and the way she softly but firmly wiggled that wouldn't allow me to look away. I found it both innocently adorable and highly arousing at the same time. Take me out to the ball game, to be sure.

"In Texas, a political speech is sometimes referred to as a Longhorn: one that makes two good points, but they are a long way apart and have a lot of bull in between." – Don't Throw Feathers at Chickens by Herring & Richter

Northwest corner of Parkwood and Warren,
in front of an office building

CHAPTER SEVEN

TUESDAY NIGHTS

N ow that I had experienced the oldest part of town, I had decided I wanted to see for myself what the "new" Frisco looked like. I had gotten more than an earful now about the strains of the "new" versus the "old" element in town, and the extent to which the burgeoning Fighting Coon debate was a reflection of that dynamic. So I knew I should also see the other side of the tracks, so to speak, especially if I was to encounter the very people tonight who would ultimately decide the issue. Besides, with the temperature projected to hit 103 that day, I wasn't exactly looking to spend a lot of time outside with a bull's eye on my Scottish skin.

I recalled Short having told me about Starwood, which I knew was close when I saw the two-story-high, burnt red brick tower just right of the Dallas North Parkway as I approached from the north. The brick tower was exactly as Short had described it, marked only by a white star enveloped by a circle. I knew at once that that meant Jerry Jones' gated country haven – Short had told me Cowboys owner Jerry Jones had developed Starwood -- was at hand.

Turning right on Lebanon and passing under the tower, I first noticed a brick building on the right, which the sign in front proclaimed to be the Starwood Montessori School. Immediately after the school grounds, I came upon Starwood. The two-way entrance and exit was buffeted by a long, tree-lined, hedge-decorated island in the middle, all leading to a guard station in front of two large, black, iron gates. I pulled to the side; within seconds, a car approached behind me, automatically opening the gate. Seeing that the guard booth was not manned, I scooted through on the other car's coattails, and I was in.

It took me roughly a millisecond to see that Starwood was a very different Frisco than the residential neighborhood north of Main Street I had first experienced over the weekend. Nowhere were the older, wooden homes, with the high weeds and the rusted pick-ups in the driveways. Passing the community center on my left, I tooled slowly around what appeared to be the beginning of a circular road. I took a left on the first street, Spanish Oaks. Huge, mostly brick homes, clearly newly constructed, lined the street. While most front lawns were fairly modest in size, the buildings that hovered over them did so with brooding grandeur. About four homes in on the left, I noticed a star on a front door. I gathered that this must be one of the homes in Starwood inhabited by a Dallas Cowboy; Short had also told me that, due to Jones having developed Starwood, several Cowboys players lived there.

I kept circling around the street as it veered to the left. Every home I passed was bigger, more lavish, more bodacious than the last. Glistening estates, many protected from passersby by locked gates and moat-like circular driveways, were lined up, one after the other. Many featured rounded passageways through which cars must pass to get to the garage in the back. Behind each lot stood a virtual forest of trees, and I could imagine the highly-manicured state of the backyards over which they presided.

I kept driving around Starwood, up one street and down the other. It didn't take me more than a few minutes to make the jump that, perhaps like Frisco itself, there were two Starwoods: one on the inside of Texas Drive, the name of the circular road I had first followed, the other on the outside.

On the inside of Texas Drive, mansions varying to a degree in size and scope, yet mansions for the most part nonetheless, were the order of the day. On the outside, the size of home was more modest, if 3,500 square feet can merit such a qualifier. At the same time, though, each was beautiful in its own right as well. In these parts of Starwood, two-story brick home after two-story brick home followed one another, like pieces of fine china lined up inside an armoir. The only notable differences were slight design variations, which appeared to repeat every few houses, and, perhaps, the shade of red of the bricks. I kept driving by one home in particular outside of which there was a brown, wooden bench, its shade and sense of invitation presenting a package more like that of a highback recliner finished with Chesterfield Bark leather, and a surrounding landscaping job, complete with eraser-shaped, chalk-white rocks lining the flower bed as meticulously as needlepoint, that rivaled any inside the unspoken border of Texas Drive.

Exiting the community out of its rear gate, I found myself on Legacy Drive, which I knew to be the street along which several major companies, including EDS, were headquartered just to the south in Plano. This was Gated Community Central. First, Lakes on Legacy, then Stonebriar, to the right. To the left, a handful more under construction, signposts all for modernized privilege and private living.

Passing the last construction site on my left and approaching on my right a taller, more commercial looking, lighter-brick building, which turned out to be the new Westin Stonebriar resort, I noticed the entrance to the Stonebriar Country Club. Listing into the driveway before the rushing cars behind me could bear down any more, I meandered my way first up, then down a slight hill while encountering a spectacular sight to my right: rolling hills of green, clearly professionally-greenskeepered grass as far as the eye could see, all bordered by rows of several stories-tall trees along either side. What I was longingly gazing at was the Stonebriar golf course, which, though I wouldn't have known it at the time, was not only championship-caliber but was soon to be joined by the latest designer creation as its high-end sibling. I next approached what appeared to be the club's main building, a limestone-constructed nod to suburban exclusivity complete with a four-column overhang for incoming visitors.

Exiting the grounds of the country club, I now better understood the Snake River Canyon-like chasm that Short had described at lunch several days prior. If this was the new Frisco, I assumed it had to be inhabited by people who were making good money, likely had grown up elsewhere and, more than likely, had well-defined expectations of a town in which to live. Among them not having the one and only high school in their adopted hometown going to battle as the Fighting Coons.

Skimer's eyes never left the wall.

"Have a seat, McDougal. Bennie with ya?"

"Haven't seen her."

"Bet she's smoking. You a smoker, McDougal?"

I was momentarily surprised by the question.

"A smoker. You light up, son?"

"Nope. Don't touch it."

"Good. Not where you wanna be. Bad breath in a bag. Don't start now, though this business will get ya thinking about it, at least. Believe me."

Skimer wheeled around just as Bennie strode in, and the two launched into a Pentagon-esque preview of my evening. We pored over the pre-published agenda with the gusto of buccaneers. Neither Skimer nor Bennie saw anything that they felt would require a story the next day. There was, of course, a caveat: until the meeting was done, it couldn't be known whether anything newsworthy was needing to be shared with the next day's Evening Outlook readers.

The sole remaining discussion item was the rundown of the school board.

"Let's start with Classen," Skimer said, and it was clear he was just getting warmed up. "He's a nut. A nut, I'm telling ya. Nut. Supposed to be the bill cow. Just another nut though."

"How so?"

"You'll see. You'll see."

"Okay. Sax?"

"Sax? Almost a nut."

"Manemin?"

"Manemin? Nut. Aggie, which should tell ya pretty much everything you need to know. Says he's not a card-carrying member, but don't you believe it."

"So he went to Texas A&M."

"What Rip here means is, Marshall, is that Aggies are a little—"

"Don't worry about that none, McDougal. You'll learn about them Texas Aggies, real quick. Let's talk Barronkoff. Piece-a-work. Watch your back."

"Will do. Mass?"

"Mass. She's okay. Just watch your grammar. She'll correct ya. Do it right in front of the others. Right there, she'll do it."

"And then there's Hurstman."

"Hurstman. She's okay. Yep. Nice lady. Bit of a nut. But a nice one."

"And then there's Stevens."

"Who?"

"Stevens. Brianna Stevens?"

Skimer looked at Bennie. "Heard of her?"

"Barely. Rip, can we—"

"Oh, yeah. Stevens. Newly-elected. Unknown quantity. That one's in your court, McDougal. Probably a nut."

Bennie looked at me and took a deep breath.

"Welcome to Tuesday nights."

I arrived early to the meeting. My first order of business was to introduce myself to as many school board members and administrators as possible. With some help from Short, and taking into account Skimer's editorial commentary, I had studied up on the school board members' bios.

Classen was a lifelong Frisco resident, a local pharmacist and an active booster of the Fighting Coon athletic program, particularly the football team. Sax was also a lifelong Frisco resident, ran a personal investment firm in town and was a huge fan of any team representing the burnt orange of his alma mater, the University of Texas. Manemin had attended the Frisco schools with Sax, ran a local oil services company and differed in views from Manemin only on their college choice.

Beyond Classen, Sax and Manemin, there were four other members of the board. Two were retired teachers, neither of whom had been raised in Frisco, Mass and Hurstman. Mass, from New Jersey, and Hurstmann, from Chicago, had come to Plano in the late 70s before moving to Frisco and teaching there, and had only retired from the classroom in recent years. The remaining two board members were homemakers – Stevens, who also served on the boards of several non-profit organizations in town, and Barronkoff, who worked part-time at a local art store.

This mix of local businessmen, retired teachers and homemakers was standard fare for school boards across the country. So was the fairly even combination of four men and three women. I assumed that Classen, given his position as president, would be my main go-to person for information. Walking into the auditorium, where several people were clustered in small circles talking before the meeting, I knew I would have to figure out who I could get to know, who I had to be wary of. The first person I looked for was Classen, whose photo I had seen several times from past articles in the paper.

"Uh, excuse me, are you Grady Classen?" I asked, having quickly spied and approached my prey.

"Yes, I am."

I was surprised at Classen's volume. He was tall, probably about 6'3", with the circumference of your average major appliance. He had a large, rounded face. His medium brown hair, having receded toward the top of his forehead, was tightly combed, his slightly darker brown mustache thick and bushy. His brown eyes were obscured by gold-rimmed bifocals. And he wore the uniform of your prototypical pharmacist: the short-sleeve, white button-down shirt, complete with the thin, black, ball-point pen in the chest pocket; the solid, pale blue tie that, even in the best of times before the long-since-occurred expansion and associated dungeoning of the waistline, was a half-foot too short; the long, brown pants that reeked of a typical busboy's in a lower middle class soup-and-sandwich joint; the black, rubbery loafers; and the black socks that, while they matched the shoes, did more to advertise the visual disconnect between the brown pants and the black shoes than anything.

"Marshall McDougal, with the Evening Outlook," I said, extending my hand. I had been careful not to call Classen "Mr. Classen" lest I generate the same "My father's name was Mr. Skimer" treatment I got from Skimer.

"Evening," Classen said, firmly grasping my hand while eyeing my tweed coat with suspicion. It was one of those handshakes where the bigger hand, in this case Classen's, accidentally engulfs the other, smaller hand, in this case mine, such that the bigger hand is essentially squeezing a set of floating fingers as lifeless as a mass of straws from a container in a fast food restaurant. I tried to quickly correct the imbalance, but Classen's hand was already gone by this point, pulled back probably more out of pity than anything.

"Glad to have ya here," he mumbled. "Bill, K.C., come meet the new Evening Outlook guy."

Over sauntered two middle-aged men, both looking friendly but equally forthright. Manemin looked the part of an investment advisor, if a small town one. His shirt was white with thin, even whiter, vertical lines, which I quickly deciphered were slightly raised in such a way to make a valiant attempt to uplift the shirt's quality but had the opposite effect because they exposed his wife-beater underneath. Sax, approaching on Manemin's left, was both tall and lanky, with surprisingly wavy, blond hair for a man his age. While Sax was graying throughout, his natural blond hair served to obscure it.

"Marshall, uh, what did say your last name was again?" Classen said, attempting an introduction. He was still mumbling, and I wondered for a moment if he was an epileptic.

"McDougal, Marshall McDougal," I said. I over-extended on both counts, essentially shaking their forearms.

"Pleasure to meet you, Marshall," Manemin said.

"Welcome to your first Frisco school board meeting," Sax added. "We'll see if we can make it worth your while tonight."

"Oh, I'm sure it will be," I said, offering my best fake laugh. "I'm looking forward to working with all of you."

"Well, hopefully you'll last longer than the last guy," Sax said, shaking his head and looking at Classen.

I tried to ignore the comment about my predecessor. The fact that my predecessor's demise was an ongoing source of comment for people was already wearing thin. Not that I was going to admit that to the school board, of course, but I was not enjoying being part of whatever game everyone but me was apparently playing.

"So tell us about yourself, Marshall," Classen said. "You a product of our fine public school system here?"

"Well, not exactly," I said, stammering a bit. "Actually, I'm from California."

"California?" Sax said.

"Yes, believe it or not I ended up all the way out here in Frisco."

Classen was getting impatient. "So where did you go to school now?"

"Well, I went to high school at Loyola High. It's a Jesuit prep school, in Los Angeles. Downtown Los Angeles, actually."

"You said a Jesuit school, a Catholic school?" Sax asked. "You didn't go to a public school? You some sort of blue-blood?"

"Well, not exactly…"

Manemin looked at Sax. "Kid says 'not exactly' a lot."

"Well—"

"You know, Marshall, I'm sure you're a good writer and all, but let me tell you we're not about the blue bloods up here. That's for Dallas down there in the big town, with all their Hockadays and all their Park Cities and all their Minks and all Cadillacs churches and all that kinda stuff," Classen said. "Up here in the country, we're just doing what we can to serve our students. Not everybody likes how we do it. Just doing the best we can."

Besides not understanding what a church would have to do with either fur coats or fancy cars, I knew I was being tested. I sensed failure; I hated failure. Here I was, the new education beat reporter, my second week on the job, trying to get to know the people on the school board I will have to cover, and the ratfuckers among them were openly questioning my credibility. Worse than being worried about my lack of experience, they're wondering aloud whether someone from my background can understand their world. That was worse, I quickly realized, because no matter how much I proved to them I could do a responsible job in covering them, I wouldn't be able to connect to them. And that would make getting the insights I would need to get the real stories that much harder.

My mind was running fast.

"I did go to public school until high school. It was just that the public school for our neighborhood scared my parents off a bit. It wasn't a bad school – in fact, my mom had actually gone there herself. It was more about having, you know, an opportunity to do something different."

"You mean to do something better."

"Not exactly…"

"So you're a Catholic, then?" Sax asked.

"Well, actually, no. I was raised Presbyterian."

"And your parents sent you to one of those Catholic schools?"

"Well, like I said, my parents saw, well, you know. An opportunity, I guess. I had a couple of older friends on our block who had gone there, and they both loved it. Seemed like a great school, and it turned out to be a great experience."

"Alright, let's lay off the new guy," Manemin said. "Marshall, you let us know what we can do to help now."

I sauntered off and settled into a seat in the auditorium. Three hours later, with the once-robust crowd now having dwindled to less than 10, I was virtually ambulatory in my seat. The board had debated issue after issue, most of which – even though it had already agreed on a budget for the following school year – revolved around money. For the most part, I had tried to follow along. My first thought was that it would have been good if someone had forced me to take a finance course. Just after 11 p.m., the agenda items mercifully exhausted, it was time for final public comments. My eyelids were gaining weight, and

I had glanced at my watch more and more frequently as the evening wore on.

An older, slight man in a light brown Cardigan sweater approached the mike. I looked over at him, and was reminded of Rexfordson approaching the mound at Frisco Field wearing a green sweater two nights before. This made me chuckle. Do these people not realize how hot it is?

"I would like to ask that the school board immediately vote on the Fighting Coon name," the man said. He was reading from prepared notes, his voice stammering. "It is an outrage that in this day and age a city like Frisco insists on using a nickname for its teams that has for years now been considered racially offensive."

I tensed up as the man returned to his seat, apparently having spoken his peace, and noticed that others in the room did the same.

"Thank you, Mr. Jordan," Classen said. "As you know, the board is not scheduled to vote on this issue until this coming school year. We will take your comments into consideration at that time."

I was aghast. This seemingly humble man had sat through three hours of discussion about facility leases and administrative leave and frozen vegetable prices, had waited until shortly before midnight to read his statement. He had been visibly nervous standing in front of the board while speaking into a microphone. He had spoken his mind, his heart. And all Classen could offer was boilerplate.

I waited until the comment section was over and started to approach Classen for a word on the man's comments.

"Understand you're the new education reporter for the Evening Outlook," said a woman's voice to my right.

I had not noticed anyone standing nearby. "Uh, yes, and what is your name?"

"Eleanor, Eleanor Barronkoff," the woman said. She was middle-aged, with sandy brown hair. Her black-rimmed reading glasses hung on a white chord around her neck. "Did you not see me participating in the discussion tonight? I mean, you are a reporter, right?"

"Hello, Eleanor," I said. "Yes, I saw you up there."

"It's German. Barronkoff, I mean. You might say I emigrated from the German Nation north of San Antonio. You oughtta get down there sometime. Ever heard of Schlitterbahn? It's a water park. Huge."

I was both surprised and confused at the thought of a large German population in Texas. "Haven't gotten down there yet," I said. "I haven't been here real long yet. I have seen some of Plano, though."

"Son," Barronkoff said, laughing. "Plano ain't Texas."

"I'm gathering that."

"So Grady told me you were here tonight. What did you think of your first school board meeting?"

"I thought it was good," I said, trying not to commit. "I thought the discussion about funding priorities was great. It allowed me to better understand where the school district is going. Helped me understand things more."

Barronkoff was watching me intently.

"So what are your thoughts on what that man at the end suggested about the Coon name?"

"Are we off the record?"

"Absolutely."

"Well, I just think that this whole nickname thing is a real challenge for us now, Marshall. I mean, the problem is, the community is wondering more and more why we are not dealing with it now. The reality is, we want to give people the majority of a school year to weigh in before we make a change assuming we even do make a change. It's a lot of history to unravel with one vote."

"And why is that a problem?"

"It's not a problem for everyone. It's only a problem for people who want the change now. But we've got a football season to play first, and we're not going to change now."

My antennae went up. "I don't understand. Why couldn't you change now? I mean, football season is two months off, right?"

"Yes, but we have uniforms to order, schedules to print. It's just not practical to make a change of this magnitude right now. So we're looking at next Spring for a vote."

"Makes sense."

I realized I had not been taking notes.

"You mind if I write this down?"

"Not at all. I just wanted to say hello and welcome you to Frisco. Let me know if I can help."

"I will. By the way when did Grady tell you about me being here?"

"In closed session."

"You talked about me in closed session? Why would you do that?"

"Oh, no reason. Let's just say Grady was interested to have met you."

With that, she was gone. I looked around, and unfortunately, so was Classen. In fact, other than the janitorial staff, I was now the last one there. Back in the newsroom, night editor Mike Farbian approached me at my desk. He had the look of a man who had been sitting on a park bench a little too long.

"How'd it go, Marshall? Anything we need to write up?"

"No, I don't think so. They mainly just talked about financial topics. Pretty boring stuff."

"Sounds good," Farbian said, sounding relieved. "I'll tell the press guys to put things to bed for the night."

"The only thing that seemed newsworthy at all was that the board doesn't plan to address the Coon nickname until after football season."

Farbian looked up from his screen.

"Was that part of the meeting?"

"No, one of the school board members told me afterward. The president told one of the speakers the board wasn't planning to vote on the name until the school year at some point, which I guess isn't news, right? But then one of the members told me afterward they were looking at springtime for a vote."

Farbian wasn't so sure. "Well, that part about a delay from this summer isn't really news. But what you're telling me is that a member of the school board told you it was because of football season?"

"Well, yeah, pretty much," I said, trying to recall the logic of the conversation. "She said they had uniforms to order, schedules to get printed. That type of thing."

"That's at least worth a brief. We don't have much time, but we should get it in."

I was surprised. "Really? I mean, I'm happy to write it up, but again, is that really news?"

"I wouldn't call it front page news, but it's at least some definition on the issue. I can't imagine the residents pushing on this would be thrilled to hear they have to wait until after football season. This is the first time the school board has put a timetable on it."

I was starting to get nervous. I was tired. I had figured my work for the night was done.

"One other thing, Mark," I said, now really forced to recall my conversation with Barronkoff more specifically. "The board member who told me this said I couldn't use her name."

Farbian paused. "Well, that's okay. We'll just attribute the comment to an unnamed school board member. Not a big deal. Yes, we always prefer a source, but sometimes you gotta go with whatcha got."

"Okay, Mark," I said, firing up my computer. I still wasn't sure this was newsworthy, but I was trusting my editor's judgment. Having seen Bennie in action, I had already become accustomed to who was boss.

Thirty minutes later, I sent a brief in for review. Farbian seemed generally comfortable with it, and with some editing the brief was on its way to the press room. It was 11:30, and now I was beyond tired. Tuesday nights, I could already tell, were going to be a bear. Which was no surprise, really. They had been my least favorite night of the week since my pledge semester, when it was line-up night. As in the pledges line up, are called maggots, are told in no uncertain terms to keep their eyes on the light then proceed to be berated until the actives got tired or passed out. Whichever came first.

"10:00 Tuesday – no dates" was how it went, and even after you went active you never quite got over Tuesday nights.

Six and a half hours later, the phone rang. The alarm had not been set to go off for another hour. I was still, for all intents and purposes, comatose.

"Hello," I offered through a filter of gravel.

"McDougal, Skimer," the voice of a clearly more awake person than me bellowed into the phone. "We got problems. Meet me in my office at 7:30."

I was soon marching toward Skimer's door, a wrist-slapped student reporting to the principal's office.

"McDougal, have a seat," Skimer said, barely looking up. "Here's the deal. I got a member of the school board who's livid, see. She's claiming she's been misquoted after a conversation with you last night. I'm not sitting here telling you you're wrong. I'm just telling you we got a problem. So what we need to do right now is understand what you and Eleanor Barronkoff talked about last night, okay?"

I was staring intently at Skimer. I was processing, trying to ensure I understood what was going on.

I started slowly. "Um, well…" I said, stammering. "First off, how does Eleanor Barronkoff even know what I wrote? The story doesn't come out until this afternoon, right?"

Skimer closed his eyes.

"You see, this now being the 21st century, and I know this is only Frisco, Texas and all, but there's this thing they call the Internet," he said. "It's that contraption that Al Gore says he invented a couple of years back. It means people can read the paper on their computer before they get it at home. You should try it once."

I was not amused.

"Okay, I get it," I said. "But what's the problem? I just reported on what she told me."

"If that's true, fine," Skimer said. "In fact, I'll go so far as to say, if that's true, she can suck on her own asshole. What I need to know is, is that what she said."

"Yes, it is," I persisted. I pulled out the notebook I had used the night before. "I have it right here."

Skimer scrolled through my notes.

"You can read all this? These are messier than Thornaker's."

"I do my best. It works."

"And this was on the record?" he said, leaning forward. He seemed to be hearing what he wanted to hear, that his prized recruit had done things the right way.

I froze. My alibi was starting to take on water.

"Well, she said it was off the record. But—"

"Off the record?!!" Skimer belched. He leaned back in his chair and pushed his fingers through his hair. "If it's off the record, why the hell are we printing it?"

"Well, I said it was off the record when Mark and I talked about it last night," I said. My words trailed off. I was a smelt on a hook, fighting a fight that was over before it started.

"I told him she said the information couldn't be attributed to her."

Skimer was having trouble containing himself at this point.

"McDougal, I need you to think real hard here, okay? Did she use the term, 'off the record'? Or did she say she was speaking on background? Either that, or did she say she was speaking on deep background?"

I tried to recall if Deep Throat had talked to Woodward off the record, on background or on deep background. The more I thought about it, the more confused I became.

"She said her comments were off the record," I said, steeling myself. "When I came back to the newsroom, I told Mark we couldn't use her name. He seemed fine with that, so we went with it."

Skimer was calming down now, his breathing slowing.

"So here's the problem, son. When a source tells you something is off the record, that means it's off limits. No can use. And you can't use it even if you don't use the person's name."

I was still confused. "But we didn't use her name."

"You're missing the point. You can't use the information in print at all. You wanna take that comment and go talk to some other board members to see if they would react to it or confirm it on the record, fine. Hell, even if they wanted to go on background or deep background or something, that might work. But you ran a story based on one off the record comment. Can't do that."

Sigh. I understood now. I could only offer a faint defense.

"Well, I would have asked someone about it, but there was no one else there at the time. Everyone else had gone home."

"Then you shouldn't have run the story. Look, I'll talk to Farbian when he gets in later. But you gotta be straight when we wanna know what you got or what you don't got. You think you got enough for something, let us know. You don't, tell us that, too. You don't think you got enough and we do, you push back. Give-and-take, all the way. Only way a newsroom survives."

I sat quietly for a moment.

"Understood, Mr. Skimer," I said. "How about I call Eleanor Barronkoff and apologize?"

"Would be good for starters. Ya gotta gain these people's trust, you know? She needs to know she can trust what she tells you. She's a real bitch, that Barronkoff, okay? Or I guess the word these days is bioch. Or something like that. Whatever all y'alls call it out there, in here, she's a bitch to me. A real big one. You just don't want her to know you think it."

I got up to leave. I had been away from the newsroom for all of eight hours. I was exhausted. And it was now apparent I had crashed and burned in my first attempt to cover a school board meeting. Worse yet, the coffee truck was still more than 90 minutes off.

Skimer could see my pain. "Don't worry about it, kid," he said. "Live and learn. This was a blip, yes. But you gotta stay on it. Rather have you over-reach than under-reach in general. Well, within reason, right? Just don't get down about it."

He glanced out toward the newsroom just as Bennie walked by.

"Hey Bennie, what time is it?"

"Time to write some news stories, Rip."

"That it is, that it is."

At this very moment for me, that was a tall order. As my favorite high school English lit teacher used to love saying, right at the point at which things in the book we were reading started to turn: and so, the thick plottens.

That it was, that it was.

My chosen road back toward self-esteem was to placate my pleading veins with caffeine, the only annoyance being the lack of an available needle. Skimer had given me what I both needed and deserved – a real-life reporter's lesson in both the art and science of determining how and when information from various sources could and should be used. It's not like I hadn't learned the difference in J-school. Which made my screw-up even worse.

"Hello, Eleanor Barronkoff."

"Eleanor, Marshall McDougal."

"Good morning."

The greeting was short and curt.

"Uh, well, I'm calling to apologize about the story in the paper today."

Silence.

"I understand you've spoken with Mr. Skimer and, well, I learned a lesson here, Eleanor," I continued. "I understand now that off the record means off the record. I had thought it would be okay to use what you said as long as I didn't use your name, which of course I didn't. I never would have used your name, which is important that you understand that."

"Marshall, I appreciate that you didn't use my name. But here's what you probably don't understand. The fact that it is now public record that we are waiting to vote on the name change until spring is going to be a problem for us."

She was right. I didn't understand.

"Why is that?"

"Well, before I tell you, we are off the record, right?"

"Yes, off the record."

"You're sure now, right?"

"Yes."

"Alright, so the issue is pressure, ok? We, meaning the board, are under enormous pressure to change the nickname. Enormous, Marshall. It's not that the nickname is meant to be hurtful, or be offensive to anyone. It's just been that way for a long time, right? In a few years, I'm talking a hundred years. One hundred.

"The issue is that the town is changing. It's trying to attract businesses. It's building new gated communities. There's a lot going on here. Perhaps more to the point, there's a lot of people with a lot of money on the line here, okay? And the name is being looked at as an albatross. Succotash, I know. It's just succotash."

"Okay, so I understand that. So why not just change it now and get it over with? I seem to be asking this question a lot."

"It's not that simple. We represent the entire community, and there is a part of the community in Frisco that does not want to be pushed around just for the sake of progress. It's probably a minority at this point, but it's a loud minority."

"And they're that loud?"

"Let's just say there are more than a handful of people around here who look at this as a way to save the soul of the town, okay? I mean, Frisco has been here for a hundred years. And it's gonna be here another hundred. And to them Frisco means the Fighting Coons."

"I'm beginning to understand more and more each side here. But the one thing I still don't get is whether it's going to be a major problem if you just do the vote. I mean, just do the vote and move on."

"The reason, Marshall, is that the implication of your statement is that the vote is a done deal. It might be ultimately, but not everyone on the board is up for the change, ok?"

I paused. "I need to ask you something," I said. "What is your position on this? I guess I haven't formally asked that."

"I was wondering when you'd ask. My answer is that I continue to weigh all the options."

"So you're not willing to commit either way?"

"I continue to weigh all the options."

I had taken things about as far as they were going to go.

"Well, I'm sure we'll get another chance to talk about this, Eleanor. I do apologize for the story. I assure you I will be more careful."

"I appreciate that, Marshall. Rookie mistake, I get it. Just don't let it happen again. I'm not in your business, but there's an old saying that I think goes something like this. Doctors bury their mistakes. Lawyers send theirs to jail. A journalist makes a mistake, it's on the front page for all to see. Do I assume correctly we understand each other?"

"Yes."

"And we were off the record, right?"

"Yes."

"Good morning, Mr. McDougal, my name is Norma Taylor."

I could count on one hand the number of times I had been referred to as "Mr. McDougal."

"Have we met?"

"Well, you don't know me, but I know you," Norma Taylor said. "Well, I know your name, at least, from this morning's paper."

I wasn't biting.

"I'd like to talk with you about the Frisco Coon issue," she continued. "I've got a lot to say on it, as you may know."

"I haven't come across your name."

"Oh, you will," she said, laughing. "You will as long as you get in the middle of the Fighting Coons."

I was starting to bite.

"So tell me what your involvement is."

"Be glad to. If you are about to start covering this thing for the paper, there are some things you need to know."

"And what are those things?"

"Again, why don't we get together and talk in person. I understand if you're busy. But let's put it this way: if you don't see me now, you're still going to see me later."

"I'm not sure what you mean."

"What I mean is, if the board is saying they're not going to vote on the name until next spring because they want to protect their fannies through football season, then they're going to have to deal with me at every school board meeting from now until then."

Her decibel level had gone up throughout the statement, which I was still trying to classify as promise or threat. "Okay, but if you are so upset with the board about this, why were you not at last night's meeting?"

"I wasn't at last night's meeting because I didn't think the board

125

was going to talk about the Coon nickname. I do have a life to live, you know."

"Well, they didn't—"

"Yeah, yeah, they didn't plan it, but it just came up," she said. "I know how it works. Mr. McDougal, I'm here to tell you there is a growing chorus of people in this town who are growing more and more impatient with the board's refusal to make this change, a change that I will tell you is long overdue. And right or wrong, I have become the loudest voice on this fine topic among these people, who by the way are all homeowners and taxpayers. So if you want to learn about what's going on here, about what's really going on here, we need to talk."

"Okay, Norma Taylor, if you are the voice of the homeowners like you say you are, then yes we should get together. How about we meet at Scotty P's on Preston. A week from Monday after the Fourth of July. Noon-ish."

"I'll be there."

"Okay."

"And Marshall?"

"Yes."

"You won't be sorry."

"Doesn't sound like it."

"I'll see you soon, Marshall."

With that, we hung up. I was intrigued. Barronkoff had said my story was going to cause a reaction, and she was right.

I was already beginning to hate her, but the bitch was still right.

CHAPTER EIGHT

COMPANY COUNTY

The next day, for a reason unbeknownst to anyone around her, Costin decided some folks in the newsroom had accents, while others didn't. That was fine by me. I had already decided the back-and-forth banter of the newsroom was among my favorite pastimes of the journalist's day.

"I don't notice 'em," she said. "I just don't. I don't think I have one even."

"Really?" I said. I was bordering on incredulous. "No offense Tanya, but you've got a pretty big one. No offense."

"None taikin," she said.

"You can cut it pretty close sometimes, too," Meesbruggan said. "East Texas accent's different than West Texas."

"I'll take West Texas, any day, "Costin said. "Like a rooster knows it's mornin'."

"But sometimes you have one, Ted, and then sometimes you don't," I said. "I don't get that."

"Probably because I'm from here in the city," Meesbruggan said. "But it comes out in certain situations. You get me all upset, or outta town 'round here, it all comes out. Remember, Dallas is probably more cosmopolitan than you think, what with all these corporate headquarters bringing in all these folks from all over. It's not like down there in Houston, where the business is much more insular. You still got a lot more folks down there riding around with shotguns in their trucks."

"Hey."

"Sorry Jan."

I looked at Bennie. "I thought you were from Louisiana though, right?"

"Yeah, well," she said. "I am. But I've spent a lotta days down there all those times Daddy had to go out on those rigs in Galveston Bay. Houston's a good town. Good people. They just got more guns."

"Look at me," Meesbruggan continued. "Me and the wife spend lots of time out in Santa Fe. You've got all sorts of folks out there, people from all over with the second homes like us, even though ours is modest by comparison. It's kind of like Phoenix, except with actual culture. Nobody's from there, either. But you know about that, Marshall, right? No one's really from L.A."

"Well, I know that's the popular perception, but it's really not true," I said. "My family's second-generation. Third including my father's side if you count Up North. Most of my friends are second, third, fourth generation California, if not L.A."

"That's gotta be an exception," Bennie said.

"No, it's really not. I mean, I'm sure lots of people move there, which I guess explains why you can't get anywhere on the freeway. But really. I can count on one hand the number of Hollywood people I've ever really met."

"So it's not all about Hollyweird, either, huh?"

"Nope, not at all."

"Funny how we all have perceptions about other places," Bennie said. "Could have fooled me. Of course, I always thought Dallas was pretty snobby, being from South Louisiana.

"Oh wait. That one turned out to be right on."

"Marshall, you figured out this whole raccoon thing yet?"

Cleary Costin was more interested in my business than hers.

"Meaning?"

"Meaning why Frisco even goes by the Coons in the first place."

I hadn't really thought about that.

"This oughta be good," Bennie said.

"The legend is part of the deal," Meesbruggan said. "Something about some railroad exec for the Frisco line doing an inspection tour sometime during the late 1800s. He arrives at one of the stations, I think maybe way up there in Missouri. And he notices a raccoon hide tacked onto the depot. The locals explained that he was drying it because he was selling raccoon hides to support his family."

"And then he paid for it," Costin said. "Two dollars, I believe. Right on the spot."

"Next thing you know the Frisco line's got a new logo," Meesbruggan continued. "Same one you see today. Look at it. It's a raccoon hide. It's stretched out."

"So that's it?" Bennie asked. "I can't remember the details."

"Well, that may be it, Jan, yes," Meesbruggan said. "But there's the other story, too."

"This is the one I like," Costin said.

"Some kid," Meesbruggan said. "Just some kid. He shows up to a school board meeting with a pet raccoon. I mean, he's got this coon, his pet coon, on a leash. We're talking like 75 years ago, somewhere in the 20s, ok? Long time ago. They're trying to decide what to call the high school teams. He suggested the school nickname be the Coons after his pet raccoon. That's the raccoon he brought to the meeting."

"Didn't I say that already?"

"What?"

"The business editor may know his stocks but he can't tell a story, can he?" said Costin, now increasingly animated.

Meesbruggan hung his head.

"Ted, I'm disappointed. Will, whaddya think about that?"

Everyone looked at Will.

Will was William Thornaker, the Evening Outlook's police reporter. Skimer had pointed him out a couple of times, and my approaches had been met with a polite-yet-firm sense of detachment as expressed in something that most closely resembled a clearing of the throat. It wasn't that he had been rude; it was more that he clearly preferred to go it alone, and Bennie had whispered to me I should consider it a strong endorsement that my introduction had produced an audible response. Ever since this first encounter, I had found myself unable to stop looking in his direction; the more he remained distant from the rest of the newsroom, the more drawn in I became. And then there was the "Thizziz-Will-y-emm Thorne-a-ker-at-the-Eva-neeng-Out-a-luook" drawl that he would greet callers or receivers with on the phone, and if I didn't know any better I would have thought I was sitting across a computer terminal from a carburetor.

But it wasn't Thornaker's strange-uncle-at-Thanksgiving-dinner-like presence in the newsroom that had caught my attention. It was his appearance. He showed up in the newsroom each morning with his trademark white, short-sleeve button-down shirt, and if it didn't look so clean every day I would swear it was the same one. Then there was the tie, the one-and-the-same daily tie, overly thick at brick-width, diagonally-striped crimson-and-royal-blue, and I was convinced – though I had yet to secure proof – that it was a clip-on.

But the real story was the hair. I had never before, nor have I since, encountered a human head of hair more voluntarily smothered in liquid. I wasn't sure if it was a mouse or a gel, but either way it would typically be so over-applied that its sheer volume would prompt it to move around Thornaker's head as he moved like a running stream. Sometimes the excess would actually run into his ears, where it would gather and then start flowing out and then downward depending on the degree of the tilt of his head, a bubbling sauce seeping from a simmering pot, a slow-yet-steady ooze, the haystacks of hair sprouting from inside each ear a mound of moss softly rippling at the mercy of a shifting tide.

Thornaker looked up. The receiver rested on his shoulder, no doubt gathering jelly by the moment, and the thought shot through me that I hoped I would never have to use it.

"Dell," he rasped under his breath before wheeling his chair around, and it was without question the slowest utterance of a one-syllable word I had ever heard.

"Excellent call, Will," stated Meesbruggan, matter-of-factly. "They're reporting this week, and folks think they'll be looking real good, especially on the profit side."

"Didn't they just announce some deal with EDS?" Clarke asked, emerging from the photo lab. My ears perked up.

"Yeah Pat, a go-to-market alliance, coupla months back. They're going great, at least from everything I can tell. They're fixin' to report their 10th straight quarter of record new contract sales. That's how you foresee things like future revenue and earnings growth. Not bad for a company a lot of people weren't so sure about a few years back."

"I guess they've really come a long way back," Clarke said.

"Where did they go?" I asked, taking mental notes for my next audience with Mr. Sapphire.

"Well Marshall you've got to start at the beginning to understand EDS," Meesbruggan said. "EDS is the company that got Plano and Collin County on the roll it's on. Lot of pride in these parts for that place. But then they got sold to GM back in '84 I think, and next thing you know 'ol Ross was gone. GM spun 'em off in '96 and it was a great time. In the meantime Gerstner and IBM had gotten real big into IT Services, which is basically the industry that Perot and EDS invented. So things were a bit tough in recent years. But they brought this new guy in a coupla years back, and now they're heading back where they belong. We've got two different neighbors on our street that work there."

Bennie leaned in. "Yeah, I gotta admit it was pretty cool what they did with Y2K."

"Good story, though I didn't have much of a New Year's Eve," Meesbruggan said, laughing.

"No rockin' eve for Ted?"

"Nope. Well, not in that way. How soon we forget about all the hand-wringing when EDS took a shot and invited the press from all over town to come and see how they'd handle the changeover for all their clients that were depending on them. It was unbelievable. Not a thing went wrong. They had balls to do that, I'm telling you that right now, though I'm sorry for the term. That was not too long ago, really, but it already seems like a memory. I mean, we all thought the world was gonna end just because of some silly computer thing. Then, nothing."

"Buncha Nervous Nellies, in my mind," Costin said.

"I was kinda disappointed nothing happened," Bennie admitted. "Better story that way."

"So were a lot of people. Except the shareholders, of course," Clarke said. "Yeah that was quite an evening Ted. Thought I'd seen it all until I saw that NASA control room they've got over there. You talk about unbelievable. Remember that great shot I got of the CEO with all those big computer screens behind him? And then they win the Navy contract to boot."

"Gusher," Meesbruggan said. "That was the word they used. You talk about future earnings? Just look at that one. Biggest IT contract ever. Texas-sized doesn't even describe it. Yep, EDS is back, no doubt."

"Wonder if they still have any of those hooker stickers around," Bennie said.

"Now, Jan," Costin said.

"Hey, it is what it is, right?" Bennie said. "I think it's hysterical. Too bad we could never do a story on 'em. Now that'd be a good story."

"Yeah, that's right. Would be a good story. I remember that," Clarke said. "I found out about it from my brother. He worked there forever."

"So what's the story?" I asked.

"It's pretty basic," Clarke said. "Used to be up a little ways on Preston from EDS there were a bunch of, well, whorehouses. They'd been there since the old Preston Trail. I mean, whaddya think there was along the trail, right? And liquor joints, too. Anyway there were still some there, and this is just a few years back now. And the funny thing was, every now and then you'd drive by, and if you know the EDS sticker that was on every EDSer's car, you always knew if one of 'em was inside. The sticker gave 'em away."

"Why'd they have to have the sticker on their car?" I said. "I mean, just take it off."

"Not on your life," Bennie said. "You wanna get on that campus they've got down there, you have that sticker. Used to be in the old days where they'd have armed guards waving folks in. No stickers? Yeah, and this is the place that's still got those things that'll shoot up in the air in the entrances to block people from entering. Like if there's an attack on the campus or something."

"What?"

"Well, that's the legend, at least," she said. "Lotta legend over there. Lotta legend."

I looked up just in time to notice a group of men quietly filing into the conference room. I quickly realized the final two were among those I had run into on my way to Baldwin Park.

"Who are those guys?"

Meesbruggan glanced over.

"Don't know. Pat?"

"Don't know. Don't like it, though."

"How come?"

"Just don't like it. Men in suits don't belong in newsrooms. Nothing good ever comes of that."

"Should we be worried?"

"What do you think?"

Everyone stopped typing for a moment and looked around.

Silence.

"Worried about what?"

"Nothing, Marshall, nothing," Clarke said. "Men in suits just make reporters nervous. Last time we saw that, well. Let's just say those of us still here are the lucky ones. That's all."

Back we all went to the tappity-tap-tap of the afternoon. At one point I swear I noticed Thornaker looking at me out of the corner of my eye, prompting me to spend the next half hour wondering if my fascination had been too obvious.

Time to write some news stories. And try not to think about men in suits.

"Hi Marshall. It's Sabrina."

My reaction was more snort than greeting.

"You okay?"

"Um, yes, I'm fine. How are you?"

"I'm fine. Did I wake you? It is 10:30, you know."

"No, no," I said. "Just getting some things done around the apartment." I was, of course, lying.

Sabrina didn't hesitate.

"So what are you doing today? It is the Fourth of July, after all."

"No plans," I said, waking up now. I wondered how Sabrina had gotten my number, and realized I didn't care.

"Well, I wondered if you might want to join us at our annual Fourth of July celebration," Sabrina said. "It's something we do every year, though we've changed things around recently since Daddy bought the Double Dip. But it's great fun. I'd love for you to join us."

Sounds good. And I even promise I won't say anything stupid."

"Well, now don't go making promises you're not sure you can keep."

"Point taken."

"So here's the plan. We meet at The Abbey for dinner, then go up onto the roof of the Double Dip and watch the fireworks. They've got some great ones over at Stonebriar Country Club, and we can see them just great from the roof. Sound good?"

"I've never been to The Abbey, but I think I know where it is. When should I meet you there?"

"6. It won't get dark really until 8 or 9 so we'll have plenty of time for dinner. Just time to hang out."

The Abbey lay at the foot of the Frisco water tower across the street from the Double Dip. I could remain skeptical all I wanted about this town. Yet I approached full of resolve for a better outcome.

"Well, hello Mr. Journalist," Sabrina said, looking up at me as I entered. "And a Happy Fourth to you."

"And I'm only five minutes late. Not too bad."

"Welcome to the Abbey. You'll love this place. Used to be a church, back at the turn of the last century. It was one of the first buildings in Frisco."

I began checking things out. The restaurant was casual, filled with family diners, and featured three rooms, with the largest one being in the middle. A salad bar anchored the back end of the middle room. I didn't see an altar, but wondered if the raised wooden entryway at the east entrance had served that purpose.

"Marshall, good to see you again," shouted a voice from a long wooden table to the right.

"You remember Daddy," Sabrina said, motioning toward me.

"I sure do. Best custard I ever had."

"Can't argue with that," Mr. Sapphire said, laughing.

"Daddy is obviously very proud of the Double Dip," Sabrina said. "We used to spend all day on the Fourth at the house barbequing, and it was fun and all. You know, corn and fruit, fruit and corn, the typical Fourth of July stuff, that kind of thing. But then when Daddy retired from EDS and bought the Double Dip, we realized we could see the fireworks from the roof. So we decided to come down here and eat instead. Besides, even by our standards it's pretty hot out there today."

"Great idea," I said, noting that the high temperature that day had been predicted to be 98, which now seemed categorically low to me judging by the horizontal Nile of sweat flowing steadily above my belly button by virtue of having spent all of two minutes in the direct sunlight.

"I'm pretty sure I've never watched fireworks from the roof of a custard shop. First time for everything."

Sabrina took me by the arm. "Marshall, this is my mother, my brother Harry and my brother Jack. And over here, this is my uncle

Chuck and my aunt Jean, and at the end that is my great-aunt Mary Jane."

I dutifully went around the table and greeted everyone, the candidate openly courting the votes of the electorate.

"So Sabrina tells us you want to be a journalist," Sabrina's mother said.

I caught myself. "Yes, ma'am, and proud to be one. It's all I've ever wanted to do."

"And you came all the way here from California to do it?"

"Well, yes, but I'm glad I did," I said, forcing the words out.

"Well, that's just amazing to me that someone would come all this way. You must be very committed to what you do."

"I am, yes."

"I remember talking to some reporters a couple of times at EDS," Mr. Sapphire broke in. "Those guys never seemed to get it all right, I gotta tell ya. Hopefully you'll have more luck, right son?"

"Well, I'm going to work real hard at it. I've already had a couple of things come up and bite me, but I'm learning every day."

"I don't suppose that would be because of the Frisco Coon story."

I cocked my head to the left. The comment had come from Harry.

"You read the story?"

"Yeah I read it. And I can't believe we're even talking about changing our nickname from the Coons. C'mon."

Deep breath. I hadn't been prepared to have this conversation over Fourth of July dinner.

"Me, neither," Jack chimed in. "What a joke, you know? How long have we had that nickname, a hundred years? It's not meant to hurt anyone. Gimme a break."

"I don't know how I feel about it quite yet, being the new guy and all," I said. I was trying to steer clear of the discussion. "I'm just getting up to speed on what the whole debate is all about."

Mr. Sapphire looked at his sons.

"What the boys are saying is that it's hard for the town to go through this, because everyone here knows how long the little critter has been our mascot," he said. "Now when a town is changing like

Frisco is, well, all bets are off on what stays and what goes. I really think we need to keep an open mind on this one, though you can see I may be the only person at the table who believes that."

Sabrina had been silent for too long. "I just think the name is fine. There's no reason for anyone to be offended by a name like that."

I hadn't known Sabrina felt that way.

"You know me. Once a Frisco girl, always a Frisco girl."

"Let's eat," Mr. Sapphire said. "We got fireworks to look at."

I scanned the menu. The religious theme from the former church was front and center. The salad section was entitled, "Angelic Salads," the sandwich section "Divine Sandwiches." Then there were the pasta section, "Congregations Pasta"; the seafood section, "Heavenly Seafood"; and the meat and chicken section, "Inspirational Favorites."

Welcome to the Bible Belt, Marshall McDougal.

"What looks good, Marshall?" Mr. Sapphire asked.

"Well, I'm just trying to figure out the difference between chicken fried steak and chicken fried chicken," I said. "I mean, if it's steak, how can it be chicken? And if you're chicken and you're being fried, isn't it redundant to be chicken fried chicken?"

"So we're gonna need to educate you about the finer points of Texas-style frying. Here's the deal, okay. In both cases, the chicken is what the food is being fried in. Chicken juice, basically. So you can have chicken fried steak or chicken fried chicken."

"But isn't chicken always fried in chicken juice?" I said. "And with chicken fried steak, aren't you mixing apples and oranges by cooking steak in chicken sauce? I mean, if you want steak, why would you fry it in chicken?"

"That's a fair question," Mr. Sapphire said, nodding his head. "Sabrina?"

I smiled. There was never any absence of entertainment with Sabrina around. And I could see where she got her personality.

"I'll take chicken fried steak," I said upon my turn to order. "Extra chicken juice."

"You learn fast," Mr. Sapphire said. "The sign of a good reporter, I'm sure."

"Hope so."

The ensuing dinner was more a roast than a meal. The subjects up for discussion ranged from A-Rod's new contract to join the Texas Rangers to the allegedly vast cultural differences between Texas and Oklahoma to, most humorously to everyone but Harry and Jack, the brothers' allegedly questionable hygiene. All subjects, in my view, more enjoyable than that of the Frisco Fighting Coons.

"Sun's going down," Mr. Sapphire announced, looking through the stained glass. "Who wants to see some fireworks?"

I was more than up for that. Every year growing up for as long as I could remember, the Fourth of July meant attending the annual parade in Pacific Palisades just up the hill from Santa Monica with my family. We climbed up the side ladder atop the Double Dip. Beyond the water tower just to the west, there were no tall buildings to inhibit the view.

"Not bad, huh Marshall?" Mr. Sapphire asked. He pointed to the south. "That's EDS' headquarters down there," he said. "Spent a lotta days and nights in that place."

"Sabrina says you were with the company for a long time."

"Yeah, you might say that. Started when the company was run by Ross. You know he started it with $100 from his wife? Yep, wrote down the idea for the company on the back of a pledge card. That Ross was way, way ahead of his time, I tell ya."

"That's pretty cool."

"It was a great, a great place to grow up with. We started off down in North Dallas, down there at Hillcrest and Forest. Used to run over to this great catfish spot over there on Forest and have lunch. This little hole-in-the-wall over by TI. We were still living in Bent Tree back then, so the drive to work wasn't real rough.

"I still remember the first time I met him. I was back in New York, working on an account. Hated it, because my wife here was back home in Texas and there I am getting on a plane to New York every Monday. And no offense to New York or anything, but I ain't exactly your typical Yankee. Anyway so that's back when it was all about Love Field when you didn't have all the choices you do now. None of this DFW stuff. You wanna know somethin' cool, Marshall, I'll tell ya cool. You know the DFW airport is bigger than the island of Manhattan? That's an absolute fact, if you include all the land over there we never see."

"Is that possible?"

"Done deal. That's a true Texas airport there, son. Honey, you remember that's not long after President and Mrs. Kennedy flew into Love Field. There was no DFW way back then."

Mrs. Sapphire nodded approvingly. "That's right, dear. Those famous pictures of the President and Jackie that day? The pink dress and the pill box hat? That was Love Field. Still there now. So is the original Sonny Bryans right around the corner. And those sticky old school desks they use for tables. But it's really all about DFW now. Unless you like Southwest."

"I've read so much about the JFK assassination," I said. "I'm looking forward to getting downtown and checking it all out."

"You know, son, anyone that comes to Dallas needs to do that. Though it's a real drive from up here in Frisco, with all that traffic building up on the Tollway nowadays. I could bend your ear in a big way about the political environment back then in town. Lotsa folks say that had a lot to do with it. Awful, I'm telling ya. Just awful. You can go down there right now, there's a big X in the street where the car was."

"You're kidding me."

"You can see the X, right there in Dealey Plaza. Drive under the triple overpass. Stand on the grassy knoll. Heck, the wooden fence that some folks say the real shooters were behind, it's right there! Looks exactly the same today, if you ask me."

For the first time since before encountering the raccoon water tower, I was genuinely excited about something I could see in Texas with my own two eyes.

Sabrina walked over. "Tell him more about EDS, Daddy."

"Oh, honey, I could talk about it all day long. You know that."

"It's okay. I'd like to know."

"Well, I'll leave you with the short version, as they say. So my assignment back there in New York was to put together a manual, a booklet basically, for this big financial institution. We were taking on their computer systems and the manual was supposed to explain to their IT people and our folks how to operate 'em. It was supposed to be a one-stop shop of what we were setting up for 'em. And right after I started I was in an elevator in this high-rise, and one day Ross gets in. I'd never met him, and back in those days Ross took it upon himself to meet all his employees. I'm talking all of 'em, okay? So he introduces himself to me and I do to him, and then he asks me about what I'm doing for the client, and I tell him.

"And so it's a few months later, and well I hate to say it but we weren't working for that company anymore. We hadn't done anything wrong, it was just one of those things. But I'm still commuting basically back and forth from New York and working on some other business, and one day that Ross gets in the elevator with me again. And we ride several floors down to the bottom, and I'm standing there, not really knowing what to say, just kinda minding my own business. And the doors open and Ross gets out. But just before the doors close he slices his hands inside and stops 'em. And the doors open all the way, and there I am just standing there dumbfounded still, staring at our CEO. And he looks at me and smiles and says, 'Guess no one read your booklet.' I'm telling all y'alls right now, if it hadn't been for that smile, I would've run for the hills right then and there."

Everyone was laughing but me. "Didn't that scare you? The CEO and all? Perot himself?"

"But that's just it, Marshall," Mr. Sapphire said. "Once you earned the trust you were part of a family, I tell ya. I guess I did at one point, 'cause I was there a long time."

"I think that's awesome, Daddy," Sabrina said. "Marshall, this is some of what I was telling y'all at the Wheezer game."

I was getting it now. I wanted to hear more. I had never heard of EDS before moving to Frisco. Now I was beginning to feel for the first time what it was like to live in a company town. Or at least a company county.

"Yeah, it was pretty special. Each of us had an employee number, and even as we grew larger it was like being part of a family. To me, it was always my second family."

"And Perot doesn't run the company anymore?"

"No, not for a long time now," Mr. Sapphire said, laughing. "That's a common misperception. He hasn't been with EDS for a good 10 or 15 years now. In fact, he runs his own outsourcing company now, just down the road over there on Plano Parkway. It's not too far from the EDS headquarters building. You know this is really taking me back. It was Ross that really led the move up north, up here. It was back around '85, I'm thinking. Ross got into it with the City of Dallas about expanding our offices. At some point he just decided to thumb his nose at 'em, and he up and moved us to Plano. It was nothing but fields back then. Just us and the fields. 'Round here they call it the Collin County Revolution. It all started with Ross and EDS."

"Yeah, I remember when he ran for president. I was pretty young at the time. I just remember how much he liked charts."

"Yeah, Ross loves his charts. It's amazing how much he represents the image of EDS to this day, to the common man I mean. The irony is, he wouldn't recognize the place anymore."

"Why is that?"

"Well, he would have recognized it for several years after he left, because when the next guy was running the place it was run pretty much in Ross' image still. Les had come up under Ross, and tried to maintain the family atmosphere. It wasn't always easy when we were owned by GM, but I thought Les did a pretty good job at it. I mean, we're talking about a company that has now grown to 140,000 people. We – I still say 'we' I guess – got 10,000 in Plano alone."

"And he's not there anymore?"

"No, he's been gone a couple of years now. Board forced him out and brought in a guy from the outside. And he came in and did what he was told to do, which was to cut all this fat from the company that I guess had grown over the years. The results have been good so far. Real good, in fact. But the folks there will tell you something is being lost along the way."

"Do you mean the family atmosphere?"

"You got it. I mean, we're talking about the company with the single greatest corporate war story you're ever gonna hear. Everyone 'round here knows it, but it was back around '80 I guess with the whole

Iranian hostage crisis. And two of our people were trapped in the country. They weren't doing anything wrong, just working with clients. And Ross hears they're in prison and what does he do? He sends some commandos in there on a couple of jets he bankrolled, and dammit to hell if they didn't get 'em outta there in one piece! It was so good they even made a TV movie out of it. And guess who the vice chairman of EDS is today? That's right, one of those two boys Ross got outta there."

"How did he pull that off?"

"Because he's Ross Perot, Marshall. So say what you want about EDS, and maybe they needed a fresh start there a coupla years back. No doubt IBM has taken control of the industry. But there was something special about EDS. Still is, I'd like to think."

Sabrina cut in. "Some people think EDS was kind of strange with their strict dress codes and all," she said. "But you always knew, if you worked hard they would take care of you. That's not really the case anymore."

"Yep, I wore the blue suit and white shirt until my last day," Mr. Sapphire said. "Tough to break old habits."

"So why did you retire?" I blurted out. I was almost annoyed that this man telling me these amazing stories about the company he loved no longer worked there.

Mr. Sapphire sighed and looked around. "You know, we worked so hard for so long on that Navy deal, and then we win it. Was last year, October to be exact. And the word came in on a Friday afternoon, late afternoon. And there we were, all up in the CEO suite celebrating and drinking champagne. I'm talking millionaires high-fiving like they'd never won a deal in their life. And this was a deal culture we'd all been working in all these years. A deal culture. And then the next thing you know they're blaring the Navy fight song over the loudspeakers for the whole building. It was the end of the day, and the employees are leaving for the weekend with the Navy fight song in their ears. Greatest thing I've ever seen."

"So why'd you leave?"

"You know Marshall, it was the holidays not long after that, and I just found myself wondering if I wanted to go through that anymore.

So I just decided. I went in one day and said, 'boys, that was my last rodeo.' Waited around 'til March, just a few months ago now, until I got my bonus. And I was done."

"Just like that?"

"Just like that. Except of course, I'd had my eye on the Double Dip all along. Spent a lot of Saturday nights in here over the years appreciating that custard, especially on those hot summer nights. So I up and bought it."

"Just like that?"

"Just like that, son. Just like that."

He let out a big smile, and I had no response. No response whatsoever. I now understood more than ever what Sabrina had meant the other night. About EDS. About a lifelong career with one company. About her dad, about family. Maybe a little bit about my father, too.

Just as I was about to offer something, anything, in the way of a final word, another shrill.

"Here we go!" Harry screamed.

"There's another one over there!" Jack offered.

"Must be the Plano city show," Mrs. Sapphire added.

I settled in for the sights and sounds one only finds on the Fourth of July. There were reds and blues and purples and greens. There were twizzlers and bursts and bursts and twizzlers, there were big ones and small ones and small ones and big ones, and the louder the boom, the higher the shrieks, including my own. I quickly got roped into a rat-a-tat-tat family tradition where whoever's turn it was had to yell out the image of what they saw in the sky before the next one went up, and before I knew it what we had seen had ranged from mouse ears and stars and bumble bees and sparklers to flowers and spikes and clown hats and hearts to confettis and galaxies and starfish and droopers to kiss marks and bows and gum drops and moons. All outdone, of course, by the occasional appearance in the technicolor cadence of what everyone had long agreed to call a Big Tex.

Looking at Mr. Sapphire participating in the game, appreciating the show, for a fleeting moment I missed being at home. Most of all, I noticed how openly Sabrina shared her enjoyment with everyone around her. Enjoyment, it seemed, which came from being around those she loved, from not only giving her enjoyment to them, but also from receiving theirs as well. I was just happy to be along for the ride.

The show ended with a bonanza of colors, the mother of all Big Texes to be sure, unlike any I had ever seen. As the family started to descend from the roof, I realized I probably would not get a moment alone with Sabrina. For the first time all evening, I felt disappointment.

I bid everyone a good night as they climbed into the family car, and made sure to thank them for their hospitality. Not knowing exactly what to do, I gave Sabrina a gentle hug and took a step back. Better to underdo than the other way around, especially with the family looking on.

"I'll see you soon, Sabrina."

"Good night, Marshall."

With that, I started walking toward the car. Just as I put the keys into the car door, I heard a rustle. Turning around, I noticed Sabrina walking my way.

"My parents said it would be okay if you drove me home. That ok?"

She always seemed to be a step ahead of me. I smiled another smile, not believing my good fortune.

"Does that mean I passed inspection?"

"With colors as flying as the ones we just saw in the sky. See what happens when you don't put your foot in your mouth?"

I followed Sabrina's directions, driving north on County Road, veering past the Warren Sports Complex, taking a right on Rogers Road and turning into the Preston Highlands tract. All brick, the homes were modest, perhaps more modest than I would have imagined for someone who was able to buy a local eatery.

"Did you grow up here?"

"Since I was a little girl, yes. Daddy looked around a few times at moving, but he always felt we had put roots down in this neighborhood. He's not one to flaunt what he's got. He never forgot where he came from, which wasn't much."

"Did he grow up around here?"

"Yep, just up the road. His daddy was a farmer, which was what people did back then in Frisco. You don't find too many of them anymore."

"Frisco is certainly changing."

"It sure is. And you've walked into the middle of it with the Coon thing. That's the symbol for folks around town as to whether we officially change or not. There are lots of people who think if we give in on the name, that our history will be gone forever. It's sad, if you ask me."

I wasn't sure what to say.

"It's okay, you don't want to get any more in the middle than you already are," she continued. "Don't worry about my brothers, by the way. If you keep writing about it, I'll keep 'em in line."

"Something tells me I'm just happy if you're on my side of anything," I said. We were parked in front of her house now. I looked at her. She was already looking at me.

Strangely for Sabrina, she didn't say a word.

"You really do have a way about you, Sabrina Sapphire," I said. I was leaning in now for effect; I sensed I was on safe ground. "I could learn a lot from someone like you."

"Someone like me?"

"Someone like you," I said. "Not someone like you. Just you."

I leaned in further. I stopped just short of her face and studied it. "Just you."

With that, I didn't have to lean any further. Sabrina had leaned the other way, and our lips had now, finally, met. The kiss was soft and quiet and long, a kiss full of purpose and of feeling and of soul. Her lips were as full and delicious as any I had ever tasted, as moist as if I had dipped my own into a ladle of rich and sugary cream.

Just when the fireworks had ended, they were back again.

"Good night, Marshall McDougal."

"Good night, Sabrina Sapphire."

And with that, she was gone, back within the comfort of the family home in which she had grown up. I watched her every move until she was inside, her wiggle leaving the same impression it had the last time, and even after she was out of sight, the sweetness of her waft still honeyed the night.

CHAPTER NINE

HAROLD BE THY NAME

Refreshed after my surprisingly eventful Fourth of July, I showed up at the office on Monday fully dialed in for my lunch meeting with Norma Taylor. Then came the morning coffee truck.

"You're meeting with Norma Taylor today?" Short asked. "Hey Mees check out here who's having lunch with Norma Taylor!"

Meesbruggan wandered over.

"Very interesting, Marshall," he said. "You sure you're ready for this, right?"

I found myself slightly insulted by the question. "Are you suggesting I can't handle her?"

"Yeah, you go ahead and think that Marshall," Short said, giggling. "Just be sure you keep your hands and feet away from her mouth."

I still didn't get it.

"What is the big deal with Norma Taylor?"

"Okay, Marshall," Meesbruggan said. "Norma Taylor is widely

seen by the community as the person who has pushed the whole Coon debate forward. Before she moved into town, it wasn't nearly as high profile as it is now."

"What exactly did she do?"

"She started by posting questions on Frisco's public Web site, right?" Short said. "It's this site that's managed by the city, you know, one of those where all sorts of information can be shared, like about community events. That was a year or so ago, and ever since she started doing that, people have talked about it more and more. Can't go to a Frisco High game now and not hear folks talking about it."

I still wasn't impressed. "So somebody starts to ask some tough questions on a city Web site, and all of a sudden she's the person who has riled everyone up in town?"

"Well, before she came around, the Coon thing was this skeleton that nobody talked about, at least not publicly," Short said. "Then Norma Taylor starts posting these questions about the nickname on the city site, and all of a sudden everyone's talking about it."

"There's no way this just came up."

"Like I said, no one talked about it in a public forum," Short said. "You can absolutely believe it has been a topic of conversation for years at the high school. In fact, the NAACP even came out here a few years ago to discuss it with the school board. But the thing was, back then, nobody outside of Frisco cared about Frisco. We were left to do what we wanted."

"Until Norma Taylor came along."

"Well, until Frisco decided to go for the money that came along with building all these private communities they're now putting in," Meesbruggan cut in. "You think Stonebriar Mall and Nordstrom and all of that want to invest in a town that's looked at as racist? Or if not racist, at least insensitive or somehow backward?"

"So it's about the money?"

"It's always about the money," Meesbruggan said, chuckling. "What Norma Taylor did was put a human face to an issue that was already brewing behind the scenes. That brought the issue out into the open."

"And I assume there are other Norma Taylors?" I asked. "I mean, if this whole thing is being driven by one person, that doesn't make it newsworthy. This town isn't that small."

"That's just it," Short said. "Norma Taylor has been successful at not just pushing the debate in public forums, but also building support. She's got all those new homeowner groups behind her now. I really think all this thing needed was a driver, and that driver was her. Serious live wire, man."

"You must be Marshall McDougal."

"And you must be Norma Taylor."

I extended my hand. "I've heard a lot about you."

"And I you."

I was taken aback at how attractive she was. She looked to be about 5'5", and her medium-length, sandy blond hair framed her strong jawbone, stopping just short of her shoulders. For a petite woman, her breasts were more than formidable, and they heaved up and down slightly from her tight frame as she spoke. She had a wide smile that exposed beautifully white teeth, and her natural laugh easily invited people in.

It didn't take long for Taylor to notice my reaction.

"Not what you expected from a rebel rouser?"

"Is that how you describe yourself?"

"Not entirely. I just feel compelled to shake things up a bit around here, that's all. If people respond to my tactics, I must be doing something right."

"Fair point. You certainly have my attention, I'll give you that."

We gathered our lunch and sat down.

"So now that you have my attention, let's hear your story."

"Okay," she said, tearing into a Cardiac fry. "Grew up in Carrolton, which if you don't know is about a half hour to the west, out by the airport. Left Texas to go to college on the East Coast, at Brown. Loved it but knew pretty quick I wasn't meant for the East Coast, at least not for too long. So I came back after getting married and having two kids, so we could raise them here."

"Here meaning Carrolton or Frisco?"

"Well, that's where things start to get interesting perhaps for you. I had some friends growing up who lived in Frisco, and I used to drive out there every now and then and see them. It was such a charming town. It was this little, charming town out in the country. So my husband and I decide to settle there after coming back to Texas. He was from the East Coast, and didn't really care where we lived as long as it was near a golf course and a highway so he could get to the office. And we have just signed the paperwork to move into this place called Starwood."

"Nice spot," I said. "Drove through there a couple of weeks ago."

"Oh yes, it's beautiful, isn't it," Taylor said. "Mind you, we're not in the middle where the mansions are and all. We're on the outside of Texas Drive, you know, with all the regular people."

"When you say the regular people, I assume you mean the regular people who can still afford to live in a place like Starwood."

"No, none of us are starving, that's true," Taylor said. "My husband makes a good living, he's an attorney, you know. And yes we are perfectly comfortable. But that doesn't mean you can sit down and not demand change when you see that it's needed."

"That's where I interrupted."

"So we've signed the papers, and we're ready to move in," Taylor continued. She was now starting to wave her arms for effect. "And I look at the newspaper – your very newspaper, in fact – and there is a story in there about the Frisco Fighting Coons beating some school in football. This is just last fall."

I was waiting for the punch line.

"The Frisco FIGHTING COONS," Taylor said, staring at me in disbelief. I could see the passion coming out of Norma Taylor now, self-described as a rebel rouser, described by others as a live wire.

"I mean, you've gotta be kidding me, right? Is this the turn of the 21st century or isn't it? I was horrified," Taylor said. "I was seriously thinking about trying to get out of our contract. I just couldn't believe I had just bought a house in a town whose lone high school used a nickname that is so obviously insulting to black people. Not to mention, I might add, to more than a few white people like me. Then we go to dinner a few days later, and somebody who lives in Dallas says, 'Oh, you're gonna be a Coon.' It was like a joke that I was the last to hear about."

"So how did you get involved?"

"I didn't hear anyone talk in town here about it at all, so I started to become concerned. That's when I went online. And basically what I said was, does anyone out there notice that this is a racial slur. I just randomly posted it to see what came up. Then I went to a homeowner meeting, and brought it up there. I was looking for a project to keep my brain going as a young mom with an Ivy League degree. I guess this was the perfect thing. I don't know. I suppose it was quite arrogant of me. 'Who do you think you are, some 33-year-old, right?' I wanted to stir things up.

"It's almost like I had gone away to school and seen what life was like on the other side. And in doing so I had learned the errors of our ways."

I finished a fry of my own. "So, okay, I get it," I said. "You're moving into town with young children and you're thinking to yourself, 'What have I done? How can I raise my children in a town like this?' Right?"

I caught myself. I had already had one problem with a source; I realized I better establish the ground rules with this one pretty quickly. Especially this one.

"Um, before you answer that, I do need to make sure we understand each other here. I would like this discussion to be on the record. Meaning that, if you don't agree, I need to know that right now. Sorry, I should have said that upfront."

Norma Taylor didn't hesitate. "I don't care if you print every word of this, and with my name all over it."

"Great. Not that I plan to print all of it, but I just need to know what's okay and what's not. You don't have any concerns about becoming a lightning rod for an emotional issue? No worries about your kids or anything?"

She shot me a look. Live wire, alright.

"Well, I admit I was a bit concerned when someone responded on the city Web site that they were going to burn a cross on my lawn, if that's what you mean."

I stopped in mid-bite.

"What? Someone said that. In public?"

"Absolutely they did. So yes, I stopped for a moment and wondered what I was getting myself into. But it didn't last long. I believe that what I'm doing is right. I'm trying to make this a better place for my kids. That's all."

I couldn't get over what I had just heard. The story I didn't want was becoming more of a story by the minute.

"Did anything ever happen?"

"No, at least not yet. But I have a feeling this thing is about to heat up big time. I've already heard several people talking about what the school board said last week. There's a lot of unrest about this."

I could sense what she was saying. I was already thinking about proposing a feature story to Skimer. The more I learned about the issue, the more I knew I had to keep pursuing it.

"Okay, so let's back up a bit. Tell me more about why you wanted to live in Frisco."

"Well, like I said it was this little country town when I was growing up. I never paid much attention to it. I can definitely tell you I had no idea their high school was called the Fighting Coons. But when I came back to Texas after a few years away, everything had changed. Frisco was where all the action was, at least for young families. They were building all of these cool new housing developments. There's parkland everywhere. It's totally master planned for families. I get my cake and eat it too, basically. I want the quiet of country life, I got it. But I want to run down the street to Super Target in five minutes and buy diapers for my kids, I got that, too. And as long as there's a Starbucks around, I'm happy."

"Sounds like a pretty compelling picture."

"Exactly. Why do you think everyone and their brother is moving out here? It's not an accident that Frisco is the fastest-growing city in Texas. The only problem is that Frisco had this little secret that's now getting out. Well, not a secret, because I don't believe anyone was trying to hide anything. It's just a, well, you know. It doesn't have a place anymore. Not today."

I could not help but think of what Sabrina and her brothers had said at dinner on the Fourth. I saw their frustration as mirroring that of many in the community, especially those who had grown up in town.

"Let me play devil's advocate," I said. "What do you say to those who say, 'What's the big deal? It's just short for raccoon. We mean no harm.' I mean, you yourself say you don't think the town means anything badly by the name, right?"

Norma Taylor thought for a minute.

"You know, I'm not so off my rocker here that I don't see that side of things," she said. "But here's the crux of it. There are lots of things in this world that at one point in time seemed fine, or at least somehow legitimate. I'm not at all saying that I would have ever supported it, but Frisco's a big baseball town, right? We've been to the Blazer games. They're great. But once upon a time, baseball only had white players. And it took awhile to give black players their chance. Maybe to some that was okay once. But time has a way of making things right. Once upon a time, everybody thought it was cool to smoke, too.

"Over time, I believe people get past their ignorance and do the right thing. This is one of those cases. I believe that."

I loved the analogy. "You sound like quite a baseball fan. I'm impressed."

"Tell me you're listening to me," Taylor said quickly. She was looking at me intently.

"This is serious business. This is where I'm choosing to raise my kids."

"Yes, I'm listening to you. I appreciate you being so open with me. And yes, I see the logic here from your side. So what's the next step for you and the homeowners here? I want to track this pretty carefully."

"That's more than I can say for the other guy."

I tightened up. Taylor noticed.

"Do you not know about the other guy?"

I gathered myself. "No, Norma, I do not, and I'm still having a bit of trouble figuring out why everyone mentions him but won't tell me the real story."

"Well, let me have the pleasure then. You see, your predecessor at the paper would not have had lunch with me today, like you have chosen to. And I appreciate that, because at least now maybe, just maybe, the new homeowners in this town will be given a proper hearing on this."

"I'm still not getting where you're going."

"Where I'm going is, the last time the Evening Outlook pretended to have an education reporter, he was the son of the head of the school board."

"WHAT?" I was furious. "What? I mean, isn't that a conflict?"

"Oh, Marshall, I'm sorry that you're only hearing this now. And yes, of course it's a conflict. But you have a chance to change things. You have a chance to report on a story that is going to come to a head in this town sooner or later. Somebody's gotta shed some light on this darkness. I mean, right? Right?"

I was having trouble getting past what Norma Taylor had just told me. I sat there for a minute, thinking through what I wanted to say. This was supposed to be about Norma Taylor and the Frisco Coons, not about me and my predecessor at the Frisco Evening Outlook. Why, I realized, did it seem like the two were becoming increasingly one and the same?

"So, if I get the drift of things here, the paper had someone covering this story who was the son of the head of the school board, and when you say that I assume you mean Grady Classen?"

"Yes, Grady's son, Gordon Bennett. He goes by G.B., which those of us on the homeowner side of things had a good laugh over when we found out people called him Gin Bomb. This is what happens when someone basically ignores you."

I was just starting to come down now.

"And I assume further then, that if this person didn't exactly give your views a real listen, it was because they go against Grady Classen's?"

"Well, I'm going to allow you to draw your own conclusions to that," Taylor said, smiling. "I take it I have your attention now?"

"Yes, Norma," I said, shaking my head. "Yes, you do."

I thanked Norma Taylor and walked outside to my car. It was another gruesome summer day in Frisco, more of a furnace blast than an afternoon.

My head down, I fumbled for my keys.

"And a mighty fine afternoon to you, Mister Marshall."

"Sammy? Seriously. Scared the shit outta me."

Sammy said nothing; he was more looking through me than at me.

"About the Blazer game ..."

"Making yourself right at home here in Frisco, I see. That's nice for you."

"Well, trying to. You know. Sammy, you ok? What are you doing out here, anyway? If this is about the $200, I haven't had—"

Sammy laughed.

"No worries, Mister Marshall, you keep your money now. We'll just need to be sure that road trip's our little secret, right? I mean, our paper wouldn't wanna think their new star reporter has a gambling problem, now would they?"

I was now more perplexed than anything. "Um, I'm still not sure I understand."

"Well, let me explain it to you this way."

Sammy was now, for the first time, looking at me.

"Let's just say there are more than a few people in this town that don't like it that things are, shall we say, taking a change for the worse. Miss Norma has lots of interesting things to say, and I'm here to tell ya I don't mind looking at her. Back home in Lake Providence, well there's not a lot to look at like that. You know what I'm sayin'. Not even at the big crawfish boil. But don't believe everything she says, that's it."

Now I was more concerned than anything. The irritation was giving way to fear. Sammy noticed.

"No big deal," he said, moving more to the left.

I moved to insert my key in the lock.

"Sammy, I don't know what the hell's going on here, but how do you know I was just having lunch with Norma Taylor?"

I glanced around to all sides, wondering if others were around. Norma Taylor, for one, had already pulled away.

"Oh, just a lucky guess," Sammy said. "Though I'm thinking maybe I need to keep my eyes out. You know, for my Sabrina. I mean, looked like you and Miss Norma were enjoying yourselves a little too much in there. Looked like you thought of it as your first Texas nooner."

He feigned surprise before I could speak. "Oh my word, you don't think I would—," he said, stopping himself in mid-sentence for effect. Then he laughed.

I didn't.

"Mister Marshall, you have yourself a good day, okay?" Sammy said, starting to walk away. "Just remember: just because a few Miss Normas raise their voices about it, that don't mean a hundred years are washed away. That's a big, wide river you're talking about crossing. That ain't right across the way like you saw there in Bossier City. That's a big, wide river. That's the Mississippi."

With that, Sammy was gone. I hopped in my car and drove off. Skimer was out of the office for the day by the time I got back to the newsroom. That was for the best, I figured. I was so disturbed with him that I did not trust what he would say to me at that point anyway. Why would Skimer not tell me that my predecessor was Grady Classen's son? Why all of the mentions of him in passing, without a proper explanation? And why the urging to cover a story that the paper has apparently suppressed in the past?

Falling onto the couch at my apartment that night, I turned to ESPN to see if I could catch a Dodger score. I was finding it hard to keep up with my favorite baseball team with the time difference. Not to mention a full-time job and a budding relationship. I had spoken with Sabrina that afternoon; she was going out of town for the weekend to visit her grandparents out at Lake Caddo. She had claimed it was the one and only natural lake in Texas, which I had refused to believe, so we had agreed to settle what she called our first fight over a movie at Stonebriar, loser buying. She had been excited to go, but had wanted to see me again. And I had wanted to see her. Out of luck on that score, I was left to look for a Dodger one.

Later that night, duly passed out on the couch now, I was again jarred awake by the sound of the rushing train nearby. I was becoming used to the "clackety clack, clackety clack" of the tracks, and had even managed to sleep through it now and again. I knew that the train crossed Main Street west of downtown and, if headed south, crossed the Dallas North Tollway just north of Stonebrook Parkway near my apartment before disappearing into the expanse of dry fields to the west. I had asked around the office about the train, and no one seemed to know much about what it carried or from where it came. The only thing folks did seem to know was that the train passed through town every afternoon and evening, and that it did so faithfully on a schedule that never seemed to change.

The train – like Sammy – was yet another token of this mysterious town into which I had settled so far from home. And for all the questions I was asking about this town, the more the answers came, the more new questions followed.

Norma Taylor was clearly trying to shape my view of the controversy. And if I allowed her MILFian appeal to get to me, she might do just that. I had to get to the other side of the story. Not sure where to begin, I decided to scour the city Web site where Taylor had chosen to voice her displeasure with the nickname. Once there, reading the postings, I understood better how emotionally charged the issue was.

But I still needed to talk to someone real, a Norma Taylor type who could speak for the citizens fighting to keep the nickname intact. I decided to meet Sabrina for lunch the following week and pick her brain on what to do. I wasn't cloddish enough to try to use her, or anyone from her family for that matter, as a source. But I thought she might know someone who was willing to talk. And I was always up for an excuse to see her anyway.

Over lunch at Scotty P's, and how great was it that Sabrina had been excited about meeting me there, Sabrina suggested I talk with her friend Teri Leiner, with whom she had attended Frisco High. Teri had not only gone to the school, but had been a cheerleader, and was a third-generation graduate. Even better, of all the people Sabrina knew, Teri was the most passionate about the Frisco Coon issue.

"But you really want to see the soul of Frisco, come with me," Sabrina said as we walked out of Scotty P's and into the smothering pillow of the afternoon.

"You mean this isn't it?"

"Well, Scotty P's has its place, of course, and there's nothing like the Double Dip – of course. But you want to see a small town in action, you gotta go see the Snow Cone Lady."

"The Snow Cone Lady."

"You got it. She runs a little snow cone stand off of Main Street. I can't believe you haven't seen it yet. Follow me there and I'll show you. Besides, it's hotter than anything out here. What better than a snow cone? Just don't tell Daddy we went there."

I had no good answer to that. But anything cold at this point sounded good. Every day I awoke, I knew it was going to be hot that day. Yet every day when I walked outside for the first time, I was somehow still surprised.

Sabrina, with me following, pulled into a parking lot on the west end of downtown. And there it was. "It" was the town snow cone stand. Though I had passed by it numerous times already, it didn't take me long to realize how I had missed the place: there wasn't much there there. The snow cone stand was essentially a snow cone shed, painted beige at one point but in need of a new coat – or three. It was small, even smaller than the Donut Palace. It was so small it reminded me of a voting booth, and I wondered how one person could move around on the inside.

Sabrina ordered, and we sat on one of the several blue and beige benches parked to the west of the stand to eat them. I wasn't sure what flavor of snow cone I was eating, but I trusted that Sabrina had chosen from among, as the sign read, "The Snow Cone Lady's Flavors." So this wasn't at all some sort of nickname that others were assigning to the woman inside – whom I had yet to see, and I still wondered if she were really in there. This was a name that the proprietor openly used for herself.

"Pretty cool, huh?" Sabrina asked, wiping a dab of turquoise from my mouth.

"Pretty cool," I said, and I had to admit, this was a pretty damn good snow cone. Then again, I was sitting in the sun on a 100-plus-degree day, in the stream of a seizing blowtorch. I was no critic.

"This stand has been here for as long as I can remember," Sabrina said. "It's just a tradition. All the kids love to come over in the summer. They hang out, and the snow cone lady treats 'em all like little kings and queens. It's great.

"Went to camp up in Kansas once and all they talked about was Cherry Lime-aids. Had one and I guess it was pretty good. But I can go to Sonic and get one of those. I mean, how many towns have their own snow cane lady? I saw a snow cone stand down in the city once. Kinda near Hillcrest and Arapaho. Was pretty hot out that day, so I thought about it. But the more I looked the more I couldn't do it. First of all, it was made out of cement. Two, you could walk inside and order. What kinda snow cone stand is that?"

I peered around Sabrina toward the small, raised window. "You're sure someone's in there, right?"

Sabrina laughed. "I'm sure, Mr. Skeptical," she said. "You think this stuff just makes itself?"

"You know, I'm already smart enough to know not to question you on things like this."

I swooped in for a kiss. "I'm a quick learner, you know. Your own dad told me that."

"Yes, I can see that. And if Daddy said it, it's true. So be nice to Teri, okay? She's one of my oldest and dearest friends. Frisco's even more in her blood than mine. And that's saying a lot."

"She's a friend of yours, she's a friend of mine. Remember, quick learner."

A few days later, I met Teri for lunch at Scotty P's, where things had now gotten to the point where I didn't even need to order.

"Teri?"

"Marshall? Hi," Teri said. "Sabrina's told me a lot about you."

We settled into our booth. I was careful to ask Teri upfront if I could take notes, to which she agreed. Sabrina had apparently explained the ground rules to Teri beforehand, so she wasn't surprised.

"So tell me about growing up in Frisco."

I was sizing her up. She was medium height, with black, shoulder-length hair. Her eyes were large, a very deep brown, almost black.

"Frisco was a wonderful place to grow up, and now it's all changing."

I could see right away this was an emotional topic.

"It's okay, Teri. I'm just trying to get to know the town better, so I can report on the Coon issue better. I'm just, you know, trying to understand."

"Well, okay. So like I said, Frisco was a great place to grow up. We used to walk and ride our bikes everywhere. It was like this little oasis out in the country."

"What was the best part?"

"It was just, you know, like you didn't feel the cares of the outside world, the real world I suppose. And it was a tight group that lived there. You could make family trees out of people going to school there. Everybody knew everybody's business."

I thought for a moment. "You know, not that I'm saying that Frisco isn't unique, but what you're describing sounds like your typical small town. Is that fair? I mean, what made Frisco different?"

"Well, I guess that's a good question," Teri said. "I think two things, okay? The first is the raccoon."

"What about it?"

"It just made us different. There's this story that some kid showed up at a meeting like a hundred years ago with his pet coon."

She stopped herself. "See, we just call it a coon. We don't mean anything by it. It's short for raccoon. That's all."

"I understand. So he shows up with his pet coon."

"Yeah, he shows up, and – at least as the story goes – he's got it on a leash, like a dog. Lots of people had coons for pets back then. I mean, they really were like dogs to some people. And smart, too. You can actually bottle feed them, you know."

"Are you serious?!" I exclaimed. Despite having heard the story already, I was enjoying Teri's version. "You can really bottle feed a raccoon?"

"You see, that's just it – I don't know if it's true, but the story says it is. And that's what makes Frisco unique. We have this story that everyone knows. You hear it from the time you're a little kid, that the kid showed up with his pet coon, and that we've been the Fighting Coons ever since. It's part of the fabric of the community. It gets passed down from generation to generation."

"So there's a lot of pride in the history?"

"Absolutely. Frisco has run on pride forever. There are lots of people in town that would do the whole taxidermy thing, you know, like get their coon stuffed after a coon hunt and put it on their wall. And it goes back to the railroad, too. We were named after a railroad, and every time that train passes through town even today, it's a reminder about who we are. About where we came from."

"Yes, I've noticed the train," I said. I paused to take a bite of my Warren Burger. "So then you grow up and become a cheerleader at the high school, right?"

"Yep. Was pretty proud of it, too. High school was probably the most fun I ever had. Everyone would go to the games. And the coon stuff would be everywhere. I mean, like the coonskip cap. How many small towns do you find where people walk around town wearing something on their head that symbolizes the town mascot? People would wear their coonskin caps to the game all the time, especially if it was cold. We would call 'em the 'Coon Crowd.'"

"You mean it actually gets cold here?" I asked, looking up from my notes. I was trying to keep the source talking.

"And then there was Homecoming," Teri said, barely noticing my attempt at humor. "I've never seen a place where it was such a big deal, especially since there is only one high school. The streets would be covered with people. The entire town would go to the homecoming dance. And coons were always part of the theme. One year it was 'Coons the World Over.' Another year it was 'Batcoon.'"

"It all sounds great," I interjected. "But I gotta ask, were there black students around? Didn't it offend them at all?"

Teri didn't hesitate. "But see, that's just it. No, they weren't. At least I didn't get the sense they were. Were there a lot of black kids in the school? No, but there were a few. And I never felt any racial tension at all. That may be hard for some people to understand, but when you grew up in Frisco you just knew we were the Fighting Coons. Everyone just knew that the nickname was short for raccoon.

"Here's the best way I can think of to tell you what I'm saying here. The student who got to be the mascot one year, she was African-American. Again, there were not a lot of black people in town, but people by and large didn't bother anyone, and again no one ever made any bones about it. So one year we're playing Whitesborough in football, and the kids from the other side were heckling the mascot, calling it a Coon and all, and she took off the head and said, 'Yeah, I am a coon – so what are ya gonna do about it?'"

"Whoa," I muttered barely audibly, writing furiously at this point. "That's unbelievable. So what happened?"

"That shut those kids up so fast, it was unbelievable," Teri said, laughing at the memory. "And remember the name of the school we were playing – Whitesborough. You think Frisco's the only town around here with history?"

"Good point. I passed a town called White Settlement on my way into town last month."

"Yeah, White Settlement. How come you guys aren't looking to do a story on that town? I mean, what's the difference?"

"Well, it's not exactly within our circulation area, you know. We are the Frisco Evening Outlook, after all."

"Yeah, I get that. Just tell me you're not here to do a hatchet job on our town. We're not bad people."

"I don't think you're bad people at all," I said, thinking of Sabrina most specifically. "In fact, I think you're a bunch of good people. But there is a story here, as long as some folks in town are raising the issue."

"So that's the second point," Teri said. "I said earlier there were two things that make Frisco different than other small towns. One, okay fine, we're the Fighting Coons, get over it already. The second thing though, is what we're doing to ourselves."

I was puzzled.

"What I mean is, we're just exploding with growth. It's out of control. We're trying so hard to attract new businesses to town, we're losing sight of who we are. And that's ultimately what's causing the problems. That's what makes us different."

"Tell me more."

"Well, it has always been this small farming town. Some people would drive their lawnmowers to the Royal. 'I'm goin' to the Rawl,' is what they'd say. People would go there at three in the afternoon. There were nicer places but the older people would go and have coffee there, with the men at one table and the women at the other. And this was as recent as the mid-90s.

"And all of a sudden, and it just seemed like overnight, there was this fast and quick influx of outsiders. They were all moving into these new private gated housing communities. We hadn't had places like that as recent as five or 10 years before that. You saw some nice homes, but not like those.

"And just in the last couple of years, it was like those people decided they had been around long enough now that they were going to try and make the town over the way they wanted. It's kind of like when a new boss comes in and says the way you've been doing this is wrong. 'But you don't understand, you haven't been here.'

"And so the nickname became what folks began arguing about. The newcomers said it was insulting, like we had meant it that way or something. The town just wants to keep that one piece of history because it made Frisco unique from every other small town. People have now started putting signs in their yard saying, 'Don't rac my coons.' They want to hold onto the little Snap-e-Jack store and the Snow Cone Lady and Brothers' Grille and everything they had come to know. Because we're not like every other small town, you know? We're not. We're Frisco, Texas. And that means something. Or at least it used to."

Teri stopped to take a breath. She had become so caught up in telling the story of her hometown that she had started to cry. Bent over scribbling notes, it took me a moment to notice.

"Pretty emotional for you, huh?"

For the first time in our encounter, Teri didn't know what to say.

"You know, if this is all so hard on people, here's what I don't understand," I said. I was stammering over my words now, wanting to say the right thing. "What I don't understand is, why the government or whoever in Frisco it is that pushed all this growth did that. Didn't they know what would happen?"

"You would think so. But you don't know what you have until it's gone, right? Frisco figured that, hey, the growth was coming anyway, so why not make the best of it and go for as much as possible?"

"The growth was coming anyway," I repeated, sensing a potential lede.

"The growth was coming," Teri continued. "But the nickname, that's the one thing that we want to hold back as our own. It means something that's hard to define. But it means something nonetheless. It just means something to us. It means we haven't lost us along the way."

We walked outside.

"Let me tell you one more story," Teri said as she piled her things in her car. "There's this older man named Harold who grew up in Frisco. His son I think is a lawyer in town now. Anyway, this man Harold, sometimes he kind of unofficially patrols neighborhoods for people. He drives like 10 miles an hour, and he has these tires tied to his car with a rope, so if he backs into anything or goes too far forward or something, the blow would be cushioned. And he just drives around, like a free security officer or something. And when he's not doing that, sometimes he rides his bike around town. You can see him riding his bike on Main Street. And the next day you'll see him driving his car 10 miles an hour with the tires. And it's this cooky little small town thing, that this man is just, you know, around. But everyone knows him, and everyone loves him, because they all know he's trying to perform a service.

"When you've got people like that around town, especially when everybody already knows each other anyway, who needs cops? I gotta tell ya, Marshall, Frisco was a pretty cool place to grow up. I just don't know what's going to happen to it next, that's all."

I stood on the baking concrete, still scribbling. I looked up, squinting into the sunshine. "Teri, I just can't thank you enough. Sabrina said you would be able to help me understand what this town is all about, and you've done just that. Thanks, and I promise I'll try to be fair."

"I appreciate that. And one more thing. Be nice to my Sabrina. She's pretty special."

"I'm trying, and I see what you're saying," I said, smiling. "Thanks again."

I turned to take a stride toward my car. I stopped and looked to each side. No Sammy. I took a deep breath, and kept walking.

I flew to my keyboard like a skimmer to a school.

The more I typed up my notes, the faster my fingers skipped across the keys. And I couldn't help but laugh as I thought about the story of the man named Harold who would ride his bike around Frisco and drive through neighborhoods with tires tied to his car.

When I was a boy, one of my favorite stories that my father would tell was when he would go to church as a young boy himself. And when it would come time each Sunday morning to recite the Lord's Prayer, he would dutifully say the words as he knew them to be. With, of course, his own unique twist. For at the part when the prayer reads, "And herald be thy name," my father, in a bout of sweet naivite, would always say, "And Harold be thy name." The funniest part of the story, which made its way to the dinner table countless times during my childhood, usually leading to howling laughter on the part of everyone at the table no matter how many times we had heard it before, was always, ultimately, the admission on my father's part that he never knew he had the words wrong – never knew that God was, in fact, not named Harold – until he was a fully grown adult.

In thinking about this story, I realized the name Harold had always been my family's touchstone for something innocent. Something that someone had been mistaken in using, but had done so with nothing but the best intentions. And so it was ironic that a man named Harold was the person who somehow iconically represented to Teri the fading innocence of her hometown.

In this sense, I had just crossed a bridge in my understanding of what this old train town was all about. The question now was, did I have enough for a story? I felt I did, and decided to ask for a meeting with Skimer to pitch it.

The next morning, Sunnivan saw me coming before I even hit the door. She always seemed to be a step ahead of me; this time would be no different.

"Mr. Skimer wants to see you, hun."

"What?"

"Mr. Skimer wants to see you. He told me to find you as soon as you got in."

"Did I do something wrong?"

I didn't want to get Eleanor Barronkoff'd again, especially pre-roach coach.

"Oh don't you worry none, Marshall," Sunnivan said. "I can tell when he's upset, and he doesn't seem upset today. Cranky. But you know."

I approached Skimer's office.

"Ah, McDougal," Skimer said.

"So I've been thinking, and that should be your first cause for concern. This whole Coon thing has me fired up, let me tell ya. Fired up. The more I think about it, I think this is a real story. You've had a couple of hiccups so far, but I think you're on to something. How your interviews going?"

"They've been great. I have a much better insight now as to what's driving both forces here. Got some great quotes on the history of Frisco and why the Coon name is so important."

"Outstanding, McDougal, just what I wanna hear. Alright then. I want you all over this story. By the end of the month I wanna splash a big, fat 'ol front page story all over this town. High time we got this story out there, and you're the guy to do it. You with me, son?"

"I'm all over it. Who do you want me to talk to?"

"First one in line is Classen. Runs that damn board, so he has to answer to the people. And I wanna know where each member of that board stands, too. Nuts need to stand up and give us an answer."

"I'm on it," I said, rising to leave.

"And one last thing, McDougal. I think you ought to get on

the phone with Austin and get some stuff from the Department of Education. I'd like to see you try and get some time with the head of education for the state. What do they have to say about this? Do they know Frisco High goes by the Fighting Coons? Do they even monitor nicknames at all? Do they care?"

"Sounds great," I said. I was halfway out into the hallway now. When your first big story hits, you want to get to it as fast as you can.

Skimer was still on a roll. "I mean, I wanna know if the Department of Education of the great Republic of Texas gives a Lincoln Log crap that the fastest growing town in the whole tootin' state is a problem for them if it's causing folks to rumble about the local high school's nickname. They don't care, they oughtta, because this is where everyone's movin', and oh by the way half the town thinks the town is backward, and the other half thinks the new folks are a little too tight in the keaster!"

"I'm on it," I started to say, but I was cut off before the words could become audible.

"Coffee truck!" someone yelled. I loved cattle call time. Less than a month on the job, and our daily ritual of journalistic bonding already seemed like a time-honored tradition. Skimer, as he appeared to be on most things, had been right. Then again, I was now looking at him differently, more critically. For someone whose paper had sat on the Frisco Coon story for too long, he seemed pretty hot on the trail at this point.

And for the Woodward of me I still wasn't sure why.

CHAPTER TEN

WAR PICTURES

That Classen was a real ratfucker. I had placed a call earlier in the day to his office; I had to settle for leaving a message. Now I had arrived a full half hour before the meeting in hopes of meeting with him. I paced in the back of the room to the point of vexation, looking repeatedly at my watch like a man waiting for a bus, but the time continued to evaporate without him in sight.

Finally, with less than five minutes to go before the meeting, with the usual suspects of community activists already filing into the meeting room, Classen appeared down at the front.

"Evening, Grady."

Classen looked entirely uninterested in stopping.

"How you," he coughed up, his blubber barely slowing its forward roll. "Understand you want to talk. Gotta get to the meeting. Don't think I'll have time to talk but we'll see."

I stood there, flat-footed. Classen knew damn well what I wanted to talk with him about. He simply didn't want to talk about it.

Barronkoff.

"Well good evening, Marshall," she said, almost mockingly. "Understand you're making progress on your big story."

I did everything I could to hide my flinch.

"How do you know I'm doing a story? Or what it might be about?"

Barronkoff giggled.

"Oh, Marshall, we may be bursting at the old seams around here, but this is still a small town in its own way," she said. "Not much goes on around here that folks don't hear about."

Bitch. "Well, I guess I'll have to be careful who I talk to, right?"

"Not a bad idea," Barronkoff said, walking away. "Not a bad idea at all."

I settled into my seat for the evening. Four hours later, I was still there, still scribbling notes on subjects ranging from latchkey kids to school lunches to teacher in-service days. Just when I thought the subject matter was going to numb all further sensation, the same man who had spoken at the previous meeting about the Frisco Coon nickname stood up again. He made virtually the same remarks he had made the last time. Made them in the same fashion.

I was compelled, but I wasn't sure why. I was careful to write down his words as well as capture his name, which I knew only as Mr. Jordan.

The moment the meeting adjourned, comfortable in my belief that I had no story to report on that night, I focused my eyes on Classen. He seemed to be aware. At one point, he looked up and in my direction, putting up one finger as if to imply he would be with me momentarily. With that assurance in hand, I began gathering my papers for the interview.

Finally, I was going to pin Classen down for a discussion on the subject at hand.

A minute later, I looked up.

No Classen!

I threw the rest of my papers in my briefcase and rushed outside to the parking lot. Classen's car was still in its regular spot. I walked back inside and looked around. The meeting room was vacant now, save the overnight cleaning crew. I looked at my watch: 11:45. Farbian was waiting.

I waited patiently for five minutes, then 10. It was almost midnight now. I was out of runway. I poked my head into the open doorway behind the school board members' chairs, where each member had an office along with the superintendent and the district's administrators. The hallway was dark. I hesitated, unsure what to do. With a start, I started down the hallway. I made a left, then a right, and now I was heading down a third hallway. I had gone too far now, had wandered too deeply into the bowels of the city's administrative interior. I had to assume that the city would not be happy with someone like me wandering down a dark hallway, let alone at midnight with no one around to control me.

I noticed a door on the left at the far end of the hallway with light shooting out from underneath. I approached carefully, measured step after measured step. I could hear voices coming from the office, and with each step it became more apparent that the conversation I was happening upon was not a pleasant one. I knew I could be seen as an intruder at this point, someone trying to eavesdrop on a private encounter. I raised my arm, my wrist palpitating, extending my knuckles toward the door. With the words "School Board President" engraved into a nameplate affixed to the door, I could see that, even in the muted light of the hallway, I had arrived at Classen's office. Even without the nameplate, though, Classen's raised voice, and that of another man, could be heard loud and clear.

"You're a bold young man, Marshall McDougal."

I wheeled around, emitting a guttural heave. I had thought I was alone. The voice had come completely out of nowhere, had cut through me, a steaming chef's knife into a mound of pooling butter.

Slowly, within two to three seconds at the outside, Eleanor Barronkoff emerged from the shadows.

"Eleanor?" I blurted out, still shaking. My eyes were still adjusting to the darkness around me, but I could see her as clearly as day now, standing no more than five feet before me.

A split second later, Classen's door swung open. Classen came barreling into the hallway. Seeing me, he tried to gather himself, but he was clearly exercised. He was sweating profusely across his forehead, and his blue dress shirt revealed Frisbee-sized sweat stains under his arms.

"Marshall," Classen said, wiping his brow. "I told y'all I was gonna talk."

"Yes, sir, but I waited, and—"

I had never been good at confrontations. While I was still wondering where Eleanor Barronkoff had come from, I knew I was the one out of bounds.

"Sir, I waited, and when you didn't come, I, well, I started looking for you," I said. "I figured maybe I was supposed to meet you in your office, that's all."

"Now Marshall, I am more than happy to talk with you in the meeting room, but I would appreciate it if you would consider this part of the building private unless invited back here," Classen said. He looked at his watch. "Especially at midnight. Last time I…mother."

"I apologize, and it won't happen again," I said. Everyone's pulse was returning to normal ranges now. I looked at Classen. Before he could force anything else out of his mouth, a figure emerged from the office and, head down, hurried past me. As the person grazed me on his way, I froze.

Sammy.

I shot a glance back at Classen so violently that I tweaked my neck. "I've had some interesting conversations with Sammy. Thought I knew him. Guess not."

I waited for a reaction; I got none.

"Marshall, I think we can all agree we've had enough for one night. Call my office in the morning and we'll set up a time to talk."

"I'd like to talk right now, Grady."

"I do need to get home. After all, past midnight, and, well, you know," Classen said, turning back toward his office. "If you'll excuse me."

I looked away. What was going on here? What was up with Sammy – and what was his relationship with Classen?

"Remember what I told you, Marshall," Barronkoff said. "Be careful who you talk to."

"You know Sammy?"

Barronkoff paused, then strode toward me. She stopped and smiled. She spoke softly.

"I just got my concealed handgun permit. Already got a spot for it. Gonna keep it right by my side. You know, that little space between the driver's seat and the console? Perfect spot, just in case of surprises. And as you know, I don't like surprises."

With that, she was gone, and – relieved now to be walking toward my car – I was not far behind. As I approached the car, I stopped. I watched and listened, for shadows, for footsteps. I put the keys into the lock and opened the door. Peering into the back seat before piling in, I started the ignition quickly and backed out of my spot. My tires screeching, my nostrils flaring, I peeled out, the fastest way back to the relative safety of the newsroom the one and only thought in my head.

I woke up the next day feeling strangely energized.

It had taken me more than an hour to fall asleep after getting home from the newsroom, and not just because the train had whizzed by, right on schedule as usual. But as I got ready for work, I realized more and more that I was in a fight. There were warning signs all around me; my choice was to back down or push forward. I had landed on the latter. To really sink my teeth into this story that Skimer was pushing me, at times against my will, to wrestle to the ground.

Skimer was my boss, and I was not about to let the sonofabitch see me stutter. I decided this must have been how Woodward kept Bradlee at bay while chasing down the story of a lifetime. This may not be the story of my lifetime, I thought, but it was a story – my story now – nonetheless.

The story, the story. I decided to take the bull by the horns and tell Skimer what had happened the night before. I also decided I wasn't going to do it alone. I wanted others to hear what I was telling him, and I wanted them to see his reaction. There seemed to be, I reasoned in a fit of suspicion, a measure of safety in numbers.

Coffee truck. I filed outside and fetched my daily dose. Skimer, Bennie and Short were all standing in a semi-circle, just a few feet away.

Bennie saw me approach. "I see no news is good news on the school front?"

"Well, depends on how you look at it," I said. "It's good news if you think I got some more quotes for my story. It's bad news if you're wondering what the head of the school board is doing screaming at stalkers like Sammy Breaux behind closed doors at midnight. Then someone's telling you about where they're gonna keep their new gun."

Short didn't sense the seriousness.

"Hey, that all sounds like good news to me," he said, laughing.

I noticed Skimer studying my face. "My office," he said, motioning me to follow him. I was less than thrilled, but went along nonetheless.

"So what's the story here?" Skimer said, closing his door behind me.

I sat down and told Skimer everything. He raised his chin.

"Son, couple of things," he said. "One, I'll talk with Barronkoff. Two, strangers approach you in parking lots referring to the person you just had lunch with, you tell me about it, you hear? Even if you know 'em."

I started to reply, but it was way too late.

"I know Breaux. Hell, the SOB works here. I don't like him much, okay? And I don't like where he comes from. You ask Bennie, she's got family from that part of Louisiana he's from. I mean, hell, I'm no fan of anything from that backwater state, but anyone from New Orleans or Baton Rouge or even Lafayette will tell ya they're real quick to point out they're from South Louisiana."

"Why is that?"

"You know, so no one thinks they're from Shreveport or something."

Skimer had accented the first syllable in Shreveport with a clarity that reeked of disdain. Why, I didn't know. What I did know by now was that Sammy, wherever he was from, was bad news, an enturbulating presence in my mix, and that the only thing I hated more than owing him $200 was the act of having gotten in his car in the first place.

I could see Skimer was ready to go off now. He had started

pacing back and forth in his office. His arms waved up and down like oil derricks.

"You're from L.A., right Marshall? Well, let me tell ya something, a little story. You know, you can find out a lot about someone over where they come from. Grew up out in East Texas. Tyler. Proud graduate of Robert E. Lee High. No Fighting Coons there. But I will tell ya, we were the Rebels when I went there. And then guess what. Few years later, had to change it out. To the Raiders. The Raiders! So I know a little something about the old ways of a nickname getting folks riled up.

"Anyway that's where the white kids went. Black kids went to John Tyler High. The Lions, if I recall. Nothing special, but I guess I had a good time out there. Then I did a couple of years over there at TJC."

"TJC…"

"Tyler Junior College. Of course, we were the Apaches, and like I kinda said there, folks think Frisco's the only place with a nickname problem. Then I get outta there and start doing what you're doing now, learning how to be a reporter. Got my first job doing obits and filling coffee cups at the 'ol Morning Telegraph. But the next thing I know I'm getting drafted, and now I've gone from these rolling hills and open land to 'Nam. And I'm here to tell ya. That was one experience I'll never forget. Don't like to talk about it much, though I guess you've seen my pictures here. So then I come back in one piece except for this big scar here from one of Charlie's bullets, and before I can get home I'm in the district and that's when I watched those boys Woodward and Bernstein do their thing. And I'm telling ya, right there I was hooked. I know I had already started out in Tyler but I got yanked out of there so fast I hadn't gotten the chance to learn too much yet. But I saw back then, up close and personal see, what the news business did when it did things right, which as we all know it doesn't always do. But it did it this time, and these crooked guys running our government were exposed for what they were.

"If I've got me a mean streak, well, I guess it comes out when I see folks trying to pull the wool over people's eyes. I just don't think that's right, that's all. So let's just say I like it when we can do what's right by the people. That's what I learned in Tyler, at least. That's what you're doing now, Marshall, and I don't know what they all taught ya out there in California. Just don't let that bloodsucking crawdad on your tail fool ya into thinking somethin' different."

Back in the newsroom. I was hammering away at the keys, the adrenaline-by-association from Skimer cornering my keyboard into a dark alley.

"Everything okay Marshall?"

I had come to realize that being a community reporter meant more time for newsroom banter.

"Just working on a story, Tanya," I said. As much as I normally liked our banter, and as pleasant a character as Costin was, I wasn't in the mood. My eyes focused on my screen; my head swirled on Sammy.

"You know, Marshall, y'all seemed right as rain first thing, but I can tell by your typing you're in a real spot of bother," Costin said, and while familiarity may breed contempt, sitting next to someone for hours on end clearly breeds familiarity with one's habits.

"Am I typing differently today?"

"Why yes you certainly are. Your typing is normally so nice, almost like you're playing a piano or something. But you're knocking the stuffing out of that poor thing like you're pounding a nail or something. Y'all gonna make a fuss over something with that story?"

Meesbruggan looked over.

"Tanya, I think Marshall's having an interesting morning," he said. "Rip really gave him one today."

"Well, bless—"

I objected vehemently, my internal angst flowing through my pores, a blast from a hose through a screen door.

"He didn't give me anything, other than a stump speech on Tyler and Shreveport."

I hesitated. "That's East Texas, right. I don't know where these places even are. Isn't Frisco already in East Texas?"

"Not really, Marshall, see…"

I was now inflicting actual bodily injury on my keyboard.

Meesbruggan tried again. "Skimer mentioned Shreveport?"

"Yeah, and he doesn't like it much."

"Well, it's no wonder. I'm just surprised he mentioned it."

"Why is that?"

Meesbruggan looked toward Skimer's office, then motioned toward Short.

"What up, Mees?" Short asked. "Hey, it's not often I get an invitation to the news desk. Must be something big. I like it."

"Skimer just brought up Shreveport with Marshall here."

Short caught himself. I had not seen this look on him before. I didn't know it was possible for him to look so concerned about anything. I felt sickness in my stomach.

Short looked over toward Skimer's office. He said nothing.

"What is it?"

"So Marshall, what Mees is talking about…what I mean is, what Rip brought up is something we don't talk about 'round here much, and there's lots of reasons for it, okay?"

"Such as?"

"It's not that simple, Marshall."

I realized no one around me was typing. I shot a glance at Thornaker. His hands flew back to his keyboard immediately.

"Marshall, what we mean is that 'Ol Rip's got a history over in Shreveport."

Meesbruggan stopped, Bennie having approached our terminals in the center of the newsroom.

"Sounds like there's a good story here," Bennie said.

"Good story," Meesbruggan said, motioning toward Skimer's empty office. "Rip brought up Shreveport with Marshall here."

"Good story, I'll say. Marshall's gotta learn what he's gotten himself into at some point, right? Be my guest, Ted. You know this one better than I do."

"That would be nice," I said. I looked at Meesbruggan with an air of expectation.

"Two words, Marshall," Meesbruggan began. "War pictures."

"You mean like the ones in Skimer's office?"

"You got it. Skimer fought in 'Nam, that's true. But that's not where the pictures come from, really. Or at least that's not what they, well, what they represent. Ya gotta understand 'ol Rip first. Yes part of it is the war, and Vietnam and the early 70s is part of it. He sees journalism as war, war between the truth and those who want to hide it. That's why he reacted so well in your interview."

Meesbruggan stopped for a breath.

"You know, when you mentioned your fascination with Watergate."

"I don't recall mentioning it."

"Oh you mentioned it alright Marshall," Meesbruggan said, smiling. "Two or three times in fact—"

"I knew it. Shoulda kept my goddamn mouth shut."

"But that's just it, Marshall, no, you shouldn't have. Because Rip was there in DC when it all came down. He was a cub reporter with the Post when it all happened, just like you're one now. I don't know whether you knew that or not. And when you mentioned Watergate and Woodward, well I don't know if Rip knows him or not but he sure as heck remembers him, and maybe one day he'll tell you about it."

I couldn't believe what I was hearing. "But he hasn't said anything yet about being at the Post, knowing I love Watergate and Woodward and all?"

"Well that's just Rip. He holds it back until he thinks someone is ready for it. He's probably just waiting for you to go to town on a big story like the one he saw Woodward and Bernstein tear into."

"He wants you to learn it for yourself, Marshall," Bennie added.

"You might say that, yes," Meesbruggan said. "I mean hey, I might have known him the longest around here, but I can't speak for him all the time. I just know how he thinks."

"Which is?"

"Which is that being a newsman nowadays is more than just a job. It's about redemption. Redemption for the newspaper as a way of life for folks, you know, back when staying connected in some old-fashioned way was still important. Redemption for making a semblance of difference still, even as everything around us gets taken away. And I ain't afraid to say I agree with him, 'cause dammit the newspaper still matters. It just matters. Always did, always will. Or at least always should. I'm fighting to keep it alive. So's Rip."

"Tell him about the other part, Mees," Short said. "You know, the past. The other part. You know. Shreveport, man."

Meesbruggan nodded. He looked over both shoulders.

"But there's another part of it that you really got to know Rip to ever see it come out. Another couple of parts."

I fixated my eyes on Meesbruggan's and lowered my voice. "Anything you can help me understand about him would be huge. I haven't exactly set the world on fire with him since I got here."

Costin laughed. "Marshall, you're doing fine with Rip. He's just testing you, okay?"

"Easy for you to say Tanya," I said, shooting Costin a quick glance.

"Go ahead Ted, give our boy here what he needs," she said.

"Okay so here's the deal. The other stuff about those war pictures is that Rip's at war. Not with anyone or anything. With himself. Rip's got a drinking problem, Marshall. Big one. Well, let me try that again. Had a drinking problem. There was a time in Dallas back in the 80s, and Rip was a rising star at the 'ol Times Herald. But then the business really started taking a dive there in the early 90s. I guess we talked about it that first day over at Scotty P's. But it's true. The industry's never really recovered from all this change going on. First it was radio and then it was TV and then it was cable. Now it's the Internet. Great business cases all, with the newspaper just kinda hanging on. That was okay for a long time, because economically speaking there was plenty to still go around. But it had become tougher and tougher for a city the size of Dallas to support two major metropolitan dailies. It was the Morning News and the Times Herald. Morning News won."

Short cut in. "Hey Marshall you're the big sports fan from La La Land. You remember the Herald Examiner out there? They had some great sportswriters back then. There was this guy Allan Malamud, he wrote this daily thing called 'Notes on a Scorecard.' Good stuff. So good that all the other sportswriters around the country knew about it, and that was before the Internet. It was just this daily kind of rambling about sports. Whatever was on his mind. Now you see papers all over the place copycatting that whole deal."

"I remember the name, yeah. But I don't ever remember reading it. We've always just gotten the Times."

"Well it folded, too. It was the end of the 80s, I think. Yeah, that's right, probably about 10-12 years back now. But the point is, even in a city as big as L.A., this is what's been happening, good longstanding dailies going away."

"I'm sorry, but what does this have to do with Rip and Shreveport?"

"Don't mind Sport, Marshall," Meesbruggan said. "It's all about sports to him, sports, sports, all the time. But sports don't count the beans."

"Count the beans?" Short exclaimed. "So you're a business writer, and that means you're a bean counter? You fooling with me, Meesbruggan!"

"Oh hell, go back to the toy department, Sport."

"I will. And you go back to your bean counting. Those of us in the toy department, we'll just keep cranking out all this fluff that people who still actually buy papers buy it for. How 'bout them beans, Mees? You know, I'd call you a beaner, but that would get me in trouble nowadays with all this Fighting Coon stuff. I'd have that Norma Taylor all over my ass right away if I did that. Actually…"

Short sauntered off, his cackling still audible even after he disappeared from sight.

"So Ted, what happened with Rip and the Times Herald? You're killing me here."

With that, the phone rang at Meesbruggan's desk.

"Meesbruggan."

He nodded. "Can I ask you to hold for a quick minute? Yes. Thanks."

"Marshall, got a hot one here. I've been waiting for this source to call back for days. Gotta talk with him. We'll finish up later."

"Can you just give me the short version?"

Meesbruggan sighed.

"There is no long version, really. Times Herald went under. Unless you could pick up a job at the Morning News, there weren't too many jobs. And let's face it, we weren't exactly making the big bucks in the first place, so it's not like we all had a lot of cushion to fall back on.

"So at one point Rip gets the job up here to run the place. Couple of 2-3 years later. And he calls me and offers me the job as business editor, and so now he's dragging me up here to Frisco to help this old rag pick up the pieces and become a real newspaper again. Don't get me wrong. Me and the wife were thrilled. We had this place down there by Belt Line and Central. It was okay, but even back then it was getting pretty worn. Next thing I know I'm able to buy into this new place out in Allen. It's not one of those McMansions like they got going in all over down there in the city now, but it's new and clean and the plumbing's not breaking down every five minutes, right? Think I may have told you that before.

"But I figured it was my last chance in this business, and it wasn't real easy when we got here. So Skip dug his heels in and started fighting to get things right. And it took him awhile, with some help from Jan and me and Will here and the others, but we started to turn that corner."

"Yes, but Shreveport?"

"Gotta get this Marshall."

"Wait...Shreveport?"

"Thanks Morty. Sorry about that. So let's dig into this..."

I almost fell forward out of my chair. I could taste it.

I stared blankly at Meesbruggan and leaned back. This was a lot more than I thought I'd get out of this morning, and I wasn't sure I was ready for it all. I looked at Thornaker. I was shocked when he didn't turn away.

"Shreveport..." he muttered, shaking his head. "Shreveport."

"Excuse me? Will?"

No response. Thornaker was back at his keyboard. Even if they were the same word, they were two words from Thornaker in one gulp. I was thirsting for more, but the mirage faded as quickly as it had appeared.

"McDougal!"

JOHN CLENDENING

It had been less than an hour since our last conversation. Now Skimer was calling me back into his office. In the interim I had learned some highly personal details about his past, none of which I figured he wanted me to know about, and as I entered his office they – and what to do with them – were still flying throughout my head like white flakes in a small snow globe.

Skimer leaned to his right and barked into the hallway for Bennie to join us. A minute later, a silky layer of carcinogen still encircling her from her hourly visit to the back lot, she strode in.

"Okay, listen. I ain't here to play hide the weenie. Where are we on this Coon story?"

I looked at Bennie, who hadn't been with us in the last meeting. She looked back at me, her fingertips so deeply orange they were almost chestnut, and I could tell she wished she were still outside.

"So fine, let's get on with it," Skimer went on. "Now, don't you worry none about that Sammy Breaux there out back or Eleanor Barronkoff being a nut. I think you have anything to worry about, I set people straight behind the scenes. I mean, it's street fightin', ain't it?"

"But Rip, if you're talking to folks behind the scenes as you say, don't I need to know about that? I mean, what if you're hearing things that I need to know about?"

"Fair questions, McDougal. Don't worry about it. You do your job, and I'll do mine. If mine means that sometimes I need to make a phone call telling people to get the hell out of the way so my new reporter can chase a legitimate story down, then that's what it means. If it means I need to tell people to go varmint hunting, then so be it. You report and write, and I'll run good old-fashioned interference as I think I need to."

"Fair enough, Rip," I said, rising from the chair. "I'll keep at it."

About to exit Skimer's office, I stopped myself.

"Mr. Skimer, then I need to ask you another question."

"Yes?"

"What I don't understand is why you want this story so badly now, when from what I can gather the paper hasn't covered it too much before. And I know who my predecessor was, if that explains anything."

Skimer was nodding now. "Okay, so first off I'm impressed. Jan

182

and I had an over-under going on how long it would take you to figure that one out. I'm pretty sure this means Bennie wins. I wasn't sure you had it in ya, but she said I was wrong. Turns out she was right."

"Thank you. I think."

"As far as where you're going here, so I get it. Why have the son of the head of the school board of all people on the story, which is a clear conflict of interest, and then you or anyone else for that matter? That's where I'm gonna low-key this.

"Let's just say that as the town grows up, this paper needs to, too. There used to be a certain way of doing things, and as much as I complain about that I was sometimes as guilty as the next guy. I mean, we weren't exactly innocent bystanders, right Jan? Wasn't too long ago we were still doing that damn 'Coon-of-the-week' thing.

"In the old Frisco, it wasn't a big deal to have the son of the head of the school board cover the school board, even if that Gin Bomb is a horse's ass. He's like a canker sore on a lip, see? Can't see it on the outside. But it's there, and it's eatin' ya up the whole time. Might be okay for awhile. Just don't bite into something sweet. Sting like a hornet. But things have started to change around here as this whole Coon thing heats up, and we couldn't stand for that anymore. So we made the change, and that's where you come in."

"Meaning?"

"Meaning that's where this old henhouse of a paper is finally fixin' to grow some real cajones. We needed some new blood, some new hungry kid like you who didn't have an agenda around here other than to come in and shake things up. And now I can see y'all are doing just that."

"I suppose I am, Mr. Skimer, yes. But really, I'm just doing my job."

"You're only doing your job, that's right," Skimer said. He sat back and looked at the war pictures on his walls. I wondered what he was thinking. He took a deep breath and looked at me.

"But I'll tell ya this. There are times in this life when you get to a bridge, okay? And the bridge is narrow and creaky, and it looks too dangerous to even think about crossing it. And sometimes the bridge is wide and looks easy, but the water under it is rushing on by real quick, and it's spilling every which way. So what do you do? You wanna get to the other side, you wanna see what's there, if you wanna grow as a person and see new things, I reckon you find a way to get across. You just find a way, that's all. It's the road less traveled, son. You don't take a chance, you always think you have all the answers.

"And that's a real shame. You don't see what the answers are, you're not even sure what questions there are. Biggest shame of all."

A part of me felt like I should kick down the locker room door and charge out onto the field. Another part of me understood Skimer was trying to impart a valuable lesson, and that I should take a deep breath and take it in.

"I understand. I'll keep pushing. Thanks boss."

"One last thing, McDougal."

"Yeah boss."

"I hear one more time about anybody out there trying to intimidate my new reporter, you just tell 'em to stay outta your chili. They want a war, son, they got one. I'm here to tell ya this whole thing really frosts me good. But it's all just mice nuts, ya hear? So don't you worry none son, because you're gonna get your Woodward moment see, and this paper's gonna be better for it. And so is this town. We good?"

I hit the phones right away. By the end of the day – holding the phone in full Woodward-Redfordness all the while – I had called every Frisco school board member for a comment on the issue. My mission was to see who came down on what side. I only got through to two of the seven, but the two to whom I got through – Barronkoff and Brianna Stevens – each granted me on-the-record interviews on the Fighting Coons issue. Barronkoff still wouldn't commit to a position on the issue, as I had come to expect.

Stevens, on the other hand, surprised me by saying that, while she wanted to see how the debate played out in the community, she had concerns about a nickname that "could be perceived as an inhibitor to the future growth of the city." While not a firm position, Stevens had essentially tipped her hand toward the Norma Taylor camp.

I was on a roll now, and I knew it. My final call of the day was to the Department of Education. I got through to the state superintendent's administrative assistant, and immediately started to sweet talk her. One of the first things I had learned, and thankfully I seemed good at it, was to charm the gatekeeper.

"I'm sure Dr. Jones would be happy to talk with you," his assistant said. "Depending on his schedule, of course."

"When do you think he might be free?"

"Well, it looks like August 12 might work. Do you mean to come here or talk with him on the phone?"

It hadn't occurred to me that interviewing the head of education for all of Texas in person was an option.

"Wow. I would very much like to meet him and all. But I'm fairly sure my editor needs me to talk with him a bit earlier than that."

"Okay, let me have our PR person, Geoff Braun, get back to you, okay? You should really be talking with him, anyway. But you seemed nice, so, well, you know. You should talk with him. I will have him call you."

An hour later, the phone rang.

"McDougal."

"Mr. McDougal, Geoff Braun with the state department of education. How are we today?"

Braum's voice was overly enthusiastic, and it took me a aback. "I'm good, how are you?"

"Well, I'm just doing fine, thanks for asking. Understand you want to talk with Dr. Jones."

"Yes, that would be great. We're doing a story on the Frisco Coon nickname controversy, and we'd like to see what Mr. Jones thinks about it. Dr. Jones."

The silence on the other end of the line was deafening.

"Mr. McDougal, what paper did you say you were at again?"

"The Frisco Evening Outlook?" I said. I was tensing up now, which might have explained why I phrased my answer in the form of a question.

"And that's a daily paper?"

"Yes, sir, it is. Well, except for Sunday. Well, what I mean is, we publish both weekend papers on Friday night."

"I'm sorry?"

"Never mind. We'd really like to spend a few minutes with Dr. Jones."

"Well, we do appreciate the call and all. And I'd be happy to speak for the superintendent."

I shook my head. "I'd very much like to talk with the superintendent himself, if that's okay."

"Well, I'm sure you can understand that he's a very busy man. The state superintendent's position is that it really is up to the local communities and school boards to work through these issues on their own. Is there anything else we can do for you, Mr. McDougal?"

I shook my head. "No, that will about do it, thank you."

"And thank you, Mr. McDougal. You call again now."

Five minutes later, I was still stewing.

"They'll never talk to you about it."

"Clearly."

"The state is just being the state," Meesbruggan said. "The last thing it wants to do is get caught up in some story like the Frisco Coons. If there's anything they don't want to touch, it's racism. Real or perceived. Either."

"Yeah, well, shouldn't they want to? I mean, why not take a position?"

"Because it's not good business. They'll sit back and watch this all play out. Then at the right time, they'll swoop in and take the credit if things go their way. If not, they'll blast the other side to make themselves look good. It's just politics."

"Just politics?" I said. I was a cross now between mild amusement and building disgust.

"Yep, just politics," Meesbruggan said. "You're going to have to make this happen inside Frisco itself, I'm afraid. Big state."

I grudgingly admitted Meesbruggan was right. As the days went on, I continued making phone calls to the board members, hoping to check the box with each of them so I could get the story done. The story Skimer wanted was to focus on the school board itself – how did each member look at the issue, what would be the deciding factor for their vote? The board was on record now as pushing off the vote until after football season. If that was true, Skimer didn't want to wait until after football season to pin people down.

By week's end, I had reached all but one member of the board – Classen himself. I had left three messages now, and with each message I had grown more impatient. So had Skimer, who, as I looked up, was now standing next to my desk.

"McDougal, we have resolution," he said. "Just spoke with Classen. Says he would prefer not to wade in. Feels since he's head of the board, no matter what he says, he will be seen as trying to drive the board in that direction. Doesn't wanna be in that position."

"Yes, but isn't that what the head of the school board is voted in to do – lead on the tough issues?"

"Yes, it is, and that's why I told Classen to go varmint hunting, just like I said," Skimer said. "When I told him I thought he'd be able to track down a fighting coon pretty quick, well, let's just say he didn't like that much."

"What did he say?"

"He said I was so blunt my bluntness probably blunts his bluntness. Thought that was a pretty nice complement myself."

I was confused. "So what does this all mean?"

"Means Classen has spoken. Meaning he has decided not to speak," Skimer said. "Just say Classen reserved comment until the school board addresses the issue further. In and out, that's it."

"Must be nice to be able to whitewash things like that," I said.

Short wandered by. "Whitewash? Hey, how about the Frisco Fighting Whitewashers? That'll work just fine around here."

Everyone within earshot laughed. The issue was a serious one. But a little comedic relief didn't hurt, either.

"McDougal, I want that piece on my desk by close of business Monday," Skimer said. "We'll need a few days to get this one right. This is one we'll need to play carefully."

"Or?"

"Or all hell's gonna break loose, that's all. Of course, all hell's gonna break loose anyway, right?! Hey Meesbruggan, you're the business guy – how many more papers you think we'll sell that day?"

Meesbruggan laughed. "At least 10 percent more."

"Outstanding, Meesbruggan, outstanding," Skimer bellowed. "Sure could use it. Hell, that might even make up for the extra printing costs for that damn column you wrote the other day, it was so long."

That was all I needed to hear. I felt relief that I no longer needed to chase Classen down. I felt an even greater sense of excitement knowing I was getting to the good part – the writing. I had done enough reporting. Time to write a news story. And write I did, long into the evening that night. What should I lead with? What was the quote that best summed up the point I was trying to make? Retrieve this quote, place it there. Re-write that sentence, put it there. Cut and paste, cut and paste, cut and paste. Fuck you, law school!

I had barely noticed my surroundings when I happened to glance over at the wall clock. It was 9:30. The newsroom was virtually empty outside of Farbian, in his own world in full editing mode, at the other end. But I was so comfortable with this process, had become so engaged in the subject matter, I could have written all night. The fact that no one had bothered to get in my way didn't bother me in the slightest. Even if they had, I hadn't noticed.

I worked it well past midnight. The next day, I worked it again. I was obsessed with getting it right. No board member would go on record as saying which way they would vote, and the state department of education had been as worthless to date as the heavy jackets I'd brought with me from California.

Two board members, however, first Stevens and now Hurstman, said they were concerned about the nickname potentially impeding the city's ongoing growth plans. That was enough for me, and I led with their concerns as well as Norma Taylor's speaking on behalf of the new homeowners in town with a distaste for the nickname. I balanced their views with those of Sax and Manemin, who were outspoken in their support of the tradition of the nickname (while still being careful to say they would consider their votes carefully), and Sabrina's friend Teri Leiner, who represented the homeowners who had grown up in Frisco, asserted the innocence of the nickname and, as such, wanted the town to preserve its heritage to the extent still possible given the rampant growth it was experiencing – and in fact expected to continue to experience into the foreseeable future.

Finally, after several weeks of perspiration followed by more perspiration, which for once I couldn't blame on the weather, I submitted the story to Bennie for editing just before leaving the office for the weekend.

"Front page stuff," I said, announcing to Bennie that I had delivered the draft to her in-box. "Above the fold, baby."

"Just don't make me your enemy."

"Well, let's put it this way: Rip wants to stir things up with the story. You think he's gonna wanna bury it?"

"Probably not."

"Any word on timing?"

"Not yet. We need to sink our teeth into this one for a few days. We'll let you know if we have questions. It's an evergreen story, but we want it out."

With that, I was out the door. I greeted the late afternoon glare with an exhausted confidence, a feeling that I had put everything I had into the story. I wasn't sure what Bennie was going to do with it. Nor was I sure what Skimer would ultimately think of it, or when – or if – it would actually come out. Remember Woodward, I kept reminding myself: 17 stories to the Post, capped off by a one-way ticket to Montgomery.

The last Friday in July had arrived. Summer was marching on. I had become so caught up in my story I had not seen Sabrina in nearly a week, though she'd been down in Hillsboro visiting her aunt before school started again, and from what I could gather from our phone conversations seemed perfectly content to be spending a few days cruising the big local outlet mall. I was feeling the need to reconnect with her, to recharge not only my batteries, but ours. Nothing that an evening out with Frisco's Finest couldn't cure, I felt, and I – feeling like an old wheezer myself at this point – was ready to again hang out with Sabrina and watch the Wheezers give it their all.

Then I noticed it. There it was, as clear as the day that produced it, a picture painted but by a finger but a picture painted still, a scrawl across my back windshield: *Don't Rac My Coons!* The words, the same ones Teri Leiner had mentioned were on signs in front yards, were done in a stray combination of block letters and basic script. But the exclamation point was different. It was diagonal, done clearly in a hurry, and there was just something about it that I couldn't escape. It was not only crooked but bordering on sawtooth, and the point at its bottom end, likely accidentally but the effect was real still, resembled wax dripping from a candle, the sensation of which was elypsees-like in the message it seemed to send. Like the message had been sent. But it wasn't done yet. Like there was more to come.

All I could do was stare. I decided after a minute to leave it, thinking it would be good fodder with Skimer. I returned to my apartment. And I could tell something was amiss from a ways off: the very same message that had been scrawled into the grime on my rear windshield was written on my door. The part of me that had seen too many movies assumed initially that the writing had been done in blood. It was in black, so the blood could have dried, I decided, and I was careful to avoid mussing it as I turned the lock and pushed the door gently open.

Just as I did, the phone rang. I rushed for it, the chance to bring someone else in to the scene a welcome one. It was the J-School placement office at USC. The Times had called. They had kept my file. An opening for a spot on the news desk had come up. They wanted me to interview for it.

Just in time, I thought as I caught my breath. Just in time.

"Sign on a chuck wagon: Pickin' up bones to keep from starvin' Pickin' up chips to keep from freezin' Pickin' up courage to keep from leavin' ... Way out West in No-Man's land."
– Savvy Sayin's compiled by Ken Alstad

Southeast corner of Parkwood and Warren,
in front of the Homewood Suites

CHAPTER ELEVEN

GOOD STORY

As the calendar turned, the temperature was not the only thing heating up; so too were the presses, the lull of July having morphed into the buzz of August. Meesbruggan was muckraking along, having exposed a local car dealer for illegally inflating prices. Costin had published a series of profiles on a handful of the community's leading volunteers, and even Bennie had gotten into the swing of things with a guest editorial on local trash pick-up.

Short was still following every pitch at Frisco Field, and while there's no cheering in the press box of course, he was convinced this was finally the year when the Blazers were going to do their version of winning it all.

I had again noticed a group of dark-suited men streaming into a conference room. I'd asked again if anyone knew who they were, but no one seemed to want to talk about it.

In the meantime, the traditional late-summer exodus from North Texas, when anyone and everyone with the werewithal to leave town does just that, was showing signs of abating. I'd been able to navigate the Krispy Kreme drive-through in under 20 minutes for a solid month now, but the back-up was starting to again resemble 1930s bread lines.

Bennie approached us in mid-tappity-tap-tap.

"Okay, I assume you've all heard about this whole congressman thing," she said. She stopped and looked around. We had talked about it, though I don't think any of us could tell where she was heading.

"So I need someone to take the lead here and see if there is any local angle we could leverage for a story. There's more and more talk the congressman may have had something to do with it."

Silence.

"William?"

Thornaker looked up. His hair was especially lubricious today, and whatever the Long Island Iced Tea of spirits he mixed together every morning and applied to his face was, he had applied too much.

"I don't know what the local angle would be, but call the local politicos and see what they think. Maybe some of them work on committees or something with him. What's his name again?"

Still no audible response from Thornaker.

"Isn't he from California?" Bennie asked. "Marshall?"

"Yeah I think he is, but that's Northern California," I responded. I looked up at Bennie. "That's like a different state."

"Now, really," Costin said. "A different state?"

Before I could respond, Thornaker let out a grunt, and the assignment was apparently his.

The next morning. First Tuesday of the month. It had now been a week-and-a-half of anticipation later since submitting my story, and I rolled out of bed right at 7:30. Early by my standards on a school board night. But Bennie had told me there was a chance the story would run today.

My eyes barely open, my hair a fistful of barley, I parked myself in front of my computer and flicked it on. There it was, in black and white on my screen, my story, and not just my story but my story in all caps glory.

BOARD ON A "COON HUNT" WITH H.S. NICKNAME.
I gasped, my jaw trapdooring downward. THAT's the headline?!
It did not reflect the lede I had written. Not even close. I had been
very careful – exceedingly careful – to write a measured lede, one that
reflected my promises throughout my interviews.

My first thought: Sammy. My second: Barronkoff. With her in
particular, I had promised her the paper would not blow the issue out
of proportion. More specifically, I had promised her the article would
not make it appear that the board was leaning toward the change. I
could already hear the phone ringing, that condescending voice again
on the other end.

Shit.

Despite my promises, the headline, I knew as I continued to stare
at it in disbelief, did just what I had assured it would not. In a panic,
I threw on just enough to keep me from getting arrested and flew out
the door. I could have read the story online, but I was still at my core
a hard copy guy. Besides, I didn't want to just read the story. I wanted
to see the positioning of it on the page. Was it, literally, above the fold?
Did my entire story make the cut, or had it been trimmed? And, most
urgently, to what extent had Skimer and Bennie edited my carefully-
crafted copy to make it sound like the board was, indeed, leaning
toward the change?

Shit!

I barreled onto Preston Road and punched it to my now-traditional
spot. I marched toward the rack, a drunk on a bender, pinballing a
quarter into the hole. There I stood for the next several minutes, just
having woken up, not yet having brushed my teeth, in full daylight for
all rush hour drivers to see, standing on the sidewalk as they whizzed
by, my neck moving from right to left, from left to right, like the old
Smith-Corona typewriter my father had passed down to me before he
finally bought me my first Mac.

The more I read, the more confused I became. My story had
been left remarkably intact. I was particularly pleased that my lede
had been kept entirely the same, and the only significant change
I could glean was the moving around of a handful of paragraphs.

Normally, for most reporters, this would be cause for celebration. But for me, standing amid the exhaust alongside Preston Road, it was the opposite. I felt betrayed. I had not known how the headline would read. Reporters rarely know what headline a copy editor will place over their cherished words, an age-old source of friction in the newsroom.

This headline did not capture my story. Not even close.

Shit.

Settling back into my apartment now, I paced back and forth. I was sipping, slowly on purpose, my latte, not because I had discovered its nirvana but more so for its calming effects on my nerves. I could already envision Classen going berserk. And that bitch Barronkoff. She always seemed to be lurking about when I least expected it. Was I going to turn the corner and find her standing there waiting for me? And what of Sammy, supposedly my first Texas friend? If he and Classen were in cahoots, which appeared to be the case despite their yelling match in Classen's office, how long would it be before he resurfaced yet again?

Then I truly panicked.

Teri.

Teri and her heartfelt stories of what it had been like to grow up in Frisco. She had been so forthright in her opinion that the nickname had never meant anything other than to honor the city's connection to the raccoon, had never meant harm to anyone. That the nickname was now seen by many in town as the symbol for the innocence Frisco was losing – an innocence some were desperate to maintain. What was she to think of me? Would she feel double-crossed, like she had been set up? She was quoted by name in the story, and I knew I would have to answer to her.

Ring. Its scream shot my hand upward, and within a split second hot coffee and steamed milk were spreading like lava across my hand.

"Hello?! McDougal, yes?"

I had answered the phone like I was at the office, and in my mind I was. I was wearing my distress in my voice. The pain from the lava was just starting to register; the only question was whether it would compare to that of the other shoe dropping, which from what I could gather in my samba was about to occur.

"Well, good morning." My heart sank.

"Hi, Sabrina."

"Interesting story in the paper today, Marshall."

I was furiously applying pressure to my hand yet trying to listen intently, trying to determine Sabrina's tone.

"Yeah. I'm not sure what to say."

"What do you mean?"

"I mean that you were the one who set me up to talk with Teri, and I can't imagine she's real thrilled with the story."

"I would think not."

"But you gotta understand, that I really did try to write a balanced story. If you read the story, it doesn't reflect the headline at all."

Before Sabrina could respond, a click.

"Hold on, someone's trying to get through. Can't wait to hear this one."

"Hello?" My blood pressure was rising again.

"Marshall, Norma Taylor, how are you?"

Norma Taylor. Here was the one person whom I felt certain would be thrilled with the story. I felt a flush of relief wash over me.

"Hi, Norma. So whaddya think?"

I had blurted the words out at least two or three octaves higher than normal, and even a quick squirt of urine flowing down my thigh gave me little reason for pause.

"Marshall McDougal and the Evening Outlook, I didn't know all y'alls had it in ya," Taylor said, laughing. "You better believe I'm pleased. And so are the other homeowners I'm hearing from. Nobody's gotten their paper at home yet but once this thing hit the Web it started spreading pretty quick. That slowpoke school board can expect a big crowd tonight, Marshall, you can count on that. This is exactly what we needed to bring this thing back from the ashes. Rebel rousin', that's what I call it! Woo-hoo!"

"Thanks, Norma," I said. I was dancing on the head of a pin, vacillating between apologizing for the story on one line while accepting congratulations for it on the other. "I gotta go back to this other call. Hold on one sec."

I switched back to Sabrina.

"Hi. That was the head of the homeowners' group. She's thrilled with the story."

"Well, I'm glad someone is."

"Does that mean you don't like it? I mean, really don't like it?"

"Well. You know why I don't. I guess my bigger concern is Teri and repairing my friendship with her."

"I tried to be fair."

"You know, it's not often you set up a friend for a real newspaper interview, like never really, and then the interview is part of a story that goes against what you and your friend believe to be right. I'm sorry Marshall but you're gonna have to go with me on this one, okay? I mean, do you think the story is fair?"

"Yes, I do. But what you don't understand is that I didn't write—"

"I know, I know, you didn't write the story, the editors did," Sabrina cut in. Now she was getting angry.

Another click. My heart rate continued to yo-yo.

"Another call, hold on."

"Marshall, Eleanor Barronkoff."

I closed my eyes and girded.

"Good morning, Eleanor. I assume you're calling about the story?"

"You could say that."

"First off let me say I worked very hard for this story to be fair and balanced," I said, trying to cut her off at the pass.

"Oh, that's just great, Marshall, but let me ask you this: who on the school board told you we were on a 'coon hunt' for the nickname? You're joking, right?"

"Eleanor, I don't write the head—"

"Marshall, I assume you will stand up for this story. And my advice to you is to be ready to defend both yourself and your employer tonight."

I clenched. "What do you mean by that?"

"What I mean is, expect half the town to be there tonight, because this is plain old tabloid crap. Yellow journalism is what I believe they used to call it. And I'm not going to sit there and have my constituents think I'm on a 'coon hunt' for some nickname, because to some of them that means I'm on a 'coon hunt' for their way of life. You know the story, which is that we're going to look at this after the football season. Has that not become crystal clear?"

"And I say that in the story, Eleanor."

"Yes, but where, in the 90th paragraph? C'mon, Marshall, this is a hatchet job, and you and your folks at the Evening Outrage – that's what we call that rag of yours when it pulls stunts like this – know it, too. I hope you're happy with all the extra papers you're gonna sell today."

"Eleanor, I—"

"Marshall, I will see you tonight. But I'm here to tell you – do not, I repeat do not, expect to use me as a source for any other story. This is two strikes, Marshall McDougal, and what you'll learn about me is that if I feel that someone's after me, I won't give them a third one. As far as I'm concerned, you're already out."

I stood silently, too stunned to respond.

"And one last thing, Marshall McDougal. I assume this conversation is off the record, right? You understand what that means, right?"

"Yes, Eleanor."

With that, there was a firm click. I laid the phone down softly on the coffee table and leaned over, allowing my head to sink slowly into my hands. Several minutes later, the pounding in my head beginning to resemble that of the neighborhood train, I still sat, motionless, listening only to my own breathing, and I swear I could hear an "I told you so" from my father all the way from California.

Sabrina.

Sabrina!

I had completely forgotten that she was still on the other line. Frantically, I grabbed the phone and pressed the talk button.

Dial tone. I pressed it again. She must be on the other line, I thought. I pressed it again.

Dial tone.

"Dammit!"

I pounded her number out on the keypad again.

"Dammit...dammit!"

My body was like a vertical funnel into which sands of stress were being filled. As it piled toward the top it rose from my upper back to my shoulders to my neck to my temples. All that remained was a celebral hemorrhage.

"Hello?"

I caught myself with a start. "Uh, hello, Mr. Sapphire? Uh, yes, it's Marshall, Marshall McDougal. Is Sabrina home, we were just on the other—"

"Marshall, quite a stir you've created. I like it, son. That's what this town needs, a little stirring."

I took another deep breath. "Wow, thank you, Mr. Sapphire. I did work hard at it. I don't gather your daughter likes it much, though. I don't think she likes me much, either."

Mr. Sapphire laughed. "Oh, son, she'll get over it. Hold on a minute, let me get 'er for ya."

"Hello?"

"Sabrina, it's Marshall." I didn't wait for a response. "I'm so sorry I left you on hold. It was one of the board members on the other line, and things got ugly. You think you didn't like the story, you should have heard her. I'm really sorry."

Sabrina remained silent. This is not something I had experienced before, and I didn't like it.

"Sabrina?"

"Yes, Marshall."

"Are you ok?"

Silence.

"Are we okay?" I mean, I don't care about the story, alright? You're more important to me than that."

"Yes, Marshall, we're okay," Sabrina said, breaking the silence. "We're more than okay."

"Really? What? Are you sure?"

"I'm sorry, Marshall, I think I just panicked about Teri's reaction, especially since I introduced you guys. I guess if you read what she said, she doesn't sound bad."

"Honestly, I tried to do a fair job with this. I really did. It's just that it's this big hot button issue in town, so almost no matter what I do I'm going to make somebody mad. But I don't want that someone to be you."

"Oh, you reporter types always know the right thing to say. So when am I going to see you again, Mr. Hot Button?"

"How about tomorrow. That is if I make it through tonight's school board meeting."

Sabrina laughed. "Oh, you'll make it through just fine. People are going to be mad. Just let 'em."

I was in full exhale now. And I was now more convinced than ever of the power of Sabrina Sapphire. I had just had the most stressful morning of my professional career, yet I was now feeling great.

Another click. Barronkoff, again? And what about Norma Taylor? Hadn't she been on the other line at some point? Shit.

Bennie. She and Skimer wanted me to report to the paper early that day.

"I do anything wrong?"

"No, no, Marshall. Great job on the story. Good story. We're getting a lot of calls here. We just want to make sure you're fully prepared for what you're gonna deal with tonight. Good story."

A couple of hours later, I was there, Woodward strolling into the Post newsroom after catching his latest fish. I had gone on a mind-clearing run over at Warren. I was feeling good.

Sunnivan breezed by.

"We having fun yet, Marshall?!"

"Awesome possum, Lane, awesome possum."

I smiled and kept walking. I bypassed my desk and reported directly to Skimer's office. Bennie was already there. Skimer closed the door behind me.

"Okay, first off, nice job, kid. Good story," Skimer said, starting to pace. The solider stopped for a moment, a war photo in his sights.

"But here's the thing, see. That whole school board thing tonight is gonna be a mess, a real mess. We're getting calls from every which way asking what time the meeting starts, if this Coon thing is on the agenda. Apparently people don't read past the first two sentences in news stories anymore, thanks to that damn USA Today and the TV." He pronounced "TV" with the accent on the first syllable as opposed to accenting the last one, which was the only way I had ever heard it pronounced. I had noticed that people in Texas did this a lot, most notably when saying the word "insurance," which dumbfounded me even more than the "TV" thing.

Bennie chimed in. The act was hyperventilating cop, calm cop; her role, thankfully for both of us, was clear.

"Marshall, if there is a big crowd at the meeting tonight, expect lots of them to want to say their peace on this whole thing to the board. That's going to require you to be in full reporting mode, because we'll want to report on everything tomorrow. We want to make sure you're up for this, that you understand what you're getting yourself into. That's all."

I didn't hesitate. "No, I can handle it fine, and if this is news tonight, then let's cover it. Let's do it."

"Good, kid, good," Skimer said. "No backing down, that's it. If some people don't like that we're on this story, tell 'em to tell it to the folks who decided we were all gonna be Fighting Coons in the first place. Either that, or tell it to the school board. We're not making this stuff up. This stuff's real, and we're just doing our job. That's it."

"Works for me, Rip," I said. "My only issue is defending a headline I didn't write. Folks don't understand that reporters don't write headlines. If you look at the headline and then read the story—"

"Nor do they have to know who does what around here," Skimer said, and I knew right away where he was going. "Your job, Marshall, is to represent this newspaper. We may not be The Old Gray Lady, okay, but we're still a real newspaper and this story shows we can do the job when we need to. You didn't write that head, that's nobody's business who doesn't know or care how a newsroom works. The Frisco Evening Outlook's headline is your headline. We all on the same page here, Mr. McDougal?"

"Yes sir, yes we are," Marshall said. I realized I needed to tow the party line, no matter who or what I encountered that night.

"Thank you for joining me in this teachable moment," Skimer said. He looked at Bennie and strode off.

"You ok Marshall?"

"No problem."

"You sure?"

"Yep."

I wasn't sure if I was, really, but if there was time to consider the alternative in this business, that was news to me.

It didn't take long to see I was in for an eventful evening.

Typically before school board meetings, the parking lot was sparsely populated at best. But tonight was different. The parking lot was a mob scene. Cars circled about looking for the preciously few empty spots. People milled about on the sidewalk. There was a circus air to the atmosphere. I gave up on the lot and found a spot on the street. As I approached the front entrance to the building, I was shocked to hear chanting.

Entering the lobby, the chanting got increasingly louder, and I realized people were chanting the words, "Don't Rac My Coons." I craned my neck to peer through the throng of people pushing to squeeze through the lobby doors into the auditorium. I could see a group of about 25 people congregating about halfway down the left side aisle chanting the words. They were chanting quite quickly, and clapping their hands twice between "Rac" and "My," such that the chant came off like a school cheer. There was little cheer, however, either in their voices or on their faces. I decided to take a low profile, finding a spot in the rear of the room against the back wall.

I had not seen the auditorium like this before. On a given school board night no more than a fourth of the 100 or so seats in the auditorium were filled. Tonight, not only was each seat filled, the room was standing-room-only. I studied backs of heads from row to row, looking for people I might know, and it occurred to me that if the room were to take on any more people safety could become a problem, particularly given the state of mind of the people scattered throughout it. With a start, I recognized him even from the back. Sammy. I tried to turn away when I saw him turn in my general direction, but it was too late. He raised his eyebrows, and as he nodded his head up and down, the more a glimmer of a grin emerged from the sides of his mouth, the more the baseness seeped through.

Suddenly a hush fell over the crowd. The air was that of a watershed night, a watershed moment, in the long history of a proud but festering town. The school board members, led by Classen, had started to file into the room and take their seats, and it occurred to me that, no matter how slowly he was moving, Classen still had this futile rush to him, a harried New Yorker late for another subway. Seated now, he looked up to address the crowd. He had the look of someone who had just swallowed a porcupine. Just as he started to lean into the microphone, the chant, which had momentarily subsided, began again.

It was louder, louder now. Classen at first tried to speak over it, but he was wallpaper at this point, one of those peeving noises that you're not sure where it's coming from but peeving still, like a running toilet.

The crowd sensed his weakness. The chants went on.

"Don't Rac...My Coons!

Don't Rac...My Coons!

Don't Rac...My Coons!"

Just then, Classen looked toward the back of the room. Despite the physical distance between us, which was likely about 50 feet, he caught my eye. He fixated on me for several moments, and the focus grew more and more intense as each moment, interminably, went on. I took a deep breath, knowing full well that I had now probably secured my first professional enemy. Or, given Barronkoff's histrionics from that morning, my second. I recalled learning in J-school that every journalist will, sooner or later, be sued over something he or she writes.

I did not recall learning in J-school that every journalist will, sooner or later, make enemies of public officials with whom they have to interact on a daily basis, but I wished I had.

I looked away, hoping a detached reaction would call Classen off. Finally, he asked for quiet.

Once. Twice. Three times. I assumed he would want to give the nickname defenders as much air time as possible. But the crowd only somewhat grudgingly listened, prompting the chants to gain steam yet again.

"Don't Rac...My Coons!
Don't Rac...My Coons!
Don't Rac...My Coons!"

Out of nowhere a shriek louder than even the chanting of two dozen stopped everything in its tracks.

"Enough cheerleading! Let's get to the point here, okay?!"

It was Norma Taylor, seated in the front row toward the right corner.

The chanting stopped. Everyone in the room was looking at Taylor. She returned the collective glare, virtually daring anyone to question her resolve.

Classen tried again to break the ice. "Can we please—"

As piercing as Taylor's scream had been, another shriek suddenly emerged from another part of the room, this time the middle left.

"Stay out of this town, lady!"

I leaned forward. I realized this woman was the same woman whom I had interviewed several weeks earlier as her home was burning. She was standing now, too.

Taylor didn't hesitate to reach for her ammunition – her acerbit wit.

"Why don't you get out of this town? Frisco ain't what it used to be, and neither are you."

The crowd murmured. Classen tried in vain again to regain control – something he had never really had at all.

"Ladies and gentlemen—"

The woman screaming at Taylor wasn't done. "This town was just fine until people like you came in!"

Classen persevered, and things were getting so bad now that I actually began rooting for him.

"Ladies and gentlemen, please, let's start the meeting. The board understands this issue is an important one, and I assure you we will consider all options in due course."

That wasn't nearly enough for Taylor.

"That's it?" She was standing again. "That's all you have to say?"

Classen might as well have been wiping his forehead with baby oil. The temperature had hit 101 again that day, and even though the sun was going down it was still at least 95. Whatever air conditioning system the Frisco school board had once invested in for its headquarters building was not doing what it was supposed to do. The room was, in essence at this point, a sauna.

"As you know, Norma, we have said we will take the issue under consideration after the football season. We have lots of other decisions to make between now and when the school year starts. And we do have a football season to play, which is something I'm sure we can all agree on."

Taylor stood there, shaking her head. Before she could respond, the man whom I had seen stand up at several consecutive meetings stood up a few feet away. His hands were shaking yet again.

"Dr. Classen, it is unacceptable to me that this school board will not take action on this issue. This will not go away, no matter how hard you try to make it so. Our town needs closure."

The man was speaking from the heart; the entire room was listening. People could see that this man was not grandstanding, was not used to talking in public. Likely in his mid 50s, he was a small man, no taller than 5'5", and was both balding and bespectacled. When framed against the super-charged environment he was standing in the middle of, he exuded a deep sense of humility.

"Thank you, Harold," Classen said, and I froze.

Was this Harold? The man whom Teri had described as riding his bike around town to check on people's safety when they are out of town? The man that, to Teri, represented the Frisco that she grew up in, that she used to know, that she hoped would somehow survive?

I couldn't get over it. I would have predicted someone who had been in Frisco for a long time would have been prone to want to safeguard the name. Perhaps, I realized, I should not have assumed that. Perhaps, I thought as I tried to capture the man's words in my notepad, I should not assume the other way around either – that if you were new to town, that meant you were automatically against the name. And then I remembered that the woman who had just challenged Taylor, who had implied by her remarks that she was a Frisco lifer, had only recently moved to Texas after fleeing Oklahoma City in '95.

I knew I needed to meet him; such a meeting was long overdue. This man, known to me as only Mr. Jordan until now, had spoken to the board several times in my presence, and not once had I taken the time to try to get to know him. This man, my very own Deep Throat, this well of knowledge about this confounding town, had been in my midst all along. My head filled with self-hatred.

Classen cupped his hand over the microphone and leaned over to talk with Sax. Several board members moved in, and after a minute they were all nodding in agreement.

"The board would like to invite members of the community to speak on the Frisco Coons," Classen said, and a roar went up from the crowd. With that, a parade of citizens walked up to the microphones that had been placed in the aisles for public comments.

I stood in the back, my pen valiantly trying to keep up with the words coming from each speaker. And I was touched by the pure passion with which people spoke, touched perhaps more than a reporter should be, but I was also learning that a reporter shouldn't lose his or her humanity along the way.

Each speaker had their own, unique view about what was right or wrong about the nickname. About how relevant a high school nickname even is in a complex world. About Frisco and Dallas. About urbanization and the dissolution of the local farms. About white flight and blacks and whites living together. I was watching so much more than a local school board meeting being held in some distant suburb of some large city. I was watching a Town Hall on America, on where the country had gone and where it was going with the arrival of a new century, as everything around all of us changed.

I was watching a Town Hall on change. A Town Hall on how different people react in different ways when its ruthless march approaches.

"Members of the board, we are here to discuss not just a nickname. We are here to discuss the very soul of our town," said one woman, wearing a "Don't Rac My Coons!" T-shirt. "This conflict is about this: you are living small, so you yourself must be small. We have seen it play out with some of the new homeowner groups. They moved into their gated communities and tried to get into local politics. All I can say to that is that it pays to do a little work here first."

"Kids are going to go out and play against other schools, and with the words 'Fighting Coons' on their chests. If we continue to allow that, we are opening children up for worlds of hurt because kids get in the middle of it," said a woman who had been seated next to Norma Taylor. "I like it here, but I don't want to be part of a community that sanctions the nickname to be okay. I want people here to flinch at the name like I do. If you want the mall, if you want the increase in the tax base…and for the property values to go up, then you have to live as part of the global village that the world has become. You can't hide behind the idea that we are just using a nickname. You have to grow up."

Two hours later, the speakers were done. The words had been emotional, no matter the side. With each speaker, the moans and groans of the other side grew more and more quiet. While nothing was ultimately solved, the communal opportunity to let it all out, it seemed, had been cleansing. Frisco, Texas had needed, essentially, a timeout, a few minutes to sit back and discuss its differences with, well, itself.

Classen granted a 15-minute break before the board was to return to its planned agenda. Knowing I had just witnessed the news event of the evening, I started packing up so I could get back to the newsroom.

I watched the man named Harold rise from his chair and head toward the exit, like most of the others were preparing to do.

"Excuse me, Harold Jordan?" I asked. "Marshall McDougal, with the Evening Outlook."

"Ah, yes, hello," Harold said. He stopped to wipe the steam from his glasses. "How may I help you?"

"You may know Teri Leiner, who I interviewed for my story today. Are you the Harold she was referring to?"

"Yes, I believe I am."

"Very nice to meet you. I've heard a lot about you."

"And you. Teri speaks very highly of you. And any friend of the Sapphires can't be too bad, I guess." He was smiling now.

"I guess what I would love to understand the most is how you feel about the Coon nickname. I mean, you clearly love the town. And I assumed you would want to keep things the way they are, at least to the extent you can, if Frisco means that much to you."

Harold thought for a minute.

"You know, son, you hit the nail on the head I think. I do love Frisco. Frisco is where I was born and raised. We had a farm. It's still there now, one of the last working ones in town. I still live there today. It's the only home I've ever known."

"And the nickname? Don't you want to keep it intact?"

"I want to keep Frisco intact. Would I prefer for the name to be kept the same? If it didn't upset anyone, yes, I would. But I think we've crossed a line somewhere along the way. We're on the other side now, and life is different. At one time, in Frisco, and I'm sure in other small towns in America, it was okay to call your school the Fighting Coons. Certainly around here it was. We didn't know any different. But I understand that in many places that's just not okay anymore, and I think we need to listen to that. Because in the meantime, the debate is tearing our town apart. And that's what hurts me the most. That's why you see me at these meetings. I can't just stand off to the side anymore."

"What's your bottom line on this?"

Harold didn't hesitate.

"I choose to be one of the few that thinks the town can retain its soul, who it is, if we change the name. No one can ever take our history away. We can still be Frisco. We can still be Frisco, Texas…can't we?"

I stopped taking notes, and looked up at Harold. I could see tears welling up in the man's eyes. And I thought I loved Los Angeles.

"So you're saying, I think, that you just want a decision to be made, so the town can move on? Is that it?"

"Again, you hit the nail on the head," Harold said, starting to walk away. "I'd say you're a pretty good reporter. If you'll excuse me…"

With that, Harold turned and walked away. I couldn't help but smile when I realized he was not moving toward a car, but a bike.

In an instant, Harold had ridden off into the night. And with him, the thought occurred, so had a little bit of Frisco's soul as well.

CHAPTER TWELVE

THE LAST COON HUNT

I was so full of myself the next morning, I might as well have consumed an entire aviary.

I had published my big story and its first follow-up. Better yet, I was the toast of the coffee truck. For two days in a row now, I had the byline on the stories that were the talk of the newsroom. And, in fact, the town. Frisco's city Web site was an open wound of umbrage, bleeding emails from people on both sides of the debate, most of whom supported keeping the nickname. Then, of course, there was Norma Taylor. She was salting my in-box, peppering me with forwarded emails, claiming victory with each one, the potential leanings of the electoral college be damned.

No matter the side of the aisle they represented, the more emotion expressed, the wider, the gummier, the toothier, was Skimer's smile.

"Hey man, don't rac my Coons," Short said as I approached him at the truck.

"Hey man, don't rain on my coon hunt."

"So Marshall, what's it feel like to be in the middle of the scrum? I mean, you're like in the middle of that grasshopper storm I was in this one day down in Plano. I was walking out of that Kroger, you know, off the Tollway. One after the other came flying in. They were all slamming into the store windows. Had to be a hundred, two hundred, of 'em. Went on for five minutes. Pretty wild. That's you, man. Grasshopper Man."

"Feels great, Chris. But you know. Just writing some news stories."

"Gimme a break. Man, you're really stirring things up around here. Skimer loves that. Good story."

"Hey, there's a lot of rich material, you know?"

"Rich? Did I hear someone say rich?" Meesbruggan said, reaching for a cup.

"No, Mees, believe it or not we're not talking about the stock market," Short said. "Something much more important than that, believe it or not."

"More important than money? I doubt it."

Meesbruggan looked over at me. "Well, except for the future of our fine city. Good story today, Marshall. Good story."

"Thanks, Ted. Can't wait to see what Sammy thinks. Maybe I'll wander out back and see if he's still planning on delivering 'em, the miserable piece of shit that he is."

"You encounter him again?"

"I think so. Either way, I've had enough of him. You know him well?"

"I wouldn't say I know him well, or even at all really. But I know who he is. He's an old hired hand of Classen. Does odd things for him, this and that. Still can't believe he works here now. He's not, uh. Well, he's not...he's not right."

"Would be great to keep him away from the ballpark," Short added.

"At the ballpark?"

"Well, yeah, you know, owner's box and all."

"Owner's box?"

"Yeah."

My curiosity was quickly turning to confusion.

"You didn't hear?"

"Hear? Hear what?"

"Oh, man. Just when I think you've got this town wired already. Breaux's dad's the Trailblazers' owner, man."

"Whoa, what? You're telling me Sammy Breaux, the guy who I spent all night gambling with in Shreveport, who confronted me in the parking lot after my lunch with Norma Taylor, who I heard screaming at Classen at midnight in his office after a school board meeting, who has basically been following me around town firing shots over Sabrina and this Coon thing, is the son of the Trailblazers' owner?"

"Yep, pretty much. You didn't know that?"

"Uh, no, I missed that question on the quiz," I blurted out. My confusion had now turned to exasperation.

I looked first at Short, then at Meesbruggan. "So I guess that explains why Sabrina and I saw him at that game. Anything else I need to know?"

They looked at each other.

Silence.

Finally, a giggle from Short.

"Marshall, I just can't hold this one back, man."

"What?"

Silence.

"What?"

Silence.

"WHAT?"

The others around the coffee truck looked over.

"Calm down, Marshall," Meesbruggan said.

"Calm down? Why? Should I be calm?"

"Marshall, so there's one other thing I don't think we've told ya yet," Short said. "I didn't think you'd care, but now I think we all know ya need to."

I looked at Short. He looked at Meesbruggan.

"Oh, Marshall, you still have a lot to learn about this town," Meesbruggan said. "I guess we never really got to the other stuff we hadn't told y'all yet. 'Til now, I guess."

I took a long drag on my coffee cup. Things were both speeding up and slowing down at the same time. I studied my fellow journalists, my eyes darting back and forth between them. They had become trusted friends. Comrades, even. In a shooting fountain of mistrust, they often seemed like the shiny coins, often obscured by the spray, yet settled quietly, comfortably, at the bottom. If I was tempted to stretch the analogy I'd say one was my California, the long and lean one, the other my Texas, short and wide, and oftentimes as I watched them bicker it would occur to me there was nothing on the surface that would prompt the type of bond the two seemed to share.

"Something tells me I don't want to know any more than I already do. First off, if you're gonna tell me that Classen's son used to have my job, I already figured that one out. That's Gin Bomb, I know. Got that out of Norma Taylor."

Meesbruggan couldn't hold himself back any further.

"So, here's what it is, Marshall. Yes, Classen's son used to have your job. And yes we called him Gin Bomb, 'cause he was like a Roman candle I'm telling ya—"

"Yeah, like a Roman candle of an anus," Short interrupted. "You never know what kinda shit was gonna come flying out of him. Just hope it was purely gaseous and not a wet one. Stay out of the way, man. Upwind if you can."

Meesbruggan took a deep breath.

"Ignore our Roman candle of a mouth here, Marshall. Sport, you are freaking sick, really. Okay, so Marshall back to the topic. So Rip asked us not to tell you the deal about Gin Bomb having your job before, 'cause he wanted to see how quickly you could figure it all out for yourself. He wanted you to get to know Classen on your own terms, without any sort of, you know, pre-condition. Sorry."

"I'm sorry, too, man," Short said. He looked over his shoulder. The look on his face, I had only seen that one other time. I felt that same sickness in my stomach.

"So you already know about Gin Bomb, okay, fine. But back to the publisher," he said. He was lowering his voice now. "We're owned by a family foundation, yes. But the key is, who runs the foundation.

Marshall, the family foundation that owns us is run by Sammy Breaux's family. His father is named Sam Breaux, too. Samuel C. Breaux Sr., to be exact. The one who's been on you, and it pains me to say it but yes our esteemed colleague, is Samuel C. Breaux...*Jr.* Those guys in suits you've been asking about? Thornaker says they work for Senior. Which, by the way, is not a good sign for the future of this proud paper."

I backed up several steps and began walking in a circle. Whatever I thought I knew of this town, I knew now, I knew now more than ever, was not enough.

"Why do you think Junior got the job here?" Short asked. "I know it's just delivering papers, right? Know what? I wouldn't trust the guy to deliver milk. Milk might get there. Problem is, you don't know who or what he's gonna snatch from your house when you're not looking. Let me ask you this: you road-tripped to Shreveport with him, right? You ever wonder how a guy like that drives a Beemer? Daddy's money. Pure and simple. Pure and simple, Marshall."

I could only look up at the sky and close my eyes.

"So, let me see if I understand." I was speaking slowly, in measured tones. "The same guy who owns the paper also owns the baseball team. That doesn't sound unique, I guess. I mean, look at the Chicago Tribune and the Cubs, right? But the son of our owner has been following me, and he is a business associate of sorts with the head of the school board."

I paused for effect. "Have I missed anything now?"

"Well, I do know Junior and Gin Bomb are friends," Short said. "Not just friends, but best friends. Have been ever since high school. That's when the Breauxs moved here from Louisiana, after the old man made a boatload of money in riverboat gambling, I think."

I shook my head. The ratfuckers in my midst, it seemed, were everywhere.

"Tell you what," Short said, again lowering his voice. He looked over his shoulder again. "Why don't you meet me in the press box at the Blazer game Friday night. I have to cover the game, but it's too late that night to file a story for the weekend editions, you know, because of your favorite early deadline. So I'll have more of a chance to talk if you need to. Besides, you might run into Breaux – either of them, I guess. It might help you figure this all out. Might make you feel better. Might make you feel worse, I don't know."

"Honestly I don't know if I want to figure this all out anymore."

Later that night, I tossed and turned in a labored attempt to get to sleep. Just when I was almost out, my nightly companion paid a visit.

Clackety clack, clackety clack.

The train's call seemed louder than usual tonight, and I was once again wide awake. As I stared at the ceiling and listened, I wondered if I would get to sleep that night at all.

Sabrina and I showed up at Frisco Field on Friday night. Despite their history of futility, the Blazers had stayed in contention for the championship of the Southwest Conference Baseball League's North Division throughout the summer. With less than a week left in the season, they trailed the rival Norman Tri-B's by only a game.

"I've never been in a press box before," Sabrina purred as we walked toward the press area behind home plate.

I had never been in a press box, either. Part of me was excited to see what an actual press box was like, though Short had reminded me that the Trailblazers, as an independent team, didn't exactly have Major League standards. Once inside, Short showed us around like one would his own home. The press box was, indeed, quite modest, with seats for only three journalists. The radio play-by-play announcer sat behind a glass wall to the left, the P.A. announcer behind one to the right.

Three innings later, Seacurg put the Trailblazers up with a two-run shot to left. The way Hodgekinz was pitching, way better than the first time I saw him back in June, things were looking good for the home team.

Time to do some fishing.

"I need to run to the restroom. You need anything?"

"No, I'm good," Sabrina said. She was enjoying her unique vantage point of the action. "I'm too busy trying to read the radio announcer's lips. This is too cool."

Once out on the concourse, I made my way toward the owner's

box. I had done my homework ahead of time; I knew just where to go. I didn't know what exactly I was looking for; if I found it, I wasn't sure what I would do with it. But my curiosity had gotten the best of me.

The owner's box was not hard to pick out. There were only eight in the stadium; it was the last one down the right field line. The outside of each box had a number and a copper-colored plate with slots on the top and bottom, into which a cardboard card could be slipped horizontally. On each card read the company or individual that owned the box for that particular season. When I spotted what was on the card outside the last box, I knew I was there. SCB, Inc. I had noticed the acronym before in looking at a Trailblazer program. I had assumed it was short for "Southwest Conference Baseball," the name of the Trailblazers' league. I knew better now. I knew now that it stood for "Samuel C. Breaux." The realization, even as people filed by in both directions, kept me at a standstill for several minutes.

All of a sudden, I had a déjà vu moment. I was now starting to drip. I was close to peeking behind another curtain, another curtain behind which I was not supposed to peek. Just as I turned to walk away, I bumped into someone.

I looked up. Barronkoff?

Sammy. He looked at me and said nothing. A smile began to emerge from his face.

"Oh, my word, look who it is, and right outside the owner's box," he said. "Are we enjoying the game, good man?"

I swallowed. "Yes…the team looks good."

"Primo good," Sammy said. He smiled. "We here at the Trailblazers like for our fans to enjoy themselves. We are, after all, Frisco's Finest."

I started backing up.

"I enjoyed your stories in the paper this week," he continued. I was now a good five feet back from him. "Back home in Lake Providence, well, that's just the type of investigative reportay we like best. Goes especially well with a good coon hunt, you know? You ever eat coon?"

"Can't say that I have, Sammy. Or should I say Junior?"

"Best thing around, except of course a turkey on Thanksgiving. You ever fry a turkey in some of that peanut oil all day? Like I said, primo good. Little fried okra on the side, even better."

He licked his lips. "Even better."

"I'm actually allergic to peanuts."

"Sorry to hear that, good man. Guess we'll have to hold off on that turkey day invite, correct, Mister Marshall?

Sammy was leaking rancor. My heart was an Army fly over now, my stomach muscles hardening like pipes in winter, the only thought bordering on intellectual getting through being the latest one about why people from this part of the country insisted on pronouncing words like "Thanksgiving" with the accent on the first syllable.

"Samuel, we need to get back to the meeting."

We snapped our heads toward the owner's box. In the doorway stood an older, portly man, probably in his mid-60s. He approached Sammy with a curious caution, almost like he knew he was up to no good.

"Just talkin', Pops, just talkin'," Sammy said.

The man looked over at me.

"Good evening, young man, enjoying the game?" The question was a friendly one, clearly intended for the average fan. What he didn't know was that he was talking to one of his own employees.

I froze; this was the man I had bounced off of that day in the parking lot.

"Marshall McDougal, sir, I'm your newest reporter at the paper," I said, extending my hand. "We kind of met one day at the office. Just for a minute."

In an instant, the man's entire expression did an about-face.

"Mr. McDougal, pleasure," said the man, accepting my handshake. "Samuel Breaux. We've watched your progress at the paper very closely."

The handshake had been stiff. Comparatively, compared to the stare, it now seemed friendly and warm.

"Samuel, we must get back," the senior Breaux said, motioning his son to follow him. He turned toward me. "Mr. McDougal."

"Very nice to meet you, sir." I watched father and son walk toward the door. By the time Sammy flashed a smile before disappearing into the box I was in full recoil.

Sabrina. I hurried back to the press box.

"Did you see that play? You've been gone 20 minutes."

"Um, no."

I had never been a good liar.

"Everything okay?"

"Just some work stuff, that's all. I ran into some people I know from the school board."

Up sauntered Short.

"Sabrina, can you excuse us?" he asked. For someone who rarely appeared serious, Short had a serious look on his face.

"Sure, Chris," she said, backing up. "Marshall, something wrong? I mean, you have seemed totally distracted all evening."

"I don't know anymore."

My calm was being exposed for the fraud it was. Short and I walked outside to the concourse. "Marshall, Skimer's on his way down to see you. Seems that—"

"What?" I interrupted. "What is Skimer doing here?"

"Don't know. He just called me on my cell. Guess he's here in the stadium, in the owner's box. Says you were just up there."

"Yeah, I was just up there, that's right." I was starting to shake.

"I didn't go inside, but I was up there. I met both Breauxs. I already knew the young one hated me. Now I guess the older one does, too."

"What the heck's going on here?"

"You tell me Chris! You seem to know everything else!" I was screaming now. "What else don't I know about this town? I mean, did I do something wrong here? Why would the publisher have something against me? I've blown the doors off the only story my boss wanted me all over."

"What's going on?" said Sabrina.

"Ask Chris! And when Skimer gets here, why don't you ask him!"

For the first time in my life, I was losing control. But I couldn't stand for Sabrina to witness it. So I just started walking. And then I started walking faster. Sabrina started to follow me, but I soon lost her, the walk turning into a run. I was running full speed now, dodging passersby like would-be tacklers, just like I had always done when I was a boy leaving the Coliseum with my father. Yet now I was no longer 10 or 12 or 15, no longer in my safe haven of my boyhood home of Los Angeles, no longer playing an innocent game. I was 22 now, all grown up. I had scored a job at a daily newspaper right out of college. In a town I had never heard of before, but in a town nonetheless, and in a town with a real newspaper that was willing to actually pay me for writing news stories.

It was my dream come true, or so I had thought. But that dream was now becoming a nightmare. The Plan was turning to ash. Worse yet, I didn't know why.

I ran by the concession stands, by the bathrooms, by the Trailblazer souvenir store. Skidding into the parking lot, I ran for my car, for something familiar, for something I could trust. Seeing my Tercel, I jumped into it and bumper car'd toward the exit. I didn't know where to go. I knew only that I needed to get away, get away from the latest ambush. I was done with the half-truths.

Back at the stadium, Sabrina and Chris stood outside the press box in shock. Sabrina was demanding answers.

"Why would he freak out if his boss is coming down to talk to him?"

"Sabrina, I don't have a clue what's happening here."

"But you seem to know all the answers, right? What was that all about?"

"Sabrina?"

Sabrina and Short turned their heads.

It was Skimer…and Mr. Sapphire.

"Daddy? What are you doing here?"

"Rip?"

Mr. Sapphire and Skimer looked at each other and smiled.

I had no doubt the truck would choose whatever direction I did. But where did those roads go? I was making an on-the-go, catch-and-release decision, a potentially life-or-death guess, with no useful information in hand, and I implored the T for an answer with the desperation of a man under water for too long. I started breaking early so I could hit the turn without losing too much speed. In the darkness I quickly made out a sign on the right that Farm Road 423 was approaching. The truck was on my tail, its lights casting their net over my car with a growing vengeance.

Getting closer to the T now, I could see another number on the sign ahead contradicting what I had just seen. The road ahead was a split road. Turning left put one on Farm Road 423; turning right put one on Farm Road 720. Neither meant a thing to me. Jamming the gas pedal down again, I juked right to throw the truck off, then lurched to the left and went flying through the intersection. Should anyone be coming in either direction, my car and I would be roadkill.

I kept moving forward; so did the truck. I zoomed by the right side of a car sitting at a stop sign, the right side of my car going off the pavement. I had meant to go around the car and take a left at the intersection. But the truck had anticipated my move, and moved onto the wrong side of the road, to the car's left, to cut me off. As our two vehicles met in the intersection, the truck miscalculated the distance between us, sideswiping the back of my car. My car fishtailed and slid almost 90 degrees to the left. But the collision had not been severe, and I recovered in time to pull my car to the right and veer down the new road.

We continued ducking and dodging, two hot wheels on a plastic orange track, Farm Road 720 now our personal Indy. My cell phone had been ringing virtually non-stop since the chase began. I assumed it was Sabrina or Mr. Skimer, and at one point I had tried to wrestle it to my ear. But it had flown through the air during a turn, ricocheting off of the windshield. It was now flailing around on the floor with each gyration like a halibut hauled onboard against its will, and the more it rang the more the scope of my desperation grew.

All at once I happened to glance up at an intersection just long enough to see that I was traveling on Eldorado Parkway. I let out a scream; this was the road off of which Sabrina and her family lived. For the first time since the chase had begun, I knew where I was. I was tempted to speed directly toward the Sapphires' and take cover. But the truck was too close behind.

I had to think of something. I had to get to the Sapphires'. And I knew I had to do it fast – a quick glance at the gage revealed that I was very low on gas. I had one last shot to get away.

Think.

I approached the Dallas North Parkway and swerved right. I was heading south now. Soon I was approaching Legacy and thus the northern-most edge of the Tollway. Down the ramp I went just south of Legacy, down onto the Tollway where I could pick up some speed. I knew my car couldn't take much more than 80, and I had to assume the truck behind me could handle a much faster pace.

Think!

Just as I hit full speed in the middle lane, I went for it. Slamming on the brakes, the truck swerved around me to my left. But my timing couldn't have been better. As the truck cradled into the fast lane, with my car down to 60 now, I swung the wheel violently to the right – and up the off-ramp, all the while screaming "RATFUCKER!!!!!!!!" so loudly and for so long that I was left gasping for air. Barreling upward toward Communications Parkway, I looked in the rear-view mirror. No truck! It must have been too far over to make the adjustment. I made a left at Communications Parkway, and another left put me on the access road to the Tollway going back north. I gunned it, the shortage of gas a momentary afterthought, passing Legacy, passing Highway 121, all the way to Eldorado. Another look in the rear-view mirror. Still no truck. I took a hard right at Eldorado, passing County Road, then the Warren Sports Complex, on my right. Turning into the Sapphires' neighborhood, I took two lefts and parachuted into her driveway. In my delirium I could see figures inside scurrying about. In an instant, Sabrina came flying out of the house and up to the driver's side. I couldn't move. I had been driving with such force, with such fear in my body, that my fingers were – literally – stuck to the wheel.

Sabrina gently pried them loose and led me into the house. And I couldn't hold it in; I collapsed on the floor, finally allowing myself to let the emotions come flowing out of me. With Sabrina holding me on the floor, I wept like a baby. I had survived the single most terrifying hour and a half of my life.

The Sapphires allowed Sabrina and me our privacy. Once I was calm again, Sabrina invited them into the family room, where I told them all the story. They all fell on every word. When I was done, done re-living my horror, Mr. Sapphire was the first to break the momentary silence.

"Marshall, what would you say if I told you I think I may know who this was chasing you?"

I looked up at him. "Mr. Sapphire, I'm not sure I want to know," I said. "There's so much going through my mind right now."

"Well, son, you see, I think I can explain at least a few things. Are you sure you're up for it? I know you've had a lot of surprises, and I've got another one for ya. But I think you're gonna like this one a lot better than some of the others you've come across."

"Somehow I didn't think the surprises were quite over, anyway, Mr. Sapphire."

"Go ahead, Daddy, tell him," Sabrina said.

"You know about this?"

"I do now. One of the things I learned tonight was that you learn a lot when you hang out in the press box."

I looked at Mr. Sapphire.

"So, you see, son, remember when I talked about EDS being a deal culture? Well, I have just made a deal. I just bought the Frisco Evening Outlook from Samuel Breaux."

I continued to look at him. Then I looked at Sabrina. She was beaming. I looked back at Mr. Sapphire.

"Sir? I don't understand."

"Well, let's just say EDS was very good to me, and the Navy contract last year was the topper. That was my first act. Now it's time for the second act. I started out with the Double Dip, and that's been fun. In fact, it's been great, and Sabrina honey as soon as you're ready, I'll want you to take over if you want to. That part you didn't know."

Sabrina was overcome with emotion. She threw herself at her dad, and the two embraced.

Mr. Sapphire turned back toward me. "The paper's the other part of the second act. I've still got more in me than just selling custard. So you see, Marshall. Made it happen at EDS, and I was there a long time. Too many nights I worked too late. Too many nights I was off in some city here or there working with my clients. My family always knew they were first in my heart, but at EDS you gotta do what you gotta do. And EDS is a deal culture, like I told ya. Always has been, and no matter how much that new management tries to change things, always will be. And growing up in a deal culture, you get used to looking for the deal. Of course, you're looking for a deal that's gonna be a win-win for everyone. With the Double Dip, that was a win-win, because I was looking to pour my money into something I could keep in the family for a long time. It was my way to give back to my family for all the patience they had with me when I was working the long hours at EDS. I, well, I…"

Mr. Sapphire began to choke up. The acknowledgement, the out loud acknowledgement, of the sacrifices his family made while he pursued a career, even if much of the mission of that career was to provide for them, had gotten to this very proud man.

He gathered himself. "In this case here with the paper, this is a real win-win, too. Breaux wants out of the newspaper business. Said tonight he's been working to shut it down. Had his number crunchers with him there to prove his case. Fact is, his plan was to walk into that newsroom of yours next Friday and announce that the next day's edition was to be its last. So you only had a week left on the clock there Marshall. You and the others. Not that you knew it. Says he won't be able to make enough money in the future in this town. I think I can. If I can't, I can't. Tough business these days, I know. And yeah this whole thing about becoming a morning paper may have to happen. Better a morning paper than no paper. But I'm gonna see. So this is my way to change the world.

"But I'm doing it right here at home. You know, think global, act local, right? This town's changing, and Marshall you've seen that up close and personal now. A little too up close and personal, I reckon. But if the town is growing up, and it's growing up whether folks like it or not, it needs a real paper, not a mouthpiece for some alley bobcat who just wants to put his head in the sand like it's 1950. Last time I looked, the 50's are over and done with.

"Besides, it's about time a local family ran our local paper again. Those folks from Louisiana don't know squat about our town anyway."

He looked around. No one knew what to say. Mr. Sapphire's explanation for making a deal had turned into a soliloquy on life, family and a changing town.

He let out a victorious laugh.

"Am I taking on too much? Probably. But okay. You gonna be a bear, might as well be a grizzly."

Sabrina threw herself at her dad once again. It was a true family moment. Sabrina's brothers moved in for hugs as well. Her mother shook her head, laughing.

"You knew about this all along, didn't you?" I said, smiling.

"You kidding me?!" Mr. Sapphire interrupted. "You think I make decisions like this without her knowledge? Let me tell you something right now: you are looking at the Chairman, President and Chief Executive Officer of this family. Doesn't matter what I do. This is the person who holds this family together. Not me."

Now it was my turn to be overcome with emotion. I had known this family for all of two months. Yet I already felt like I had known them forever. And the moment I was witnessing, was in fact participating in, made me feel a pang for my own family. I realized I missed my own parents. I missed my sister. I thought back to the closest thing I could think of in my own family's history that could rival this moment. It was the night before I had started USC as a freshman. My father had taken the family to dinner at Trader Vic's in Beverly Hills. We hadn't made a practice of going to fancy restaurants as a family very often. But that is where we often went for special occasions. And my father had raised a glass to toast me, for tomorrow was the day his son was going to start college at his beloved alma mater. But the words never came out. My father, never one to showcase his emotions, had been overcome. "You're going to have so much fun," was all he could muster before bursting into tears. Followed, of course, by the other three of us at the table.

Little did we know then what I would find in my first job after college. What about all I had seen? Why had Classen been so openly hostile? Why didn't they think they could make enough money on the paper? And, ultimately, what did any of that have to do with me?

Mr. Sapphire approached Sabrina and me. Standing between us now, he draped one arm over each of our shoulders. "There's only one thing we still need to clear up, and the answer is at the paper," he said. "Marshall, now that I'm gonna be your boss and all, I need to ask you to come with me. I understand now what you've been going through. And there's some people that owe you some answers."

I was apprehensive at the thought of such a meeting. "It's okay, Marshall," Sabrina said. "I'm coming, too. Don't you worry."

Mr. Sapphire rolled his eyes in mock disbelief.

"If I had a dollar for every order I took from the females in this house, I'd be able to buy that damn baseball team, too."

"Does that mean I can come?"

"Oh, of course. Marshall, you up for it?"

"Yes, sir, Mr. Sapphire. I'm definitely up for some answers, I know that."

The three of us moved toward the door for the drive to the Evening Outlook. As we walked outside, Mrs. Sapphire came running through the doorway.

"You best get to the ballpark," she said. Her voice was trembling. She looked at me.

"What is it, Mrs. Sapphire?"

"Seems that somebody named Jim Blumb has gone off over at Frisco Field. He had a gun. There's been a shooting."

"A shooting? Who's Jim Blumb?"

Mr. Sapphire echoed the question.

"Honey, who was it that called? Anybody know who Jim Blumb is?"

"I don't know. I could barely hear what they were saying on the phone. They just called. It was a Mr. Tonaker, I think. Something like that."

"Thornaker?!"

"Yes, that's it. He just said y'all oughtta get over there pretty quick. I'm sorry, I don't know what's happened."

I stood for a moment in the driveway. And it hit me.

"Gin Bomb."

"Who?"

"Gin Bomb...Gin Bomb!"

"Who's Gin Bomb?"

"Jim Blumb is Gin Bomb. We have to go. I'll explain in the car."

"What? Who?"

"I'll explain. We gotta go. Oh...my God."

We raced toward the ballpark. Even as I told Sabrina and Mr. Sapphire as much as I knew about Gin Bomb, I couldn't get past Thornaker. What was he doing at the ballpark? How did he know to call the Sapphires'? Did he even know Mr. Sapphire had bought the paper?

As we approached the ballpark, I assumed the Blazer game long since over, the fluorescent glare of flashing blue and red police lights signaled company. I was alternatively alarmed and relieved at the thought that the police were already there. But then I saw it: the ambulance. Mr. Sapphire roared his car to a halt outside the ticket windows. We could see the commotion centered near the owner's box down the right field line, and we veered in that direction as we raced inside. As we approached, things began to slow down, my senses quickly coalescing into an emotional ball of string that I could not navigate. I was seeing things around me, though those in my midst were quickly becoming fuzzy, out-of-focus, almost spirit-like in their definition, like figurines from those cartoons from The New Yorker my father had been reading all those years. I could not hear anything, anything at all, and it was like the marionettes in my midst were living in another world, one I could make out through the fog but was not allowed to inhabit. The only sense that was magnifying was that of smell, and from inside the bubble that had suddenly engulfed me the only thing I knew was the unmistakable aroma of death had penetrated its lining. It wasn't so much a smell but a pong, and though I had never before experienced it, I knew it to be real.

Someone had been killed.

Was it Skimer? Was Skimer gone?

Who was going to teach me my craft? Without my Bradlee, how would I become Woodward?

Welcome to Frisco, Texas, Marshall McDougal.

We were still about 20 feet away from the open door of the owner's box now, the same door outside of which I had snooped, the same door into which I had watched two generations of Samuel Breauxs disappear just two hours earlier.

What, I asked myself in my daze, had happened since? I could see through the fescue that paramedics were wheeling a stretcher out into the concourse. On the stretcher lay a body under a sheet covered with random splotches of varying degrees of red and brown. There was the smell again, growing more odorous by the moment, and I could faintly hear Sabrina gasp behind me.

All of a sudden three figures emerged from the owner's box. It was two police officers – with Harold Jordan sandwiched between them.

Harold?! I rushed toward him. "Did you shoot Mr. Skimer? What happened?" I was flailing about, searching for any answer I could get my hands on.

Harold looked at me; he didn't say a word. I couldn't tell if he was a man in shock, or one at peace with himself.

I looked to my left. Breaux Sr. was emerging from the box now. His head was down, and he did not look up as police quickly ushered him away. Right behind him came the suits, the two young men whom I had seen one-too-many-times now, the ones whose occasional, out-of-place presence at the paper was now all-too-clear.

Next came Classen. Upon glancing in my direction, he suddenly lunged toward me, his sodden hands coming within inches of grazing my shirt, before being held back by the police and being dragged away.

"You…," he mouthed. I was seeing clearly now. His eyes were billiard balls, his pupils olives, and his arms bounced off his sides as he looked toward the stretcher, two like sides of beef swinging from metal hooks in a frozen warehouse.

I looked at the stretcher just as one of the policemen pulled back the sheet. And I couldn't believe it, but it was not Skimer. It was another man, a much younger one, his balding hair matted to his still-gleaming head, his eyes still open, staring skyward with a distant blankness, a splatter of black and ruby just outside his left eye that looked like a rotting raspberry. I reached my arms out to each side, grabbing for anything within arm's length. Someone responded, Sabrina I think, and it was all I could do to not collapse on the hot pavement. It was the man who had confronted me earlier that very evening, had driven me to a level of paranoia I didn't know I possessed. No one needed to identify him. I knew in an instant it was Sammy.

Another policeman emerged from the box. Behind him came another one, and then another one, and as I struggled to make sense of it all a surprise was still awaiting me. It was Skimer, right arm in a sling, riding on a second stretcher. We all rushed toward him, our concern being overtaken by a palpable sense of relief.

Mr. Sapphire got to him first. "Rip, you okay old man?"

"Never better, boss," Skimer said, and a smile began to creep through the mist of the scene around us, a smile that spoke of a man still in control, sling and all.

"What happened?" I screamed out. "What happened?"

"What happened? Well, Marshall, let me tell you something, what happened in this here box tonight is something I'm thinking might make for a pretty good news story, that's what. Ya oughta get something to write on, though you should know Thornaker's already at the office putting something together, crafty sumbitch that he is. He's textbook on nights like this."

My hand was shaking. I quickly fetched my notebook and my pen from my pocket, any good reporter's toolbox never out of arm's reach, my mind still zeroing in on Thornaker, the man who rarely spoke a decipherable word yet was always a step ahead.

"Okay, so here's the upshot. Breaux Sr. cuts the deal with Mr. Sapphire here to sell him the paper, which Marshall I'm thinking you may already know by now. Gin Bomb and Junior, they'd been out in the concourse drinking and just generally being the no-goods that they are. And they walk in and Senior tells 'em what's happened. Boss, you and Miss Sabrina had already left by that point, after Marshall here took off. Anyway I'm here to tell ya these Cajun fools, they just about lose it. Gin Bomb starts going off about how Senior promised him his job back at the paper, yeah, like that was ever gonna happen on my watch at least.

"So then Breaux tells Gin Bomb to pipe down, and Gin Bomb goes and pulls a gun out and turns it on both Junior and Senior at the same time. They're standing next to each other next to the bar, and he's wagging that thing at both of 'em. First he goes after Senior about the paper and all. Then he gets through that and goes on a bender about Junior going after his girl who just happened to be his own girl's best friend. Something about Gin Bomb's girl and how Junior buddied up to her and no matter how many times he confronted them about it and then he saw some emails and a phone number on a piece of paper and he knew they were lying even before he saw him pat her on the ass right in front of him. And it was right when Gin Bomb was looking at Junior and calling him a wolf in sheep's clothing and a liar and a cheat and all of that, and nobody in the room really felt like Gin Bomb had this one wrong, and well I thought I saw an opening so I lunge for Gin Bomb, you know, 'cause I just couldn't take him no more. And he turns toward me and shoots, and I'm down.

"All of a sudden I'm back in 'Nam and even though I'm shot, or at least I'm thinking I'm shot, I roll over behind this table. Hey, when you've been shot at as much as I have in those jungles, you know, it all comes back to you pretty fast, okay? I mean, we're talking Charlie, Charlie all over again. That's when Junior goes for Gin Bomb and they're rolling around in the suite. And the gun flies out into the doorway, where I guess 'ol Harold is standing. If I heard it right Thornaker had called him from listening to the police scanner and hearing about a problem at the ballpark. And y'all know Harold, he always seems to be around, you know? So Harold picks up the gun and, as Junior reaches for him, he fires. Just one shot. And a perfect one, right to the temple. Junior is dead, right off. I'm talking dead, boys. You could tell by the way he hit the ground. Like a tree in the forest. And Gin Bomb just runs off, and I guess folks have never seen a guy run so fast. He's gone in a flash, and I'm telling all y'alls right now we won't see the likes of him in these parts again.

"It all happened so fast, none of us knew what to do. That's when the cops showed up, and first thing they did was focus on Harold. He was still standing there holding the gun, almost like he couldn't believe he had actually shot it. And he's just looking at it, and we're not sure what he's gonna do. So the cops take the gun from him and he just sits down in a chair, and he's already 'cuffed and all, and all of a sudden I'm tellin' ya but the man starts crying. And all you can hear is him muttering something about Frisco and his town dying. He just kept repeating it…subtraction by addition, subtraction by addition, or something like that, like he was in a trance or something. It was unbelievable, I'm telling ya. Unbelievable."

We were all in shock, taking in every word, and it took a few moments for one of us to respond to what we had just heard.

"What about Classen?" I said, anything to break the silence. "What did he do?"

"Classen? Classen?! He just stood there in the corner the whole time. Didn't move a muscle. Like he was a dumbass mule, just standing there watching it all unfold. Didn't move. Never seen a man so scared in all my life. Like one of those buffalo or cattle sitting there all day in that EDS field. You know, the one they got down there on Legacy over there by Preston, you know, so they get the tax break because they got farmland? Yeah, bunch of buffalo and bulls, that's Classen."

Skimer had been talking increasingly quickly, and just when we were hanging on every word he let out a grimace. The paramedics went to tend to him, and he tried to brush them off, the proud soldier playing the part. He looked up at us, a calm starting to take over among the crowd.

"Just need a few minutes here," Skimer said. "I'm feeling good. All y'alls don't need to worry about me. Looks like maybe I got grazed. Be back on the horse in no time. Charlie didn't get me then, didn't get me now either."

I surveyed the scene around me. Just a few feet away, the police were about to haul Harold off. I looked over at him, and the moment got the best of me. I approached him, not knowing what to say. "Hear you're a good shot there Harold," I said. I wasn't sure if I meant it as a compliment or not, though I hoped he'd take it as one.

"You been coon hunting as much as me over the years, you would have hit him pretty good, too," Harold said. "Those little critters run around pretty fast, you gotta be fast. Ya just gotta be fast. I was just a little too fast this time. Instinct, I guess."

Coon hunting. The irony was not lost on me. Harold had been so passionate about the Fighting Coon issue, to the point where he had spoken in public about it. To the point of tears.

"But what about your comments about moving on, about getting past the Fighting Coon thing? And you're a coon hunter and all?"

"That's just it. Yeah, I'm a coon hunter, a proud one. A pretty good one, too, I might say. But there's a big difference between shooting at raccoons and wearing something on your sleeve that has to go. Why can't you hunt coons and want your town to grow up at the same time?"

"I don't know, Harold. I don't know."

With that, Harold was gone, hauled off by the Frisco police, likely to the closest jail, likely to be charged with murder, likely, given the presence of multiple witnesses, to be put away for the rest of his days. Meaning that, more than likely, he had hunted his last coon.

Frisco, Texas…Home of the Fighting Coons.

I walked back toward the group. Mr. Sapphire and Sabrina were talking with Skimer.

"Marshall McDougal, we were worried about ya," Skimer said. He looked me squarely in the eye. "Son, we were really worried about ya. You okay?"

"Yes, sir, Mr. Skimer. I'm sorry I ran out on you. I just couldn't figure out what was happening anymore."

"Well, we're gonna clear that up, right here and now. No more surprises, right? Well, I guess other than Jan being here, and all."

I wheeled around.

"Jan!"

"Hey, Marshall, how ya doin'?"

"I've been better. It's been an interesting evening."

"So I hear. So much for the relaxing spontaneity of your average Friday night."

Skimer jumped right in, as usual. "Okay, Marshall, so I understand you know now that Mr. Sapphire here has agreed to buy the paper from SBC, Inc., which I guess you now know has been run by the Breaux family."

Skimer stopped himself. "You know, Marshall, you never asked me about who owns this place."

"I never even thought to ask. Rookie mistake, I guess. My first of many."

"Well, that's alright. They had let me run the paper without too much interference for a few years. Even when we started losing advertisers there in recent years and cutting staff which hurt like hell to have to do. But all that started changing right about when Classen took over the school board. You see, I could see things were starting to heat up with the whole Fighting Coon thing. Hell, all you had to do was check out the city Web site, and it was Norma Taylor this and Norma Taylor that. And I decided it was time for the paper to do what papers goddamn do, which means cover the goddamn news.

"Problem is, we had Gin Bomb on the education beat. He was a pretty decent writer, but there was a clear conflict of interest there with his dad running the school board, see. So I went to Classen myself, you know, so I could keep G.B. out of the middle.

"I say, Grady, we need to move your son either to another beat or off the staff, we can't condone this kind of conflict. And you know what he tells me? He tells me that he doesn't see the conflict, and that if I have a problem with the way he runs the school board then I can take my case to Breaux. So I do that, and I come to find out Classen and Breaux are in cahoots to try and keep a lid on the whole Coon thing."

"How'd you get to that?"

"Thornaker. Thornaker, I'm tellin' ya. I just turned him loose, see, just between us girls, really. You look at that guy and you're thinking, this guy's cretinous, to say the least, right? Don't talk to no one, just sits there and mumbles all day long into that greasy phone. And you couldn't pay me enough to actually use that phone, ya know, 'cause it's a sea of oil and all, but you know what? That thing is a wand, and that Thornaker's a magician, I'm telling ya. That guys knows more people, gets more shit done, than any reporter I've ever worked with. So on the side, I had 'ol Will start lookin' around for me, see, and he's keeping me updated and all, and he's telling me that Breaux is caught up in all sorts of stuff over there in those damn casinos."

Thornaker. I could only shake my head.

"Damn riverboats," Skimer said. "So there was another problem, which I guess I need to tell ya about."

He looked at Bennie.

"Jan knows the story, and Meesbruggan, heck, he knows the story better than I do. Oh heck I'm guessing the whole newsroom knows about it by now."

"Probably true," Bennie said. "If Meesbruggan knows it, Short knows it. Mac and cheese."

"Alright then, fine. Whaddya gonna do?" Skimer said, not missing a beat. "Family ran a catfish farm. Figured I'd be running it someday, see. Good business. Had a stock pond. Some good catching. Long as you got enough of them pouches for chum. Little dog food, you know, the dry stuff. But you grow up in East Texas, you got Shreveport right around the corner. About an hour, that's all. And that's okay. But it's not okay when you're being called there for the wrong reason. Hung in there for a couple of years after things went south at the Times Herald. But that's when they started putting in those riverboats. Had to find some comfort somewhere, I guess. Family's got some land over there in Mt. Sylvan, just down the road from Tyler. Nice place along Route 110, some water out back. Bit snaky, but nothing you can't kill with a shovel, and if you don't get 'em, all those wild hogs they got running around there will. So I'm out there a few days here and there, and I end up heading over there to Shreveport. Sometimes I'd make it back, sometimes I wouldn't. And we all know what happens when someone's thinking that way. Still remember that one weekend out there during Mudbug Madness. Not sure how I ever got home from that one.

"Let's just say me and Johnnie Walker became good friends. And those times I wouldn't make it back to Mt. Sylvan? It was me and Johnnie some of those nights, just the two of us."

"And that's when you met Breaux."

"That's right, Jan. That's exactly right."

Skimer looked at us.

"You know, one of the best things about this life has been doing my thing alongside some of the best people I know, and Jan here's one of 'em."

"Thanks Rip. But you know, I've been meaning to ask you. How'd you meet Breaux anyway? I don't think I ever asked you that before."

"They had this paper out there in Tyler. So one day when I was actually seeing straight I wandered in there and asked about a job. And Breaux happened to be there looking around, because he was thinking about buying it. And he and I got to talking, and next thing I know he's buying the Frisco Evening Outlook and asking me to come run it for him. I was so happy about that I didn't know what to do with myself.

"So I run over to Shreveport for one last night out on the river. And there I am, me and Johnnie, hamming it up. And all of a sudden there's Breaux standing there looking at me. I'm thinking I've just blown my second chance. And all he says is, 'I'm looking forward to working with you.' And he's smiling. And I'm thinking, either this guy really thinks I'm a good editor, or he thinks he's got one on me. You know, so I could never turn on him or something, 'cause he'd fink me out for being a boozer. Turns out I was right on both counts."

Skimer sighed. "Good news is, I don't have no gambling problem no more. Paid off my debts a long time back now. Of course, then there's the drinking. There was a time there I didn't think I'd beat it. Devil's a powerful thing, I tell ya. Haven't had a drink since. Been six years now, almost."

Skimer looked down at his bandages. "Could use one about now though."

Mr. Sapphire was quick to fill the gap.

"Now, Marshall, I want you to know Rip here's already walked me through all this. So no surprise here. I support Rip 100 percent."

"Thanks Boss," Skimer said. "I'd say get me back to those piney woods out in East Texas! Beautiful out there. Just not ready yet. Got more to give."

"I'm sorry," I interrupted. "I still don't understand."

I was still focused on Classen and the Breauxs. Especially the Breauxs.

"Why would Classen and the Breauxs want to keep the Frisco Coon thing quiet? I mean, Classen is from Frisco, so maybe he's just tied to the name. But the Breauxs are from Louisiana, so why would they care about it?"

"Good question, Marshall, and people question why I want to pay for some kid from California to relo to Frisco," Skimer said, laughing. But he quickly grew serious again.

"You ask Meesbruggan that, he'll give you his stock answer, which in this case would be right on: money. Money, son. You see, Classen and Breaux came to think that as long as the name Coon stuck, it would somehow slow down the steamroller of growth coming into Frisco. And if that happened, they'd be able to maintain their virtual monopolies on local pharmacy business and local newspaper advertising, or what's left of it. They wanted to keep the status quo, and not because they cared about the mascot of the local high school. They wanted more money. Just wanted more money."

"And that's where the Blazers come in," Mr. Sapphire said.

"Absolutely right, boss," Skimer said. "So everything I've said so far pretty much happened before you got here, Marshall. But that's why I needed you, or someone like you. I needed someone who was young and fresh and eager to make a splash, and when we first talked on the phone, I knew that person was you. You got here, and other than showing up looking like a bank vice president or something, I knew even more I had the right guy. So did Jan here. Saw it on your first day."

"It's true, Marshall," Jan said. "That first story you wrote needed some work, sure. But young kids don't get bylines on their first day in this business. Not that I'd ever seen."

"Thank you both. I'm flattered. But I'm still unclear on the Trailblazers. What does the baseball team have to do with this?"

"Ah, the final piece of the puzzle," Skimer said. "Basically made a deal with Breaux, the senior one of course. Was a pretty good reporter in my day, if I don't say so myself. So when I got into this whole deal,

I started digging. And I find out Breaux's working deals on the side to keep the Texas League away from Frisco."

"The Texas League wants to come to Frisco? Wow. I didn't know that. But what would that do to the Trailblazers?"

"Well, it wouldn't help, I can tell you that. Fact is, it would probably be the end of 'em. Blazers were concerned that, if the Texas League were to come to Frisco, fans would lose interest in their team. Probably a fair assumption. But guess what? What would be the one thing to keep the Texas League away from Frisco? Away from the fastest-growing city in all of Texas?"

"The Fighting Coons."

Everyone wheeled around. The voice had come from over by the concession stand. Short smiled his cheeky smile. "Evenin', everyone."

"Christ, Short, you gave us a real scare there," Skimer said. "What are you still doing out here, anyway? Game's been over for awhile now."

"Well, the game's over, but tonight I think we can all agree the real action started after it ended. Anyway I thought I'd check on Marshall. Man, you talk about giving folks a scare? You okay?"

"I'm fine now, Chris. As far as I know."

"Short's right – the Fighting Coons," Skimer said. "You think the world's most famous minor league baseball system wants to bring a team into a town whose high school is called the Fighting Coons? I know the town is growing like gangbusters anyway, we all know that. It's been gathering steam for years. But things are different when it's a public sports team. They're gonna look at things a little different."

"So that's another reason for Breaux to want the paper to sit on the issue," I said, nodding my head.

But I still didn't understand. A cub reporter, I no longer was. I had learned to keep asking questions. And when one is answered, time to pose another one.

"All of that is fine, but at the end of the day, you work, or worked, for Breaux. So why wouldn't he just tell you what to do? And you said they tried to hold the gambling over your head."

Shreveport. Sammy. The wolf with the smile. The worst kind.

"Another good question, McDougal. And the answer is, gambling and drinking or no gambling and drinking, I had too much information. Besides, I told ya, six years now without a drink. So that wouldn't work. And like I said my debts are gone. So I had threatened to go public with Breaux's efforts to try and keep the Texas League away from Frisco. Could have fired me anyway I suppose, so we cut a deal of sorts. I keep quiet about the deal, but we find a soft landing for G.B. and I'm allowed to bring in a young reporter from out of town to bring the damn skeleton out of the closet. To cover the news. And when I say 'cover,' I mean 'cover,' like real newspapers do."

"And that turned out to be Marshall," Sabrina said.

"You got it."

"And what happened to Gin Bomb?" I asked.

"Went to work for Classen. Hadn't seen him for awhile before tonight, but I suspect he's been up to nothing but no good. No value-add there, none at all. And Junior? First off, God rest his soul. Hate to see that happen to anyone, even someone as gutless as him. Sorry, but the guy was worthless, a classic hanger-on. And anyone who's going behind his friend's back and fooling around with his girl, especially when the girl's his own girl's best friend? Let's just say I just don't know how you look yourself in the mirror. Like I said, gutless. And he's just been mooching off his dad's money, waiting for his turn, that's all. Just going through the motions back there in Circulation. All due respect, but that's all he was ever gonna do. He's harmless, I guess. Well, was."

"You say he was harmless and I'd like to believe that. But he had two reasons not to want me around. He was best friends with the guy whose job I took over, one. Even if he was fooling around with his girl, I suppose. And two, by chasing down the Coon story, I was fooling with his dad's interests."

Sabrina couldn't keep quiet any longer. "And his dad's interests were his interests."

"Again, you got it. Hey, you know how to write? I'm sure we can find a place for you on the staff."

Everyone laughed. It had been a heavy evening.

"This only leaves one question then," Mr. Sapphire said. "Who was it that chased Marshall halfway across Collin County tonight. Had to be Gin Bomb or Junior."

"Thought about that too, boss. Know it wasn't Junior, 'cause he was with us at the ballpark. Which is just like him, see, to always have an alibi. Could have been G.B., but he doesn't have a car."

I shook my head. "It may be better that I don't know. Not sure I want to."

Skimer looked at me.

"Son, I'm here to tell ya this whole thing is done. We're moving on. Breaux don't run this paper no more. This vote goes through on the Fighting Coon thing, the Texas League's as good as here. And it's a new day in Frisco. That means Breaux's good as gone, and probably the Blazers too, even though that hurts I guess. If he's smart, and Breaux's smart enough, he'll follow through on the sale now while he can still get something back."

"Yeah, but the school board has already said they're not voting on the issue until after football season."

"Short?"

Short looked over. "Ran into Classen at the game tonight. Said the school board would vote on the Coons sooner rather than later. In fact, he confirmed it, first meeting after the school year starts."

"Is that on the record?" Bennie asked. "I mean, is that something we can go to print with?"

"He said it is, Jan."

"Looks like it's time to write some news stories this weekend!" Skimer exclaimed. "Marshall, you up for it? You can pitch in with Thornaker by dropping off your notes at the paper on your way home. Will can take care of the rest, though you may have to translate what you wrote. He's an old pro, that Thornaker. A real pro. Still can't believe he and Harold were on the police scanner. Folks say Will's hobby is reporting, so I guess I ain't surprised to hear that's his evening entertainment.

"Anyway you'll have to get on the horn with some of the school board members this weekend, nuts and all. Classen included, much as I hate to say it. Might need to help you with that one. But we oughta have this in Monday's paper. That vote's less than two weeks off now. Town will need to know pretty quick. You think you had fun at that school board meeting last week, Marshall? This one will be an all-timer."

"Sounds great, Rip," I said, and I knew I must be feeling better to be calling Skimer Rip again.

"Ultimately, Marshall, this all's a big victory for progress, you ask me, regardless of how the vote goes. Point is, Classen has finally agreed to move the thing along. And much of that is because of you, son. I know I was pushing ya, but you ripped right into this story the way I knew you would. This old newspaperman just knew you had it in ya. That's why I brought you out here. We needed our own young Woodward. We needed outside blood to get this thing rolling. To shake this place up. To keep the school board honest. To force Breaux's hand. To get him to fish or cut bait on running this paper. The fact that he's now cut bait, well, I don't need to tell any of you what a deal that is."

Skimer stood up. He took off his glasses and rubbed his eyes. He had chased a lot of stories in his time. Some demons, too.

He looked at me. He took a long, deep breath, and slowly with his one good arm affixed his glasses back behind his ears.

"I believe in ya, Marshall. You got integrity. Built right in. Parents of yours must have done something right. You reminded me there's goodness in what we do, at least when we're in it for the right reason."

"To write news stories?"

Skimer smiled.

"To show the truth, son. To show the truth. Ain't no higher calling than that. And they can take away every damn paper there is. Just stop printing 'em forever. Would like to think they don't really want to. At least not for awhile yet. But no matter what happens to all of us ink-stained wretches, they can't take away the truth. Can never take that away."

Sabrina walked over and put her arm around me. Then Mr. Sapphire stepped forward.

"And the news gets better for all of us, Marshall," he said, looking around the room. "I want you all to be the first to know I have asked

Rip here to be publisher of this great paper. I know he's been the editor, the real guiding force, behind all the good work the paper has done, for a long time. And I want to reward him for that. Besides, I'm an IT guy, not a newspaper guy. Still trying to figure out how to run a custard shop. A daily paper? Hey, I need some help."

"Rip, I don't know what to say," I said. "I guess congratulations are in order. But who will be the new editor?"

"Oh, that was an easy one," Skimer said. He looked at Bennie.

"You?!" I exclaimed. "Jan! Congratulations. A great choice." I was genuinely pleased. From my first day, when Bennie had helped me get through my inaugural story, I had seen her skills. I had grown to trust her, and now, I knew, she trusted me.

Skimer motioned toward the doctors standing nearby. "That enough for one evening, folks?! Razzoo's still serving up rat toes? Beers on me. And soda water, I guess. No need to true up. Just belly up on my tab, if these good docs will let me."

Everyone agreed a celebratory round was in order. I chuckled to myself. It was the first time I'd heard a term starting with "rat" that was a good thing.

"One last thing, folks," Skimer said. Everyone stopped and turned around.

"So Short, what's the good news from this grand old ballpark? How did Frisco's Finest come out tonight? I mean, I was here and all, but not sure I remember."

"4-0, a three-hit shutout by Hodgekinz, with the save by Roodie," Short announced. Everyone cheered. "They're tied with four games left. Right down to the wire."

"Same old Wheezers?" I said, looking at Sabrina.

"Four games is a long time," she said. "They've still got plenty of time to mess it up."

"And if they do?"

"Same old Wheezers," she said. "It would be awful strange not to be able to say that anymore. The Wheezers have been around here for a long time."

"Some things change, some things stay the same," Mr. Sapphire said. "It's the way of the world, honey."

With that, the young and the old, the weary and the wearier, filed toward the parking lot. It had been the longest, most trying day I could remember. But if I still had my wits about me, and I wasn't entirely sure if I did, the thought occurred that maybe, just maybe, a lot of questions had been answered tonight. The answers to which might, just might, make life in Frisco, Texas a little easier.

We stopped off at the paper and headed back to the Sapphires' house. When we got there, with Mr. Sapphire having gone inside, I placed a call from the driveway to my family. When I told them all the story they followed every twist, the house of mirrors it had all turned out to be, and when I was done, the only audible sound was that of weeping. When I heard it I instinctively craned my neck forward, as if I were in the same room with the others and reacting to something they said or did, and when I heard my mom ask my father if he was okay I knew whose tears were flowing. I had already deduced it was him, anyway, the memory of Trader Vic's having lasted. The next thing I know, I'm crying, too, and then we're all crying, a group tearfest, a family moment, a family moment to remember. A family moment to remember, for the rest of my days.

"Son, we're just happy you're safe," my father said, breaking the verbal silence, which by that point seemed like it had lasted for hours. "And I just want you to know…I love you. I love you, son."

I started to respond, but my eyes welled up again. My throat begged for moisture.

"I love you, too," I said. My voice was cracking. "I…I love you, too."

I looked at Sabrina, who had not left my side, and from the look on her face, from the purity in her eyes, I felt, for the first time in what seemed like so very long, whole.

Back at my apartment later that night, I found myself staring, once again, at the ceiling. I wasn't really having trouble falling asleep; I was so wired from the events of the evening, I wasn't even trying. Besides, I was waiting for an old friend to pass by. When it did, I wasn't disappointed.

"Clackety clack, clackety clack," it went, and for the first time it wasn't a rumble, but a melody.

A mellow, medicinal melody. And to these ears, for the first time since I moved to Frisco, Texas, a melody so soft, so sweet, the machination of the engine, the screech of the whistle, the infuriation of the tracks, all so harmonious now, it left me humming along, wishing for more.

CHAPTER THIRTEEN

WHITHER THE SOUL?

*A*nd so the following Monday, the last one in August, under the byline of Marshall McDougal, Staff Writer, the Frisco Evening Outlook published a front page and above-the-fold story proclaiming that the local school board had agreed to vote on whether or not to change and remove all references to the nickname of Frisco High from the Fighting Coons to, well, anything but.

In the annals of newspaper headlines, this was but a footnote.

But for the town of Frisco, Texas, and especially to whom it had been home for generations, it was man-bites-dog stuff.

Simply put, to the locals, after three quarters of a century of doing things one way, they were now going to do things a different way. But the more people I talked with as I continued to cover the story, the more I got to know the town, the more I realized it shouldn't have been the news it was.

For the winds of change had been blowing in Frisco's direction for many years. More recently, these winds had taken on the strength of the tornadoes that occasionally roll down into Texas from the central plains on steamy Spring afternoons, those afternoons when the gale is so sheer the flags flap so hard they're like prisoners trying to flee their captor, those afternoons that move into those evenings when the sky is charcoal, when the families huddle, when the sirens wail.

And it was just a matter of time before the cuts of the jigsaw shifted about. In a physical sense, many of them already had, with the clearing of farmland and the razing of older homes making way for the new, master-planned, gated communities catering to the upwardly mobile, upper-middle class and wealthy who only a decade prior would in all likelihood not have considered Frisco for a home.

But this was an emotional shift, one done at a much deeper level. It spoke of growth but also of decline, the decline of life as it had been known for decades in a town that safeguarded its heritage, including its sense of removal from the big city only 30 miles to the south but a world away in mindset, as pridefully as a gemologist would a precious stone.

And Frisco, Texas wasn't, couldn't be, alone in this new century. Countless other smaller suburbs on the outskirts of America's cities were also being blown about by these same winds. These exurbs, these often formerly-rural towns, were being sucked inside the protruding bellies of America's cities on the heels of a range of concurrent phenomena: from the expansion of roads and highways to the suburbanization of well-paying jobs to the advances in technology that allow people to be as productive from their home office as they would be from a real one. Well-known byproducts of these changes have included longer commute times for many, as well as mazes of construction on streets not designed as throughways for large sums of traffic as the necessary amenities get built to support the new masses who, while they now live further from the city center than ever, still expect quick and easy consumption of goods and services.

What has not been talked about as much is what these changes have done to the souls of these towns. In the case of Frisco, Texas, one could make the case that its soul – regardless of the outcome of the Frisco Coon vote – was already in the rear-view mirror.

Indeed, the struggle into which I had been inserted was not, in fact, about a nickname, even when that nickname was widely considered racially insensitive.

It was about the evolving destiny of an American town.

About a town that had lived a certain way, and for the most part had been left alone to do so, for so long.

About whether there was still room for its soul along the way.

The struggle was about a town that was now more fully getting stitched into the quilt that was the America of the new century.

The question for Frisco – and to the growing legions of formerly small towns being digested by sprawl – was this: What was most important, the past or the future? For Frisco, it had seen two neighbors take different routes in managing this change, and it didn't like either one.

Its cousin to the south, Plano, had been the guinea pig for the Dallas version of sprawl that had opened up the floodgates to the north and Collin County. The result was that Plano had essentially been built out over time. This kept property values up because, in any town, space is at a premium. A home buyer at the dawn of the 21ˢᵗ century would find very little for sale in Plano, and certainly in newer West Plano where, despite the fact that the lots were modest and the back yards were often comprised of nothing more than a hopscotch court's worth of grass outside a sliding glass door, it would be a surprise to even see a "For Sale" sign.

Commercially, Plano had become Chain Central. It would be difficult to drive more than two city blocks and not find one or more Starbuck's, Chick Fil-a's, Corner Bakerys, Boston Markets or Palm Beach Tans. Frisco's cousin to the west, The Colony, had gone an entirely different way. It had kept commercial activity to a minimum compared to Plano, limiting it en masse to the maze of storefronts along the north side of the main channel of Highway 121. But the city had not built out its residential communities like Plano had, and as a result the equivalent level of commercial development had not followed.

Frisco had tried to manage the change differently.

On one hand, it had tried to embrace the changes that it knew were coming, like them or not. It had tried to do this by building out new residential communities, while at the same time building out a commercial infrastructure. It is difficult to tell, in chicken-and-egg scenarios, whether Frisco's own growth led to even more growth coming its way, or if it was just responding to what was already inevitable. Regardless of the answer, which is likely a little bit of both, some would say it both sold its soul and tried to protect it at the same time.

Which, Frisco would find out, is a very tight line to walk.

The story of Frisco and the Fighting Coons is but a parable, an examination on vicissitude. To some, the nickname was a scarlet letter; to others, a badge of honor. The battle over Frisco had become that of a town at civil war with itself. It would be bad reporting to assign one side the blue of the Union and the other the gray of the Confederacy, for no one was trying to secede from the other. In fact, it was the other way around. The newcomers to town wanted to be there, as did the lifers. They both had vested interests, financially, emotionally, or both, in the town continuing its upward spiral.

The battle, really, was about what kind of town the new Frisco, the Frisco of a new century, would be.

About what a small town is supposed to be like when it grows up.

About what a town that used to live its life in peace would need to be like in a world where political correctness – at least some of which is based on having the proper sensitivity to others in a truly heterogeneous world – was now, for the first time, a factor.

Whither the soul of Frisco, Texas?

Souls don't die easily.

To see the soul of Frisco just after the turn of the 21st century was to take a Sunday drive down Main Street on a Saturday night.

You've got the locals hunkered down with their frozen custard at the Double Dip, over their chicken fried steak at The Abbey, over their rib eye at Randy's Steakhouse, over their Tex-Mex at Manny's Grill.

You've got teenagers sitting on the benches outside of the snow cone stand at the corner of Half Main and Second next to The Depot cafe, where the Snowcone Lady is serving it up from inside.

You've got the train barnstorming by just to the west, a daily reminder of the root of the family tree.

You've got an elderly man named Harold riding around on his bike, checking on houses whose owners are out of town.

You've got folks motoring their lawnmowers to pick up some cheap Fanta at the Snappy-e-Jack.

And you've got the old downtown water tower, watching down on the activity from above. The tales this water tower could tell. It could tell of the olden days of Frisco, when Frisco was Frisco and it was the bane of the rest of the world that they couldn't share in it. It could tell of time sneaking up on its namesake town, when the world started to descend on it, and of all the changes that came as a result. And it could tell of what didn't change, of what the grandfathers who told the fathers who told the sons.

And there would always be a word about the simple glory of a hot summer's night on Main Street, where whether the scene is playing out yesterday or tomorrow, not too long ago never seems too far away.

A few weeks later, I received a call.

I had received a job offer from the L.A. Times. My return ticket to California – way sooner than expected – was in hand. Something… big? Mine for the taking.

I had come to know through the chase of my first big story that journalism was indeed my true calling. Yet I was filled with a sense of gnaw. And so I dialed the phone.

"Hi. I need to talk."

A week later, my father was there, having jumped in his car at the chance for his first-ever road trip to Texas. Besides, he told me with a wry look upon his arrival, he figured I might need the extra space to haul back whatever I had collected over the summer.

And so we talked and we talked and we talked. And then we talked some more. It was the best time I'd ever spent with my father. Just the two of us. At my apartment. Over Warren Burgers, Cardiac Fries and Dr. Peppers. In my trusty Tercel as we tooled around town, we dissected both the art and science of adding steamed milk to coffee, mowed through six-packs of Krispy Kremes, peered through the open window as we gawked over the cold case of the lone donut.

We had lived under the same roof since the day I was born, but our cohabitation had been but a mandate. I wondered why that was. My father said he didn't know any more than I did. Sometimes, we agreed, you need to go far from home in order to get closer to it.

I had assumed my father would do what he could to talk me into moving back. He didn't. He was somehow different to me now, more patient, more open, the way he listened to me describe The Plan, tell my stories of what it was like to be away from home and live out my dream, and the only time he was more parent than friend was when he admitted that he called mom upon taking one look at me to tell her the corporation had grown.

In the middle of it all we took a much-needed rest from the topic at hand, spending the day at the Texas-Oklahoma game with Sabrina and Mr. Sapphire. It was the traditional Texas-OU weekend in Dallas, for as long as anyone can remember the first one in October when the arthritic bones of the Cotton Bowl swell beyond their means in the middle of the Texas State Fair, which Mr. Sapphire insisted was somehow equidistant from both campuses, and the whole place turns upside down. I'd never seen my father have so much fun. He squeaked like a hare at every turning point in the game, and he couldn't stop talking about how the even split of the burnt orange of Texas on one side of the field and the crimson of OU on the other reminded him of the days back before '82, back when USC and UCLA would split the Coliseum, one half filled with vivid red, the other with the brightest blue you'd ever hope to see, the 50-yard-line marker the Mason-Dixon line dividing families and friends who get along just fine every other day of the year but just not that one.

And then when the game was over, when we had finally made our way out of the stadium and spilled into the griddle of the fairgrounds, my father and Mr. Sapphire proceeded to embark on a spirited debate over the relative merits of frozen custard and ice cream, Mr. Sapphire feverishly promoting the combination of the frozen custard in all its creamy splendor and whatever topping one chooses, my father insisting on that of the chocolate shavings embedded into the thick green swirl of jello-textured, mint chocolate chip, even going so far upon the winning of the oversized stuffed toad to send a shot across the bow that, and I still to this day wonder if it was the Lone Star talking more than anything, any ice cream variety needing to be puffed with air was more of a crepe than anything and that ice cream was only ice cream if placed on top of a cone and not dependent upon the nature of its accoutrements.

I knew on the spot that while they were different, beauty was in the eye of the taster, and however the debate came out, like when it comes to so many things, ice cream included, there's more than one way to get things done. In the end, they agreed to disagree, my country lawyer father waiving his right to a hearing, Mr. Sapphire, ever the closer, getting in the last word by securing the commitment of a nightcap for all at the Double Dip.

The more I watched my father engage with Mr. Sapphire, the more I watched him experience things he had never before experienced, the happier, the more content with himself he seemed to be.

Or maybe he was the same; maybe, just maybe, it was me who had changed. Maybe, just maybe, my father had been there all along.

"I'm proud of you son. You're defining your own path," he said the next day just before he drove off. "I don't know. Maybe it's time for one of us to do something different. But you'll figure out what's right. Just know we love you."

Then he put both hands on my shoulders and locked his eyes on mine, and it was Trader Vic's all over again.

"Know that I love you, son. No matter what."

Life is an accretion of moments in time. Some of them mold you, some of them define you. Others defy you. If there is ever a moment in a young man's life when you are going to cry like a baby, it's when your father, just when you think such a moment will never come, yet just when you need it the most, stands close enough to you where you can feel the broil of his breath, puts his hands on your shoulders, looks you in your eyes and tells you he loves you.

That's when he's not just your father, but also your dad.

The next day, the phone rang.

"Hi son."

"Hi dad. Where are you?"

"Somewhere east of El Paso. Ever heard of Wild Horse?"

"Been through there once, if I recall."

"Didja know El Paso is closer to L.A. than the southeastern most point of Texas? I looked it up. Hey, maybe Texas isn't so far from California after all."

I laughed. "I'd say you're right about that one, dad."

"Thanks for a great weekend, son."

And he was right. It had been a great weekend, one for the ages for the McDougal males, one filled with those moments that even in your most transient of times you know right away you will never forget.

"Hey. I just want you to know again that, whatever you decide about the paper, you have my support."

"Thanks dad," I said. "I love you."

"I love you, too."

In the end, I turned the offer down. The Times, California, they would always be there. But I still had things to do at the Evening Outlook, things to do in North Texas. The most important of which was to continue dating the one and only Sabrina Sapphire, with whom I had fallen very much in love. She had become my own brand of comfort food, like stew in winter: not only does it taste great, but it makes you feel good all over, rarely leaving you wanting even when the anticipation promises to be too much.

She had, in fact, become my light. My shining light, capable of bringing truth and love and beauty to the darkest of situations. Of intensifying their presence in the brightest. And somehow, her cup of aplomb always half full, knowing just the right mix to apply for most all of them in between.

At that point in time, not too long ago, I had come to know that something…big could be something…simple.

That there was grandeur, there was grace, there was glory even, in the simpler things of life.

Something…simple, indeed.

The mid-October morning air at the Warren Sports Complex trumpeted the dawn of relief.

The molt of summer was belatedly beginning its annual retreat, the crispness of fall just through the pass now, the solid of the caterpillar preparing to morph into the spectacularly detailed tapestry of the butterfly, perhaps one of the buckeye variety, a worn dollar bill-blend of copper and green, its brown and orange eyes on its wings, their horizontal protrusion and shape conspiring by accident to resemble the head of a tiny koala.

I was relaxing, reveling in the need for my USC sweatshirt, safeguarding my Grande Non-Fat Latte like a best man does the ring, the newest coffee addictee enjoying himself watching Sabrina's young cousin and his crymates run up and down the field.

Staring off into the distance for a moment, I had a realization: I could see, seemingly, forever. Contrary to popular belief, there were hills in Texas after all, or at the very least ridges, and I was on one. I was looking west, beyond the modern-day Levittown rows of brick homes in the foreground, toward the square patches in the distance that were dotted with water towers like a mélange of rooks and bishops randomly positioned on a panoramic chess board.

As I looked at them I remembered my chill upon the matching pair proclaiming my arrival in White Settlement, my freeze at the eyes of the raccoon. I closed my eyes, trying to picture all of the ones I'd seen since. They are dispersed throughout the landscape in these parts, markers for their towns, banners for civic achievement, like snowflakes no two created quite the same, many the old checkerboard style, some stark white rising from stray fields like magic beanstalks, others like giant thimbles with mostly beige or baby blue barrels and white tops seeming to rise from the urbanity like they had somehow volcanically erupted upward and were formed over time by the sands. We drive by them every day, paying them little heed as we go, but they are there, always there, silent partners in our day, watchful observers of our patterns, the newer, industrial-sized ones hulking, flexing, clear in their focus, the older ones, the ones with the larger tops as well but with the multitude of spindly legs below hovering over the scene like bobbing octopodes, slowing down over time but when push comes to shove still sharp as a whip.

I opened my eyes and wondered what they would say to me if I asked. What they would say of me and my time in this old train town, even if I didn't.

What they would say, at the glare of noon.

What they would say, at the chimes of midnight.

What they would say, because they could.

Then I noticed something. Could it be? Yes, I thought: water. I could see in the distance the glistening, the beautiful glistening of water, the sunlight having painted a sheen across its navy blue surface. I wondered for the briefest of hallucinogenic moments if it was the Pacific – my Pacific – that I was seeing. But I knew, even in my wettest of dreams, that that could not be.

"What's that body of water over there?" I said to Sabrina.

"Oh, that's Lake Lewisville," she said. "It's one of the biggest lakes in Texas. It's huge. Just a big bucket of fish pee. But it's huge."

I had wondered from the beginning how they survived in Texas without water, without having water be a major part of their lives. There was the Gulf of Mexico, but that was a five-hour drive to the south. Up here in Frisco, in "southern Oklahoma" as they mockingly describe Collin County down in Dallas, water was not part of daily life. There were a plethora of lakes in the area. But when you're from the ocean, lakes don't really count.

"There's so much of me that's tied to the water. I don't know. It's hard to explain. It's like I'm a different person when I look at it."

Sabrina smiled. "It means that much to you, doesn't it?"

"I guess it does. But you know, I don't think I really knew it, I mean really knew it, until I left. There's an old saying. It's something like, 'the mountains are the heart, the desert is the soul. And the ocean is emotion.' I'm not sure. Something like that."

"Well, we don't have a lot of mountains around here. Like none, really."

"I've noticed."

"There's a saying up in Colorado. Everyone from here goes there to ski in the winter. And it gets to the point where we just kind of take over, you know, in the way that Texans do? And there's this saying up there: 'If God had wanted Texans to ski, He would have given them a mountain.' I always thought that was funny."

"Any old sayings on the desert? I don't see any of those here either."

"None that I know of. I think that leaves you with Lake Lewisville."

I looked around. Slowly, purposefully. The scene was regnant. So, too, was the feeling that rushed through me next: that I was home. Right here, in Frisco, Texas, I felt at home.

The fact that I could see only Lake Lewisville and not the Pacific was, for the first time, not cause for alarm. I had endured, I had survived, I had beaten back, my first summer away from home. Thanks to the crudeness, the raw crudeness of this summer, I had seen and experienced things I never would have, learned lessons I never could have, had I stayed home, not taken the chance, not searched for my destiny with the widest lens I could grasp. And now fall, my favorite season of all, had arrived, and I was still standing, looking forward to what new was to come.

Home, I had to come to realize, was where the heart was. Deep in the heart, deep in my heart, I knew now that home was not necessarily where you were from, or even where you lived. It was, rather, how you lived. To live with dignity and respect for others, to live within a community of people while you hone your craft, whether it be teaching school or running a school board or practicing law or working as the cub reporter for the local newspaper. That was home.

And part of this was not to look at things as black or white, right or wrong. Part of this, I knew now, was that people, depending on where they came from, what they grew up with, what they knew – who they were – all looked at things differently. As long as you gave people a chance, tried to see it their way, honored the opinions of others as if they were your own, that's what was most important, because the best answer, no matter who asks the question, doesn't always come from within.

I thought of The Plan, the straight line I had etched in the damp cement of my youth.

The determination to execute it.

The naivete that I could.

When we draw up our plans in advance, we ignore the wanderings of men. You never know what a man is all about until you know him, where he came from, where he's been. Every man has his story, every story its turns, every turn its trips. We're all trailblazers, really. Blazers of our own trails, that is. None are straight. And no two are ever the same.

Gazing toward the square patches, I saw the seed.

AUTHOR'S NOTE I

GONE NUTS

This author left his native Southern California for Texas in the summer of 2000. Just when he thought the temperature would never cool, fall's grace took shape, and for the first time he thought he might stay awhile. When winter's will then proceeded to sap the green from the grass and leave it weed white, he reconsidered.

While he didn't work for the local newspaper, he was witness to local history: in March 2003, the Frisco School Board voted unanimously to change the Frisco High nickname from the Fighting Coons to the Fighting Raccoons, and immediately moved to start removing all Coons references on jerseys, stadiums and memorabilia. According to the Frisco Independent School District Web site, the board "voted that the mascot officially be the full name raccoon and not its shortened version. It was felt that this keeps the traditions of the community intact, while also being sensitive to any concerns or the potential discomfort of current and future students. Their decision was based on one thing – that it was the right thing to do."

One of the most visible changes the city made was to eliminate the "Home of the Fighting Coons" line on the Preston Road water tower. The eyes of the raccoon still peer at you as you pass by, and one can only imagine the tales it, too, could tell.

And below the raccoon is a large sticker that now reads:

Frisco High School
Home of
AAAA Softball
State Champions
2002

Life in Frisco, Texas continued to change after its teams no longer took the field as the Fighting Coons.

Beyond the replacement of the words "Home of the Fighting Coons" on the Preston Road water tower, the most visible change in town as a result of the change in Frisco High's nickname was that of the football stadium's name, which went from Coon Memorial to FISD (Frisco Independent School District) Stadium.

The gradual removal of the word "Coon" and term "Fighting Coon" from the Frisco landscape had actually begun to take place in 2002, the same year the city celebrated its centennial. A year later, Frisco opened its second high school, fittingly naming it Centennial High – complete with Titans as a seemingly non-contentious nickname – in order to commemorate the city's first 100 years. By spring of 2006 the school had graduated its first class of 400 seniors. And it would appear that many future Titans, as well as many future Fighting Raccoons, were in the pipeline. In Fall 2006, the Frisco school district reported an enrollment of 23,500 students – the ninth year in a row in which the district's enrollment grew by more than 20 percent over the previous year.

By 2010? The school district served 34,000 students. Since the beginning of the decade, 35 more schools had been opened, including four high schools. All of which reportedly made Frisco's, by percentage since 2000, the nation's fastest-growing school district.

Further change was also on the horizon for this old train town as part of its swift passageway to new century boomtown.

As part of Frisco's growth plan, the city successfully lured the Dallas Burn, the professional Major League Soccer (MLS) franchise that for years had played at the Cotton Bowl just east of downtown Dallas. Re-named FC Dallas, the team began play in 2005 at sparkly new, $65 million Pizza Hut Park on Main Street, just west of downtown. The complex features a 20,000-seat stadium, which in November of its inaugural year played host to the MLS championship game, 17 soccer fields for amateur players and a 600-seat stadium and turf field for high school soccer and football.

All the while, like the steamroller of growth toward Collin County and into Frisco that precipitated its own evolution, the Dallas North Tollway continued to expand to the north.

By the summer of 2003, The Tollway, as it is routinely called, had reached Highway 121. By the summer of 2006, it would extend as far north as Main Street. Four summers later, a drive up the Tollway would take one all the way to Highway 380 at the Prosper city line. The Tollway, a nascent construction project at the beginning of the decade, had as of its end become a seemingly endless highway into the hereafter, probably a good thing for the local populace, the size of which had mushroomed beyond 100,000.

2003 was also the year when the Texas League indeed came to Frisco with the arrival of the Frisco Roughriders, the AA affiliate of the Texas Rangers. In their inaugural season, and playing at the all-new Dr. Pepper/7Up Ballpark across the street from Stonebriar Mall, the Roughriders would win their division and go all the way to the league championship series before losing to the San Antonio Missions. By the end of the decade, the Roughriders were an institution, as much a part of the local landscape as the IKEA just to the south, the one just behind the stone wall that now proclaims in large, block letters, "WELCOME TO FRISCO."

Of course, when the air in a small town is this accelerant, when a small town is really no longer small, it's rare such change takes hold without leaving a few things behind. While the Double Dip is still going strong as of this writing, by the end of the 2000s a drive up Preston Road would reveal no Donut Palace. And with a drive down Main Street, one would discover neither The Abbey nor The Snow Cone Lady. The Abbey's building is still there, and a drive-by would leave one's pallet never the wiser, meats of all kinds frying inside in chicken juice, chicken or not. *The Snow Cone Lady? The shed is no longer there, the benches long gone. Leaving one to wonder whatever happened to her. Or if she was ever in there in the first place.*

The raccoon? As it seems to have done for so long, it continues to wreak havoc in its own, inimitable way. A news story out of Olympia, Wash. in August 2006, entitled "Psycho Killer Raccoons Terrorize Olympia," summed it up best: "We used to love the raccoons. They'd have their babies this time of year, and they were so cute. Even though we lived in the city, it was neat to have wildlife around," he said, "but this year, things changed. They went nuts."

Some would suggest this author went nuts when he left behind The Land of 73 Degrees for a place where it's usually way too hot or way too cold. For the record, while the promise of the flash of the sun over the water line still weakens him like the whiff of the scent of a long-lost love, he's still there. And when he catches his first bluebonnet sighting every spring, he catches a smile from himself.

Some would suggest Perot went nuts when he left behind the yesterday of Dallas for the tomorrow of Collin County, but even all those years later in 2008, when Plano had long since built out the wheat fields to the west, when EDS had again lost its independence, having been acquired this time by Hewlett-Packard, a drive up Preston Road to the east still offers a clear view of the castle, still mounting the flatness like a saddle, its windows still gleaming mouthwash green in the splash of a North Texas afternoon.

Some would suggest the town of Frisco, Texas went nuts in nicknaming its school teams the Fighting Coons in the first place.

Others would suggest the town of Frisco, Texas went nuts in changing the name in the end.

Regardless of where one comes out on the subject, something on which virtually everyone can agree is that life in Frisco, Texas at some point along the way changed forever.

As for this author, he says nuts are best on ice cream as long as they're not peanuts, and that they're even better when they are pecans and the ice cream variety on which they rest is frozen vanilla custard. And when you combine that with some cherries on top at the Double Dip on a hot summer night…well, let's just say that as much as things change, whether it is yesterday or tomorrow, it's nice to know that some things, some small-but-precious things, can be counted on, counted on to sound, to smell, to taste, to be, the same.

AUTHOR'S NOTE II

IN THERE ALL ALONG

News of the pending demise of the EDS headquarters building during the summer of 2018 prompted me to drive through Frisco for the first time in years, curious to see if even more change had come the town's way.

Thankfully, mercifully even, both the downtown and the raccoon water towers remain. Of course, they are surrounded by businesses ranging from a new movie theater complex to the new headquarters of the Dallas Cowboys.

Pizza Hut Park? It is now Toyota Stadium, an offshoot of the decision of Toyota Motor North America, Inc. to follow in my footsteps and relocate from Southern California to North Texas.

Scotty P's? It is gone, having been replaced by an empty storefront under construction, though I have heard that other locations can still be found.

The Double Dip? The building is there, as is the sign. The custard is not. The Double Dip apparently moved a few years ago, but didn't survive. "After the move to the new location, our sales have not justified the business overhead," it said in a message to its customers. "We are so, so grateful for your patronage and loyalty."

And then there's the Snow Cone Lady. Just when I was ready to proclaim these eateries of which I once wrote as but figments of my imagination, it turns out she never went out of business after all. She is still serving it up, the beige shed having long been replaced by a burnt red wood variation a few blocks to the west. Elated at the sight of it, I got in line, the 103-degree heat microwaving my flip flops, and took in the scene.

I first noticed that the shed was built to look like a train car, which the old beige shed was not but makes sense for an old train town. I then noticed the trim on the place. I'm tempted to say it was yellow, but when you're this hot – and the line is this long – your mind can play games. Mine did, and soon I found myself daydreaming of a shade of yellow about which I once read called yellow angel light, which apparently has something to do with the wisdom to make good decisions. Clearly it was a good decision to try one last time to find The Snow Cone Lady, not only because I finally did so but also because the Cherry-Purple Passion combination that I went for was easily the best snow cone I've ever had.

As I turned to walk away I noticed one last thing, a sign affixed to the shed. At first I thought it was a simple railroad crossing sign, one of those commonly seen at train crossings, especially level ones. And you certainly see them around Frisco. But when I looked closer I realized that the sign said something different. "Snow Cone Crossing," it said, and in an instant I realized that I had struck gold. Just about everything that had once caught my fancy in this town had changed over the years, the search for its soul elusive as it crossed over from small to big. But not The Snow Cone Lady. She was in there all along.

ABOUT THE AUTHOR

John Clendening is a former award-winning journalist who now works in corporate communications. He is also a writer whose passion is to share stories that touch people's hearts. Clendening lives in Dallas with his wife, Jean, and their seven children – five humans and two canines.

CPSIA information can be obtained
at www.ICGtesting.com
Printed in the USA
LVHW040831291118
598485LV00001B/28

9 781532 056833